OUT OF THE CHUTE

A.R.Donenfeld-Vernoux

Acknowledgements

Without the help of the Orange County Advance Novel Group, this book would never have been possible.

Thank you especially Dirk and Gregg who took the entire journey with me, and also to Lynn and Bill, for your time, insights and suggestions that make everything better.

Disclaimer:

Dedication:

To those with skills no longer valued, no matter how hard they worked or how much blood and sweat they gave to jobs they believed were going to be there for them forever
—and then weren't.

Time to go beyond the shock and fantasy and learn to live in the real world.

Time to listen to the call of survival as it speaks over the deafening, grinding roar of the rat-wheel to success.

When reality sets in, it's time:
 to reconstruct priorities,
 take stock of emotions,
 accept failures,
 forgive those who've hurt,
 forgive yourself for hurting others,
 accept mistakes,
 grieve for those lost, and
 live in appreciation for the gift of each new day.

And, most important of all—understand life's most valuable message: what seems like the end is only a new beginning in disguise.

It All Starts Here

A silver white handlebar mustache doesn't even begin to cover his smile as the nurse hands the pink wrapped bundle to the man. He's tall, portly, bald— wearing a double breasted pin striped suit with a carnation boutonniere. Elegant. Important looking.

He leans over, folds back a corner of the bunting swaddling the newborn. Blue eyes try to focus and stare from a round rosey face framed with damp blonde curls. Another girl—his sixth. He likes girls, takes his daughters to the office and out to lunch with his cronies, teaches them how to fish and play golf. Smiling, he touches the soft skin of her cheek, something resembling a smile, but is probably just gas, shows toothless gums.

"Well aren't you a fancy lady," he declares and holds the baby just a little tighter against his chest, bends over to rub his nose against the soft fringe above her ear, inhales the sweet smell of a newborn life, well worth the trip from his law office to the hospital.

He hands the infant back to the nurse, kisses his new trophy wife on her forehead, and leaves to go back to his office.

As soon as he's out the door, the nurse fills in the birth certificate clipped to the board she's holding: "Fancy Lady." Oh well, she thinks, people are naming their children all kinds of funny stuff these days. Gone are the days of good old fashioned names like Mary, Susan, Helen or Sally.

1

Fast Forward Fifty Years

The broken down 1968 Chevy pick-up races north on the I-90, while Fancy Lady tries to avoid the busted spring in the torn passenger seat that's been poking her in the ass. Her dog, Tug, half on her lap and half on the floor, looks out the window with disinterest.

Janice Joplin belts out "Me and Bobby McGee" while the horse trailer behind dances to its own song in high Santa Ana winds. Fancy wonders if her brain is addled. All she can think is—what the hell am I doing here? Where has my life gone? The swaying jolts from the trailer haven't knocked any sense into her.

The man behind the wheel holds a toxic fascination. Crap! I've lost my mind! I'd follow him anywhere. Of that she is more or less sure. At least for the moment. Of the rest of her life—not so much.

They're on their way to a jackpot team roping in Merced. Not one of the finer garden spots of California, she shortly finds. Should have been on guard once they passed the Harris Ranch feed lots pungent smell of too many cattle penned in too small a place. Acrid. Made her nose tingle, eyes run. It's a harbinger of turkey ranches to come.

Fancy Lady had a brief introduction to where they were going and what would happen. Her cowboy drew hard on his Camel. As the smoke spiraled out of the corner of his mouth, his voice growled. "Jackpot roping consists of teams of two cowboys on horseback 'n scared shitless steers. The cowboys pay a fee to enter the roping...covers the cost of the arena, the critters to rope and prize money for the winners.

"Idea is, one cowboy ropes the cow by its head or horns...he's the header. 'T'other ropes either or both hind legs...he's the heeler. The ropes are pulled taut and the steer 'stretched' 'til it stops moving. Team with the shortest time wins." He takes a deep drag. Looks over at her for the first time in a while. Only a short look. "You got it?"

She got it. The header goes first, and woe betide the heeler who misses if the header has a good clean catch. The cow just runs and stops when it can't run any longer. Poor cow. The team has no time in the contest for the round.

Fred. The driver's name is Fred. He was a bull rider for years. Hitch, his father, claims he was tossed on his head one time too many. Maybe his dad's right.

Fred is one of the most attractive men Fancy Lady ever saw. Not handsome, but rugged. Craggy carved face and brooding, almost black eyes. A shock of black hair shot through with gray, and a profile she thought she'd die for. He's a genetic throwback to his Native American great-grandmother. He's also the town drunk.

They found each other in the Mustang Saloon. She's drowning sorrows in a large rum and Coke, not too much rum, heavy on the Coke. Fred's sitting in the corner of the bar hanging his head over his vodka and grapefruit. It would be hard to paint a more vivid picture of dejection. He's fifty years old and still hanging out at the bar in the town he was born in. Never got too far from home.

Call it pheromones, call it lust, call it whatever you will, but the first time Fancy set eyes on him she went weak in the knees. Maybe it's just the time of her life. Top executive out of work— new consulting business struggling, huge salary gone. No jetting back and forth to Europe first class like she was used to. It's a bad time to be alone. Age fifty. Menopausal. More crap!

3

She grew up in a small town and couldn't wait to get out—like moving to big cities, getting up at six AM, donning woman-warrior-business-suits, pantyhose, high heels, war paint and grabbing her weapons of Gucci handbag and briefcase for battle with…men. Thirty years of hard work and unceasing push, push, push. Talk about driven! And she was good at what she did. High power entertainment attorney, moved over to business affairs in a fast moving company, then studio executive. Business suits upped to French designer and shirts custom made with monogrammed cuffs. She'd learned to shoot the cuffs to show the tiny embroidered letters like the guys did. Hot shit!

But suddenly it was over. Corporate perks and salary gone. She looks down at her sweatshirt, jeans and dusty cowboy boots. She's out on her own. Or is it just free?

She's even beginning to think and speak differently. Her East Coast accent, her lawyer-like phrasing are slipping slowly away like the rest of her past, re-emerging from time to time to shock her into recognition of their loss as the chameleon effect of the automatic blending in with surroundings take over.

Friday afternoon, as the cowboys say, she's "goin' down the road." In this case they're goin' "up" the road north from Santa Maria. The road's empty, the wind's up, Fred's concentrating straight ahead. At best he's taciturn. At worst he can go hours without a single word, grunt or sound. His horse is actually better company. More communicative. Fancy knows when the horse wants: hay, oats or water. No clue what Fred wants, other than seemingly to be left alone. But then—why is she here?

She tries to start a conversation. Gets a few grunts. Gives up. He lights an unfiltered Camel. She lights a filtered Kent. The horse moves in the trailer and its swaying movement translates through the hitch into the pick-up. She turns in the seat— looks at Fred's profile. Memories of high school, driving with the handsome cool guy, flood back. There's something James Dean-morose about Fred. Rage and frustration seep from his pores.

4

He's the poster boy for melancholy. *What's he thinking about?* She burns to know. When she asks, the answer's always something like, "nothin' much," or "just trying to figure what time we'll get there," or "wonderin' if we should stop and eat along the way."

But that couldn't be it, could it? Wasn't there some deep despair roiling around behind those dark eyes? She's positive he has more to say. In those rare moments when he's talkative, he's well informed, very bright. He's a college graduate, an avid reader. He reads the newspaper from cover to cover and loves Time, Newsweek and National Geographic.

They pull off at the next exit. "Need gas," is all he says. She watches his lanky frame, broad shoulders and narrow hips in ancient Wranglers as he heads into the station to pre-pay. Down at the heels Roper boots. His dusty black Stetson's seen more than a few too many rodeos, but his face beneath compels her to him.

Town gossip is he grows and deals grass. Could be. Always has money and never seems to work. Home is his father's ranch in a tiny cottage badly in need of everything— roof, paint, kitchen, new plumbing. A herd of feral cats keep the mouse population to a minimum but also take to using the house as a repository for dead things. Not her favorite place to visit.

He's made a reservation in advance and they check into a small, clean motel close to the roping. There's one jackpot that night, two on Saturday and one on Sunday before they're on the road again.

Next stop—the arena parking area. Takes his horse, Rosie, out to feed and water.

She gets a nice rubdown before saddling up.

Rosie's truly one of the homeliest animals around. Her face is unattractive enough but it gets worse as she wiggles her lips in bizarre ways. Her hide is mottled strawberry with funky patches of white and gray. Fancy thinks of the horse in a rhyme, 'Rosie, Rosie Ugly Posey'. If anyone but Fred gets near she whinnies like she's about to be slaughtered. Rosie knows Fancy as someone who throws her a flake of hay from time to time so she accepts her, but her wide frightened eyes still follow closely. Who knows what the woman might do?

Fred's partner arrives in another pick-up, horse trailer behind. The two animals greet each other. Friends. Every night his partner insists on tying the horses on opposite sides of a trailer. Every morning one of the horses has chewed through its rope and the two are standing amiably together. They never run away, they just like hanging out side by side. Fred's partner refuses to learn. Stubborn. The horses never give up either. Every morning they're together, no matter how they're left the night before. Lost a lot of ropes that way.

The two cowboys have little to say to each other. They nod and do their work.

Fancy sits on the tailgate of Fred's truck with Tug, her treasured friend. Woman and dog sit silently, watch trucks and trailers fill the lot. There's a circuit of jackpot roping up and down the I-90 and the I-5 where winning counts towards standing in the Professional Rodeo Cowboys Association. The top guys compete at the National Finals Rodeo in Las Vegas every December.

They greet the occupants of the truck next to them, a team of grandfather and teenage grandson roping together. The boy wants to be a professional cowboy and his grandfather goes along. Wants to help the boy attain his dream. When the introductions go around, she introduces herself as just 'Fancy'. She's hated her name all her life and figures Fancy Lady is too much, Fancy by itself is bad enough.

Soon the lot fills. Fred and his partner sign up and pin their team number on their backs. Since it's a PRCA sanctioned event, they have to wear cowboy hats out of the chute and western shirts rather than tee-shirts. The hats can fly off during the event as long as they start out with them on.

The horses warm up in the arena. This culture starts at a very early age. A five year old girl races one of the big quarter horses 'round and 'round to warm him up. Her father yells over the rail,

"Slow down, darn you! Don't wear him out now." He turns to Fancy, "That little hellion loves speed. Got no idea what she's going to be like in a few years." He shakes his head and she sees pride in his eyes.

His son and roping partner steps next to him. The boy yells to the little girl, "Sissy, get off that horse and do it now!" She pulls over to the rail. Maybe she isn't even five. Her legs barely make it across the saddle to stirrups pulled up as far as they can go. Her hair's in braids with pink bows, she's wearing a pink shirt and fuchsia kids Ropers. There's determination in her eyes and freckles across her nose. Her brother lifts her off the saddle and over the rail, handing her to their father.

Talking to Fancy, the father puts her down. "Her mother won't come, scares her to watch, but this 'uns been riding almost two years now." He looks down and puts his hand on her shoulder, pulls her against his leg. "Can't get her to ride her pony…not big or fast enough for her. She'll be a barrel racer for sure."

The little girl looks up with serious blue eyes. "No way." She puts her hands on her hips and moves a bit away from her father. "I'm gonna be a header."

Later, Fancy sees her with another brother, maybe a year or two older. The two of them set up a plastic steer's head and toss ropes at it over and over with amazing accuracy. They keep it up for the entire weekend.

The roping begins. The riders wait in the chutes for the steers to come out of their pens. The steer must break the barrier rope before the riders or they suffer a penalty. The time it takes for them to stop the steer is crucial. The header rides alongside the animal and throws the rope. A clean catch is over both horns; a one-horn catch is difficult as it can fall off. The heeler is behind throwing to catch both hind hooves. One will suffice as long as the rope stays put.

Dust flies up from the arena surface. This is the dry part of

California, high semi-arid and almost desert. A water truck sprinkles the surface to try and keep the dust to a minimum but it doesn't last and has to be done over and over. The sun beats down mercilessly during the days. Fancy pours water on her neck scarf from time to time but it dries quicker than the dust. Her wide brim western hat gives some relief. She slathers her face and arms with sunscreen. Tug climbs down from the bleachers and finds a shady spot under the truck.

This evening, each team has seven steers. Best total time wins. After the second run the lights go on but shadows shroud the arena floor. Without the sun, it begins to get evening desert cool.

A small stand serves hotdogs, hamburgers and fries. They eat a bag of chips with homemade meatloaf sandwiches on baguettes Fancy brought along. Tug has some meatloaf too. Fred has a beer, Fancy a diet Coke. His partner eats one of the hamburgers and oily fries from the stand. The smell of grease mixes with horse, manure, hay and sweaty men. Oddly, she decides she likes it.

Back at the truck, Tug looks up with questions in his eyes and Fancy remembers to fill a bowl with water for him. He knows to stay in the truck bed and doesn't need to be tied down. He's eyeing an Australian Heeler in another pick-up a way down the line, but they don't bark, they just look at each other. Gentlemen.

Walking back to the stands, there's a commotion. Men vault over the railing into the arena. Fancy peers through the crowd. A horse is down, rider not in sight. There's a familiar whinny, the sound Rosie makes when she's deathly afraid. The next thing Fancy knows is she's over the top of the rail and racing on the arena dirt with no idea how she got there. She helps Fred up. He's a bit groggy and dirty. Blood courses down his cheek. He shoves her off and runs to Rosie. She's still on the ground but trying to get up and shaking her head. He reaches her and she stops howling when she sees him. He bends down, hand on her shoulder and checks her legs. She lies quiet for him.

8

"It's okay girl, nothing's broken. You just had a spill. Come on, you can do it." And he gentles her up letting her get her balance leaning on his shoulder. When she stands, she lifts one hoof off the ground and he looks at it. There's a cut above the hock. He feels all around the leg and pats her flank. "Come on girl, just a scratch. Let's get it taken care of." His voice is as soft and caressing as the hand he keeps on her. The horse shakes her head as if she knows what he's said. He slowly leads Rosie out of the arena without a look or a nod in Fancy's direction. She stands alone in the center of the arena.

His partner tosses a look with raised brows. Fred answers "…must 'a stepped in a hole and stumbled…hard to see with all them shadows." He looks down and the melancholy look is back. He pats the horse on her flank, rubs her gently; feeling for pain, injury. "Nothing broken, but she may have a sprain. We'll see." His partner nods.

Fred brings a drop light out of the storage box in the truck and puts it on the ground near the horse. Then he rummages for alcohol and a rag to rub her leg down. Rosie isn't pleased but she seems to know he's taking care of her; lets him do what he wants.

Blood still trickles down Fred's face, now staining his collar. He won't let anyone take care of him until he makes sure Rosie's all right.

One of the other cowboys comes over. Turns out he's the local vet. He hunkers down next to Fred and they feel Rosie all over and up and down her legs.

The vet's voice is kindly "Don't need to worry much 'bout her. Just sprained it during her fall. Should be okay for tomorrow…put some liniment and wrap it good." He pats Fred on the shoulder, "…see how she walks in the morning…and let your woman fix that cut." He nods towards the blood on Fred's face. "Don't want infection." Fred mumbles something unintelligible and finishes tending to Rosie.

Later, Fancy cleans the blood off—a surface scalp cut.

9

They go for dinner at the local watering hole. She has one rum and diet Coke, Fred has six vodkas and grapefruit juice. At dinner he never says a word, just stares down into his drink, showing his wonderful profile. He wants a seventh vodka and grapefruit, but she steers him out of the joint and back to the motel.

He barely undresses before crashing on the bed. She spoons his naked body, drapes her arm over his chest. He was too tired to shower and when her nose presses against his neck she smells his sweat and Rosie's mixed with dust and liniment.

Fancy thinks back to something one of her friends said in the midst of a divorce, "I've never felt so alone in my life, so abandoned, as sleeping next to a man who doesn't seem to care I'm there."

Her mind unconsciously skitters to recall the men she's spooned in the past: attorneys, executives, even an actor or two. International. Cultured. Intellectuals chock full of charm, character and chat.

Fancy can't for the life of her figure out what the hell she's doing with a drunken cowboy with skid marks on his tighty-whities and no conversation to speak of.

Time Off

Fancy is one pissed off woman. Attorney, company executive, top level. Worked her professional ass off at the last two gigs, made them profitable with her sweat and muscle and both sold out from under her. Her pay-off? A bad attitude and a grave dislike for corporate culture. But she still has to shell out for the bills, support herself, her employees, her family, the various friends they bring along. Lots of hands out wanting something.

She was offered several jobs with other big companies. Not in a pigs eye, was all she could think. She was done with corporations and lack of control over her own life. Instead, she decided to do what any less than semi-cogent woman that angry might do: buy a ranch...when she's never even been on one.

Fancy stands under the weeping willow in the middle of her acreage. Four fenced corrals spread out on one side, a comfortable house with 2500 square feet of mostly high wood ceilings and open space on the other. She likes the great room kitchen combo, it was instant attraction with commanding control of her surroundings. Control is the most important. A front porch looks out over the lawn sweeping down to the willow where she stands, paddocks beyond.

She fell in love with the ranch at the sight of the tall, lacy willow gracing the entrance. There was something both majestic and comforting about the unassailable presence of the imposing tree at the center of the spread.

11

Off to the left are the stables, room for four horses and overhang roof to give shade. She imagined sitting there afternoons, putting back a cold one, telling tall stories while the rest of the world goes by.

Further along is another building, the far end a two bedroom guest cottage, next a garage big enough for trucks or camper if she wants. The part closest to the entrance will be Fancy's office. Three rooms and a toilet.

The idea of sitting in a corner of the largest room, her desk facing a sliding glass door where she can see tall green grass waving in the breeze, trees a far cry from Central Park, pink roses along the fence line, makes her quiet. She smiles. She hasn't done that in a long while.

The ranch gives her space to carry on a consulting business. She gets paid and clients get the use of her fertile brain for a lot less than the cost of putting her on salary. And the best part is, she doesn't give a rat's patootie if they take her advice or not. The pleasure of consulting—"Here's what I think you should do. Take it or leave it." Fancy can sit in her office, look out at the ranch, and wear her jeans and boots while she doles out expensive advice.

There are times when even the highest priced executives need time off to re-group and figure out what they want to do next. Fancy's life was always orderly, pointed in one direction—up. She never had time to try new things. Time to re-visit the past, explore the present, think about the future, and take stock of what a middle-age woman can do with the rest of her life.

Not that her plans include being a rancher—raising cattle or horses. She likes horses well enough, just not enough to ride them like she did when she was younger. Now her like is limited to throwing a flake of hay at them and making sure they have water. She'll hold reins at rodeos and team roping. More than that, she leaves to the cowboys.

The ranch is in the Santa Isabella Valley. Known only as 'the Valley', by the time she arrives, the area is famous for good wines and movie star ranches.

The Valley is also home to cowboys and Indians. She knows the correct term is 'Native Americans', but linked with 'cowboys' it hurts the ear, no matter how PC it might be. A Reservation is down the road. The Santa Isabella Valley is starting to come into its own as wine country, but ranches and horses are the local stock in trade.

And then, there's the Mustang Saloon. Fancy spots a ramshackle dark brown wooden building with a front porch and railing that looks like horses should be hitched to it. 'Fern bars' obviously not welcome.

She pulls her silver Mercedes into a spot bracketed by dusty trucks, all populated by big dogs. Tongues lolling out the sides of their mouths, the four pawed passengers ignore the strange closed silver vehicle where a very well groomed Soft Coated Wheaten Terrier looks out a window, nose pressed close. Poor Tug.

The sound of honky-tonk piano drifts out through the open door along with smoke, loud conversation and laughter. After all the western movies Fancy's seen, she's finally going into a 'real' cowboy bar. As she enters, she hears a New York City Detective friend's voice in her mind telling her, "Fancy, you love to go into places I wouldn't get within a mile of without my gun drawn." Hmmm. *Is this one of those places?* She certainly hopes so.

As she makes her way through plaid and striped western-yoke-shirted-shoulders to the bar, conversation stops. Everyone turns to look at the stranger in town. She's dead pan and orders a red wine. The bartender, a young woman with a pretty round face and long straight blonde hair, looks horrified. "Do you really want red wine? It comes from a box!" *In the middle of the wine country?*

Fancy's a bit taken aback. "Okay, thanks for the warning. Make that a rum and coke."

The bartender, Polly, introduces herself as she serves the drink. "You new in town?" she asks.

"Yes, just bought a place out on Salsepuedes."

"Okay then, welcome to the Mustang Saloon. Don't mind the cowboys, they're just havin' a good time." She motions to a young man, probably mid to late twenties, dressed in ratty jeans and a wrinkled, holey and dirty tee-shirt. "This here's Raul. He does gardening if you need some help 'round the place."

He switches his beer from his right hand to his left and shakes. "Good to meet you. Where's your place at?" And just like that, Fancy is a member of the community.

Polly tells her Raul travels with a giant, shaggy, rough-coated grey-brown dog—Rocko. Fancy noticed the dog when she parked her car and thought immediately of a Lurcher, the descendant of ancient dogs used for poaching the royal estates, part sight hound like an Irish Wolfhound, and part shepherd or terrier, reputed to be both smart and loyal. Rocko looked the part as he sat behind the wheel in Raul's truck, paws on the steering wheel, patiently waiting for his master while he checked out the goings and comings at the Mustang. She learns the local legend has Rocko driving the truck home when Raul has a few too many beers. Probably does, Fancy thinks as she sips her drink.

The smoke's as thick in the Mustang as the laughter and bonhomie. Also testosterone. Everyone smokes and Fancy peers through the billowing clouds to check out the other denizens bellied up to the bar. *Damn, they're really cowboys.* Coming from New York, the only actual cowboys she's seen was when the rodeo was at Madison Square Garden.

Takes her a few visits to the Mustang to learn the local terminology: the cowboys and ranchers are 'hats' and the businessmen are 'suits.' The bar is filled with hats, most of them cowboy, some baseball. Wrangler jeans are the uniform. And tight, too. Fancy's never seen so many attractive man-butts in one place before, good looking rugged men, for the most part wearing western shirts outlining broad muscled backs, and dusty black or tan Stetsons or Resistols. Yup, she's landed in testosterone town!

In the background Johnny Cash is working to be heard over the din. As she gets used to the noise and the smoke and can finally tear her eyes off the tight jeans, she notices the bar takes up the front left part of the saloon. On the right are a few tables

14

straggling towards the back of the room—mostly filled by a large pool table and players. Behind the bar area a few more tables crowd near an upright piano. The walls are dark wood; entire ceiling filled with dollar bills and business cards tacked in place, an occasional pair of skivvies nailed near the cards, a hat or some small toys.

As soon as she orders a second round, her business card joins the others. The other bartender, Jack, has a process for making the cards stick. The bar turns quiet as he takes a tack, puts it through the card first, then the dollar, holds a block of wood against the tack and heaves it all together up to the ceiling. The wood falls to the floor, the tack stays, card and dollar in place. A round of applause breaks out, then the conversation starts up again. Fancy leans over the bar, "Good going! Can I buy you a drink?"

Jack smiles, "Don't mind if I do. Thanks!'

"Make one for Polly too, please."

Everyone seems to be having a good time, even the loud yelling is good natured until the conversation stops again. The distinctive sound of Harleys rumble and bark in through the open door, taking precedence over the juke box and voices.

Here it comes, Fancy thinks, we're going to get killed in a rumble between cowboys and bikers. She looks around for help. Polly is deep in conversation with a guy wearing a black hat with feathers and a long braid hanging down his neck. The two are almost nose to nose across the bar and from their body language they're oblivious to the imminent arrival of the wild bunch.

Three bikers enter the bar dressed in black leathers. Shoulder to shoulder they stand inside, in front of the doorway. Appraising the action. Red and white checked café curtains bracket the door and frame the tall, broad, silent men. Cotton neckerchiefs rolled into head bands keep long straggly hair in place as they stand, feet planted apart, hands fisted at their sides. Cigarette smoke wreathes them like movie magic smoke. To Fancy, the stance is menacing. First there's silence. Ominous? Then the yelling and laughing start again. They fold into the crowd, bikers and cowboys slapping each other on the shoulder or back, man-hugs all around as they shove into the bar to order beers.

Fancy lets out a breath she hadn't realized she was holding. Who knew cowboys and bikers got along? What other things can a city woman learn in this western town in the back of beyond?

At that moment, Fancy understands, bizarre as it was, she's probably made a good decision. And she hasn't understood yet the name of the road where the ranch is situated is a corruption of the Spanish phrase *'salir se puedes'* meaning 'get out if you can'.

Old Stories New Places

Three weeks after Fancy moves into the ranch, she's on the front porch, feet propped on a porch rail, looking out over her new home. Tug is asleep next to her on the love seat with his nose against her hip. A balloon of local red wine, a nice Merlot, rests on the table by her chair.

Her new two-tone blue Lucchese ostrich boots, are still tenderfoot clean, embroidered snip toes spread apart to frame the weeping willow in the middle of the lawn leading to the pastures below. She's been discovering certain ranch facts that never occurred to her. The water bill to keep the lawn green is more than a thousand dollars a month. The cost of the gardener and crew close to the same. Takes a lot of work and more money to keep a ranch looking good.

Just as she's enjoying the view, the sky turns ominous. Looks up. Dark clouds coming up from over the mountain. Rain? The Valley has been in drought for several years. Rain is much needed. Might even drop the water bill some.

The first drops begin to fall. Maybe change the Luccheses for something a tad more practical? Like rain boots? She picks up the cushions from the wicker porch furniture and brings them inside, stacking them by the door. Calls for Tug to come in and sees he's already next to the recliner where she watches television. Smart dog.

An hour later, the few drops have turned into a torrent. A major storm is filling the wells, the nearby lake and the creeks with much needed rain. Wanting to enjoy this first real downpour in her new home, Fancy puts on a slicker and hat. A strange notion hits her. She wants to dance in the rain. Outside in the roundabout, she pirouettes, jumps, and does a few rock n' roll moves she remembers from American Bandstand. Hands raised to the sky, mindless of water sliding into the arms of her slicker she dances her way toward the weeping willow. Stops. Oh-oh! Slithering snake-like down the hill on the slick grass a stream has formed across the lawn through the pastures to the ranches below. In the few minutes she watches, the stream grows with mountain run-off bleeding across the highway. Several small geysers sputter to life on the lawn, spouting more water to join in the flow. She's never seen anything like that before.

Running over to the guest cottage and office, she realizes water is pouring from the street around the corners of the lower buildings to join the deluge. Even a New York lawyer can see water stacking up against the side of the outbuildings. It needs to be diverted into the pastures or it will eventually flood inside. The main house is safe, it's perched on a decent sized rise. At least she hopes it's safe. Everything else is on lowland.

No more dancing for Fancy, she's alone on the ranch, dog no help. She drags a shovel from the barn and goes to work. Three hours and four ditches later, Fancy looks at her hands. Palms blistered and bleeding, wrapped with old kitchen towels. Back screaming in pain. Shoveling is not exactly what she had in mind when she thought of ranch living. Mud from head to toe. But she looks back in pride to survey her work. Barn, stable, office and cottage all have neat trenches dug, diverting the swift water now channeled across her ranch into a fast running stream. No more stacking.

Tired and grumpy, she makes her way back up the hill towards the house. Before she clears the willow, a man in a hat and raincoat, carrying an umbrella stops her. "You the owner of this ranch?"

"Yes," she replies, "I'm Fancy. Who are you, may I ask?"

Strange, he's come on to her property. Not usual to pass the gate without asking unless he's a Jehovah's Witness. She hopes not.

"I have the ranch next door and I'm going to sue your ass."

Maybe a Witness would have been better? "Sorry, I don't understand. What do you mean?"

He brandishes the umbrella and points at the water rushing across the pastures. "See all those leaves, they're going onto my property. I won't have your leaves dumped on my lawn. You come and take them away, and do it now."

Fancy nods her head a few times, deep in thought. "Exactly which leaves are you talking about, sir? Please show me."

"The ones from your ranch." His voice is rising as he points in several directions. Agitated. "All those leaves."

"Oh, I see. How about those other leaves, the ones from the ranches up the road, or across from the mountain. Those leaves the running water has brought to my ranch. Do I have to get rid of those too?" It's taking every bit of patience not to knock the old guy on his keester, but she manages to keep her cool.

"Well, I don't know about those leaves, but I think you should take them all because they come from your ranch."

That was it. The last straw of the day. Fancy loses it. "Well how about you just get off my ranch and take your stupid claims with you. If you got a problem with leaves, then get a lawyer and sue not only me, but every other ranch this flow passes through before it gets to you."

"Don't you sass me young lady...and you aren't very Fancy!"

At that, she starts to laugh. Almost crazy like. She's covered in mud dripping off her slicker, her hair is wet, water has dripped down her back, into her boots and her hands hurt. It's the laugh that does it. The man looks at her like she's a lunatic about to attack him. Pretty close to right. He turns and runs off through the side gate to his property. Fancy is still laughing when he slams his door.

Two hours later she's had a hot shower, shared two hamburgers and a baked potato with Tug, and started a fire in the stone fireplace. The living room is warm; wood smoke softens the air and reminds her of her grandfather's house. He liked a wood fire and liked it even more with a grandkid snuggled on his lap.

She misses him and her grandmother. Both of them long gone. Folks. He a carpenter and farmer, she a redheaded Irish lass who managed to birth eight kids. Their memory meant home. Grandpa with his long handlebar moustache, suspenders, thinning hair and brilliant blue eyes refusing to fade with age, singing "Old Dan Tucker" and beating time on his knee. Grandma, standing in the arch to the kitchen, hands clasped under flowered apron as she looked on with pride and love in her eyes for her man. He worked their farm for years, backbreaking work, Grandma working at his side until she went to cook their meals, take care of the kids.

Fancy looks into the flames. She's happy even though her back and hands are sore. She's put a good days work behind her. She props her feet up and raises the glass of wine as she thinks back to another time. Her other life. The one she admits she fled from.

***

The rack of lamb a tiny pile of bones in front of her; a glass of Bourgogne warms in her hand. The first class section of TWA flight number 861, non-stop from Los Angeles to Paris.

The stewardess leans over solicitously as she removes the plate. "Miss Burns, are you all right? Do you want anything else?"

Most of the stews regularly working first class on TWA 861 know Fancy by name. She takes these 747's across the ocean many times a year. Once she tried to count how many times she's taken this particular flight, gave up, probably close to a hundred.

The plane jumps as it hits an air pocket, but she doesn't give it a second thought. She feels as safe as if she were home in bed, sometimes even safer.

She's always polite. "Thanks, I'm fine. I'll finish this glass and try to get a little shut eye." As executive of a television studio, she's on her way to spend a week in Cannes. Negotiate with television broadcasters.

Meal and tablecloth swept away; wine glass refilled. Time to close her eyes and relax on the long flight, almost eleven hours in the air with a nine hour time change. By arrival time almost one day is lost. Please let me just close my eyes and chill, she tells herself. It's been hectic right up to boarding the plane.

Fancy is very good at her job and knows it. There's nothing to worry about. Now it's time to relax with no telephone to interrupt. This is her sacred time, a time to treasure where thoughts come quietly. This is the only time in her busy schedule she can enjoy some peace and quiet.

Gently, the stewardess shakes her shoulder. "Miss Burns, we'll be landing soon at Charles de Gaulle in Paris. Would you like some coffee or some champagne? Perhaps a heated croissant with a little jam and some juice?"

On the way to the toilet to freshen up, she straightens the skirt of the designer suit, shoots the monogrammed French cuffs of the custom made shirt so they peek out of the jacket sleeves the correct length and stands tall as she strides down the aisle. A woman in complete control. Or so she believed in those days. Funny how life can cut you off at the knees without a by-your-leave or a warning.

Tug's woofing in his sleep snaps her from her reverie. Fancy looks over at her rain boots and slicker dripping dry across the room in the pantry. Still caked with mud. Tomorrow she'll have to hose them off. She hears the whirring and occasional clank of the washing machine going though its cycles with her muddy jeans, socks and shirt. Almost time for the dryer. Her eyes clear as she looks around her, the ranch house, the fire, the dog. Her life now. Certainly different from what she'd been used to. She stretches, one hand at her side to release some of the ache in her back. Her hands are so sore she can hardly move them, she looks and see blisters have formed on her palms.

Which life is better? Might think about that tomorrow.

21

The Mustang Saloon

The Mustang Saloon is Fancy's home away from home. Friends know if they can't find her at the ranch, they call the Mustang and either she's there, or whoever's tending bar knows where to find her.

The Mustang is the hub of the town. Its owners are the center of local social life, plan town events, festivals, weddings, holiday parties—unofficial social directors. No one's alone in Santa Isabella as long as they can crawl or drag themselves to the Mustang. It's the place where you find a recommendation for a good plumber, gardener, and electrician; learn who's a badass, who's a cheater. Find a new lover or just dump the old one. There are no secrets at the Mustang.

Sunday afternoons raucous honky-tonk music fills the valley air. A piano, singer, fiddle and guitar player can make a lot of noise with the "Orange Blossom Express." The singer belts out every country song ever played on Nashville radio in the last fifty years. She also knows some that weren't. The bar is crowded on Sundays, the pool table pushed over in a corner and those who are inclined, dance in the postage size space. The decibels between the music and the yelling at the bar is so loud, customers almost require earplugs to survive.

Those who can't take the noise and smoke retire to the few tables on the porch, lean back and put their boots up on the railing to enjoy the sunset and the clear Valley air. Locals perch on the

22

railings, sit on the steps, crowd around the tables. Everyone knows everyone else and moves from one table to the next. Typical Sunday afternoon in Santa Isabella.

Fancy's at the bar with a girlfriend, Sybil, who's at the ranch visiting from Los Angeles. They're enjoying the sights—tight Wranglers that is, and watching people try to dance on the miniscule dance floor.

Sybil shouts in Fancy's ear, "What's the name of the song they're playing?"

Fancy answers, "You Piss Me Off You Fuckin' Jerk."

Sybil's face turns bright red, "How could you say that to me? What have I ever done to make you so angry?"

The noise level in the bar is even louder than usual. Fancy's laughing so hard she can hardly speak as she leans back towards Sybil, "That's the name of the song." Her answer is a bit garbled, she's close to hysteria.

Sybil shouts back, "I can't hear you. Why are you so mad at me?"

"…not mad!...name of song?"

"What's wrong with asking the name of the song?"

"That *is* the name of the song."

"What's the name of the song?"

"You Piss Me Off You Fuckin' Jerk."

"There you go again. What's wrong with you? …and stop laughing! It's not funny!"

By now Fancy's head is on the bar, tears running down her cheeks and she's convulsed with laughter. All she can do is wave and put her palm up.

Sybil's furious, her anger clear as she yells over the music and chatter. "Answer me! Stop laughing and don't treat me like that." She's grabbed Fancy's arm and starts shaking her.

People at the bar start to turn around. A fight? Between two chicks? Hard to get much attention over the din of the music. But Sybil is loud!

One of the cowboys has been listening to the whole shebang. Leans over. Touches Sybil on the shoulder. Gently. "M'am, is there some problem? ...can I help?"

"All I did was ask the name of a song and she's swearing and insulting me."

Several others within earshot turn to see what's going on.

The cowboy looks perplexed. "You mean the last song the band played?"

"Yes."

"It's called 'You Piss Me Off You Fuckin' Jerk.' Was that the one?"

Sybil looks at him with hate. "Oh, damn! You too?" By now Fancy is outright crying, hiccoughing, can't catch her breath.

Just then, the band takes a break. The cowboy looks bemused as he takes Sybil's hand, "I'm sorry m'am, I didn't mean no harm, but that *is* the name of the song." The onlookers catch on. They know the song well.

She gulps. "Oh. I see." At least she has the good grace to turn red and laugh with the rest of them.

New Friends

If Fancy wants a change from the Mustang, she's off to the south on the San Rodrigo Pass. Sundays in the canyon at Divine Towne Tavern with the band playing outside is a cool place to hang. Everyone sits around on tree stumps or old picnic tables, eats tri-tip sandwiches and drinks beer. The crowd includes a passel of bikers and their spiffed up and spit shined hogs, families, cowboys and Yuppies from Los Angeles. You wouldn't think it, but everyone gets along just fine enjoying the music and the cool air in the hot summer afternoons.

Friend Ruth and Fancy are at Tavern when a cool dude in soft looking leathers sidles up to Ruth and says with a knightly bow and flourish. "Might the pretty lady with the long dark hair care to come and see the old Indian caves up the road? It happens I have an extra helmet for a rider."

She looks at him for a moment. Handsome. Very. "Sorry, I wouldn't want to leave my girlfriend alone."

Fancy motions to her. "Don't worry about me. I'm fine here if you want to go with him."

"You sure?" Ruth looks around the crowd, more bikers than usual. She looks back, worried. "Will you be OK?"

Fancy knows Ruth's been dying to ride on the back of one of those big hogs—doesn't want to hold her back. "Go, go. I'm fine." Fancy's making shooing hand motions to send her on her way.

Ruth smiles back at the dude and off they go.

Fancy's sitting at a long weathered wood picnic table nodding to the music and watching the crowd. Next thing a voice at her right shoulder asks, "This seat taken?"

Fancy looks up and there is a skinny biker, tats from fingers to ears that she can see, stringy no-color hair, leather vest with no shirt and headband. Leather wristband with spikes, lots of scary skull and sword silver rings. "No," she says, "take a seat—yours if you want it." And she turns back to the band.

The guy sits down next to her and politely says, "Thank you m'am. 'Preciate it."

After a few minutes, he starts up a conversation. What he doesn't know is, Fancy enjoys a chat with anyone. Her business entailed talking to people from around the world. She has no prejudice against how a person looks, only against how they act, and the skithery looking dude has been real polite, so, when he asks, "You from around here?" She's quick to answer that she's down from Santa Isabella.

For the next hour and a half the two are deep in conversation. She learns all about him, his mother, how his house had been damaged in the last fire, his brothers, and how to make a good peach pie. They trade recipes, gardening tips, where's the best place to eat for a reasonable price in town. He owns an auto repair shop, married with several kids. Both new buddies are happy with each other and their afternoon. No involvement. Friendly talk is all they want. He buys her a beer. She buys a tri-tip sandwich and they share.

Ruth shows up and takes one look at who Fancy's been hanging out with and freaks. "Oh my god, are you all right?" Her eyes widen as she looks at the biker.

"Relax, I'm fine. Actually, more than fine. My friend and I have been having a lovely time. Real nice afternoon." Fancy turns and smiles at her new buddy, he smiles back, minus a couple a teeth. She couldn't care less, learned early on to look beyond the cover.

26

With that, the biker shakes hands with Ruth. "Pleased ta' meet you m'am, we've passed a real pleasant afternoon." Then he gets up, nods to Fancy and reaches over to give her a friendly little hug. "Good ta' spend time with you. Been a real pleasure with such a friendly lady. I'll leave you to your friend now."

Fancy returns the hug and adds, "I've enjoyed it too. Thanks for the company, and I'm going to try that peach pie recipe." As he leaves, she turns to Ruth. "So, how'd your afternoon go?"

Ruth looks a bit wired. Ignores the question. "Are you sure you're OK? That was one real strange looking dude."

"Don't worry, I'm fine…said I reminded him of his mother. He's polite, a pleasant conversationalist and a real gentleman once you get past the tats and the biker garb…owns an auto repair shop south of here."

"I can't leave you anywhere without you getting into some kind of trouble." Ruth's now harrumphing.

"So, how was your ride?"

"It was okay at first. We rode all around the mountain, great views and fun. He has a beautiful bike."

"What was the 'after the first' part?"

"Tried to make out with me in the caves. We had a bit of a tussle…but he got over it."

"…and you were worried about me?"

Mustang Concierge Service

Fancy has to go to the hospital for minor surgery. The doctor releases her a day earlier than her ride expects and she has no way home, a goodly distance. Friday afternoon, no one around to fetch her. She calls the Mustang and explains her dilemma. Ten minutes later Polly calls her back. "Elevator Paul's repairing an elevator at your hospital and will come to take you home when he finishes.

Sure enough, an hour or so later, Paul pokes his head into Fancy's room. "Ready to go?" When she nods, he wheels her and her bag out of the hospital, makes room amidst all the tools and packs her into the repair truck for the ride home. Such service!

The Mustang can handle any emergency. Got a flat tire? Call the Mustang. Need to plan a wedding? Call the Mustang. They aren't too great with funerals. With that you're on your own.

Pretty good at mating needs, could be horse stud service, dog studs or just wanting a man around for chores. Any kind of chores. Any kind of man.

Of course, that's where she found Fred.

Yeah, she knew he was the town drunk. But when he lifted his face up to her and started talking in the strange way he had, almost like he was talking to himself, she listened. Flattered? Usually he only talked to the guys, that is, if he talked at all.

He talks, she looks him over. Hands gnarled, calloused, face could use a shave, not too much beard, what she sees is shot with

28

silver. Needs a haircut. Blue and red jacket has PRCA logo which she learns stands for Professional Rodeo Cowboy Association. She looks down, worn Roper boots. Even more worn jeans and dusty black hat that's seen more than a few good years too many. Feather in the band. She sniffs. He doesn't smell bad. Actually doesn't smell like much of anything other than tobacco and a faint whiff of soap or aftershave…must be soap. That's the first good sign.

She realizes she hasn't heard a word he said until he pokes her arm. "Want 'nother?" He points to her empty glass.

"Yeah, okay. Sure."

He motions to Polly. "Get us each another one."

Polly looks at Fancy, "Same?"

"Usual. Shot of Bacardi dark with diet back, glass of ice." Polly well knows what she drinks but it gives her something to say, to try and remember what he was talking about. Didn't matter much, soon as the drinks come, he's back to morose, looking into his glass as it empties. Fancy has no idea how to speak to this man. What to say. She finishes her drink. Might as well go home.

As she slides off the bar stool, his hand reaches out and lightly holds her arm. "Want to go for dinner tomorrow? Meet you at the Saddle-Up Barn at six?"

The Mustang has just become the place where Fancy Lady loses her mind. Surely everyone needs their very own mid-life crisis? She has hers at fifty, kicks over the traces and come close to running away to join the circus. Well, not exactly, but close. Like any good filly, she's galloping to freedom, shaking her head and letting her tail fly free in the wind.

She nods assent to Fred as she leaves.

Haulin' Mercedes

Fancy's office is simple, just her and a half-day secretary to manage her consulting business. Part time bookkeeper comes once a week and does the books, taxes, and payroll.

The ranch isn't a working ranch. A couple of sheep, a very angry steer, keep the grass down in the pastures during rainy season. She feeds them hay and oats and likes the way they greet her when she walks down the hill from the house to the office. The sheep like to have their noses patted, the steer glares at her. Every morning she assures him she was not the one who cut his balls off. He never seems to believe her.

The ranch inherited Myrtle, a red and white polka-dot goat. A woman left her to board. Never picked her up. Never paid for board. Every once in a while Fancy gets an e-mail with more excuses, promising to pay board, pick up the goat. Last one she answered with a terse, "Don't bother. Now she's my goat." Never heard back.

Myrtle follows her wherever she goes. Spends most days in the office where Fancy can keep an eye on her. Myrtle is good company and generally well behaved. She has one bad habit—likes to eat Fancy's beautiful roses, dozens of them, one bush at each upright fence post around the pastures. Whenever Myrtle's wandering the ranch, Fancy watches her. As soon as she's not looking, Myrtle sidles over to one of the roses, takes a cautious nibble until she's caught. Fancy keeps a fly swatter on her desk, runs out howling and swats the rose thief on the nose. Damn goat!

When Fancy bought the ranch, she had a Mercedes. Not a great vehicle to haul hay for all the critters. Take things to the dump. Go camping.

But she loves that car. The last piece of her corporate status accoutrement. Everyone in Hollywood who's anyone at least has a Mercedes, and not one of the small cheap ones. 420 SEL or, even better 560 SEL. Diesel's for the tree huggers.

Since she moved to the Valley, those who were 'friends' solely for her business status don't bother with her anymore. It took less than an hour for the word to get around the industry she was no longer a studio exec. Forming your own consulting company quickly translates into being fired. Everyone understood the new owner brought in their own management. With the job, the title, and the big company behind gone, her power went—*Pouf!*

Couldn't do much for anyone, no more favors, big expense account gone with the wind. Nothing to be gained by being friends with her. *Kapow!* Just like in the comics. Dropped like a hot potato. Or, the more Fancy thought about it, she was now treated like two day old fish left out in the heat too long. Interesting. Entertaining. And somewhat of a relief in an odd and quirky way. She no longer had to spend time with people she wasn't overly fond of. Didn't have to laugh at stale jokes.

And best of all, didn't have to go to parties where everyone was impressing each other about how well they were doing. Most of her business career she sent her assistants to those parties, now she no longer had to dodge them. Some invitations had been hard to slither out of.

She always had good intuition, took about ten seconds max to figure out who tried to curry favor, who wanted something she might arrange. Early on, she learned how to assess the quantum of interest. To gauge in advance how big the favor might be. Job for a nephew? Financing of a series? Introductions? Didn't matter.

Easy to tell once you learn the signs. Actors were the worst, desperation could drip from their pores. She had a creed she lived by and never deviated from:

- NEVER date actors under any circumstances, aspiring writers next on the no-no list.
- Don't screw your clients and don't let the clients screw you...both literally and figuratively.
- Never discuss sexual orientation, religion or politics with business associates or clients.
- The best deals are when both sides are just a little unhappy
- Friends are not made in business unless they are from a sector you don't deal with.

When she moved from New York to L.A. it took a while to understand her new Volkswagon Rabbit was an unacceptable ride. When she took it to meetings, no one would ride with her. They told her to park and ride in their new Beemers, Mercedes or Jags. Another New York lawyer friend convinced her to buy a Mercedes so she wouldn't be a pariah. Amazing how fast everyone decided it was okay to ride in her new silver Mercedes 420 SEL. Fancy sniffed and thought how shallow the creeps were.

Once on the ranch, she could ditch the Mercedes. Didn't have to worry about being scorned by the doormen at the Beverly Hills Hotel when she handed over her keys. The studio security kiosks always seemed to raise the barrier faster for Bentleys, but her Mercedes was enough to do the trick.

Once she got used to the Mercedes, she enjoyed its grab on the California Freeways and the purr of its engine, so quiet it was hard to keep to the speed limit. Sometimes at night, roads empty, she'd open it up for a few minutes—just to clean the engine out, she'd convince herself, as she sped along at a smooth hundred-twenty MPH, the car cruising steady and sweet as a jet crossing the blue Atlantic.

Time for one last trip in the Mercedes with two girl friends, Polly and Maria. Maria's husband hauled their 5th wheeler up to St. Louis Obisbo, parked it in a campground, took off with his truck to visit some buddies. Left the ladies to their own devices. Fancy and the women arrive in the Mercedes and after their luggage is out of the trunk, she backs it almost under the 5th wheeler's overhead extension and the kingpin to fasten in a truck bed. Looks like the 5th wheeler could be hitched up to the Mercedes if it had a plate to secure the kingpin. Maybe hidden in the trunk?

The women sit out at night in front of a fire and knock back rum and cokes, laughing and telling stories. Pretty near every night some poor soul comes by, stands and looks at the Mercedes, scratches his head and walks away.

Couple or three lookey-loos actually ask how the 'little ladies' got the 5th wheeler to the site with the Mercedes. Want to know how and where the trailer plate and kingpin fit. Fancy waxes knowledgeable about a plate in the trunk, welding extra supports to the underpinning of the car and fitting the trunk lid so it slides back far enough to accommodate the kingpin. Even has a few guys believing her.

The other women sit by the fire, listening to her spiel—trying not to laugh. Waiting for some guy smart enough to ask to see how it works. Fancy's prepared for that too, has the whole trunk packed with her dirty clothes, bras and panties on top. No guy is tough enough to get her to move them aside just to see a plate. Never gets that far anyway, her patter is too good.

Once they return to Santa Isabella, the Mercedes goes away and a candy apple red Chevrolet Suburban takes its place. Hard for her to believe at first, but she falls in love with the vehicle. Pulls a horse trailer right smart. Sleeps in it, Tug curled next to her, goes camping with the girls and their families. Manages to stuff fishing poles, cooler, small barbeque and clothes enough for a week or two.

One time they go to a water park and she spends the whole time on the water slide with the kids. It's so much fun she finally

33

manages to get Tug to go down the slide with her. Soon as he hits bottom, he's not pleased, shaking water out of his nose, rubbing his ears in the grass. She towels him dry, cleans water out of his orifices, but he keeps his distance the rest of the day. He must have forgiven her as he sleeps next to her at night in the Suburban, same as always. She puts her arms around him, her face in the soft ruff around his neck, dry but still redolent of water park chorine. Dogs aren't like people; they'll forgive anything for those they love.

Disaster is imminent. A client is in town and needs Fancy to meet him at one of the studios. Mercedes gone, should she rent one? Image is everything in L.A.. Naw! Inspiration hits. She drags a hose out into the dirt in front of the office, makes a big mud puddle and leaves it for an hour or two, then drives the Suburban through the puddle. Fast—several times. Mud splashing high onto the cherry red paint. Lets it dry. Walks on the edges of the puddle with her Lucceses. Leaves mud on them too. Goes to her meeting in western hat, jeans, silver buckle and fringe jacket. Almost like a real rancher. Looks that way at least.

Studio security ushered her in faster than in the Mercedes. The European client loved the huge vehicle, admiring the vast dash, plush leather seats, pulled and poked all the levers, saw how the seats folded, made into a bed. Impressed.

So were the car hops at the client's hotel. Vied for a minute about who would get to park it when they went inside for a drink and a discussion of their meeting.

Laughing all the way back from Beverly Hills, Fancy congratulates herself. Figures she's due an Oscar. Damned if she hasn't found out a secret—a California rancher has better snob status than a New York lawyer or a studio exec with a Bentley.

Who'da thought street cred increased with mud!

Horseshoes

Fancy's ranch has a stretch of land behind the stables— four stalls long on one side, maybe fifteen feet wide to the fence along the street on the other. Weeds and dirt, old tires, rolls of wire fencing, all left by the prior owner. Fancy ignores the mess, pretends not to see it in vain hopes it will go away. Still, it's one of those things that annoy her every time she passes it—at least several times a day.

A neighbor, Adam, stops by one Sunday. "…been noticing those rolls of fencing behind the stable over there." He points to Fancy's pet peeve. "I need to extend a pasture, those 'ud work. What'cha want for 'em?"

Within minutes the deal is made. An eyesore removed. Few bucks in the kick. Good deal all around.

No sooner has Adam's truck passed out the gate when Raul stops by.

"Fancy, I'm taking a load to the dump, want me to take those old tires? No use for them here, just dirt collectors."

"Fabulous. I'll pay the dump fee." And off go the tires. No excuse left to not clean up the area. Fancy rolls a large garbage can over, plastic bags, work gloves and starts the dirty job.

Half hour into her work, a grey truck pulls up. Jim sticks his head out. "What's up? Need a hand?" Big smile on his face as he ambles over, pulling on work gloves.

While later, another truck pulls up. This time it's Smiley.

35

"Hey, Fancy, can I give you a hand? I'm hiding out for a few hours. My wife's family is in town, and I don't want them hunting me down at the Mustang."

The two men set to work. Fancy goes in the house, comes back with an ice chest of cold beer, stack of ham and cheese sandwiches. Two more guys have joined Jim and Smiley. She's glad she made extra sandwiches.

She knows something's up, just not exactly what it is. "What's with all you guys? Don't you work enough during the week."

Jim looks a little sheepish. "Tell the truth, we've been looking at this nice little strip for some time. Thought it would make a perfect place for horseshoes."

"Jim found out Adam needed fencing, remembered seeing the rolls behind the stable, thought they'd do the trick. Adam called Raul, told him he'd picked up the fencing; Raul's turn to come for the tires."

"So, since the tires and fencing were gone, you just thought you'd stop by and see if I could use a little help?"

Jim has a little more color in his face then when he started. He's shuffling his feet.

"We didn't think you'd mind. Long as we kept the area clean, no beer cans or cigarette stubs or nothing." Smiley to the rescue.

Fancy can't help laughing. She has just become proud owner of the local horseshoe pit. Seems everyone came prepared. Adam arranges a pit on one end of the strip, another about forty feet away. Bags of sand hauled over and dumped in. Metal stakes banged with a sledge hammer into each pit. Within an hour the game has started. Three more trucks pull into the driveway, lining up in front of the stable.

Truck dogs, hesitant at first, sniff and introduce their rear ends to the ranch dogs, showing them they are friend not foe. Soon a small pack is circling the ranch; the ranch cats have taken to the roofs—watching with disgust.

Every Wednesday and Friday the trucks pull into the driveway, park, drivers take out their coolers and beers, horseshoes, and the game begins. There are regulars and visitors. If a visitor gets out of hand, the regulars throw him out or get him to quiet down.

One afternoon one of the visitors gets pushy with a regular. Not quite a fight, but stupid drunk handsy stuff that can easily turn into an all out scuffle. Tug doesn't like it. No way. The one being pushed is a nice big friendly guy with an equally friendly female Golden. Tug backs up, gives the visitor a warning growl or two. Jerk pays no heed, pushes the regular again, more serious this time. Tug launches himself on the drunk jerk, bites his ass and hangs on. The guy screams, jumps around trying to swat the terrier off but Tug hangs in there, swinging from his jaws.

Jim steps in, grabs Tug and pulls him off. Keeps him close, tucked under his arm.

The visitor is red faced and brandishing the iron rake for smoothing the pits that was resting against the stable wall. "Give me that fucking mutt. I'll kill him right here. I swear!"

Another regular, the local cowboy Tug was defending, takes his champion from Jim, holding him tight against his chest. "Listen you asshole, Tug was protecting me from you, stupid. You'll have to come through me to get to this brave guy." With that, two more of the other regulars stand at his side, ready to defend Tug, now official Keeper of the Peace—Dog Sheriff.

Soon there's a line of guys against the drunk.

Smiley steps forward, not smiling, "I think you need to pick up your shoes and leave. Now. ...and don't come back."

The guy shuffles a bit, starts to protest, sees too many angry looking eyes.

As he pulls out of the driveway, he rolls down his window, sticks his head out and yells, "Fuck you all and your stupid game anyway. Won't find me playing here anymore." The truck spins out of the driveway amid laughter and a forest of raised middle fingers.

***

Christy is Fancy's friend from L.A.. Tall, beautiful, long dark hair and a figure that can make a man cry. She knows how to dress—knows how to tease. She also likes to have fun.

Christy and Fancy like to visit the local casino late at night. Around midnight they look at each other, nod, and hit the road. They can sit at their favorite machines, all full up with money. Good time to hit a few jackpots. Two hours and they go home, usually with a little jingle in their pockets. They sit on the porch, look at the stars, sip some red wine and laugh.

When Christy's Beemer pulls into the driveway to spend the next weekend, she dodges trucks lined in front of the stable. Hauling her suitcase into her room she calls back to Fancy. "What's with all the trucks and guys standing behind the stable?"

Sighing, Fancy explains the horseshoe pits. "Now all the guys come two days a week and play horseshoes. Doesn't bother me much, I just leave them to their game."

"You don't play with them?

"No, I've got no idea how to play…doesn't appeal."

"Mind if I go see what's going on? Looks like fun to me."

"Go for it. Plenty of male pulchritude to scope out. Watch out." She cocks an eyebrow and smiles.

With that, Christy's out the door.

Two hours later, she's back. Red patent leather flats covered with dust, big smile on her face.

"So, ya have fun?"

"Yeah, I did. Good game and lots of fun. It reminded me of when I was a kid and played bocce ball with my father. The guys showed me how to play. We changed teams so I got the knack of it…they invited me to stay and play again Wednesday. Do you mind?"

"Not at all, stay as long as you like." Fancy's happy for the company. She and Christy don't get on each other's nerves. Both like to hang out at the Mustang, go for dinner, stop at the casino, and at home, respect each other's privacy. Best buddies.

The next day, unexpected, the guys are back at the pit. One of the local ZZ Top look-alikes knocks on the door. "Hope you don't mind, Fancy. We thought we'd get in an extra day playing shoes. If it's all right with you?"

"Sure, go ahead. Doesn't bother me."

"…uh, and…uh…is Christy around? Thought she might like a few more lessons?"

After they've been playing for a while, Fancy ambles on down to see what is really going on. Seems the guys are taking turns teaching Christy how to pitch. 'Teaching' means standing behind her, left hand on her waist, right hand reaching around to hold her arm as she pitches. Just happens the pitching arm brushes her overly endowed breastworks on the way. Or, in other words, the guys cop a feel.

When Fancy watches, Christy winks at her and rolls her eyes. Smart gal.

Jim calls out. "Come on Fancy, let me show you how to play. Then you can join us."

"No thanks. Not really my thing, but you all go ahead." Not a snowballs chance in hell, she thinks.

When Christy gets back to the house, the two of them laugh. "Sure, I know what they're doing. But I don't care; I get the lessons."

Christy becomes a semi regular at horseshoes, the cowboys entranced by the beautiful willowy woman who plays a mean game of shoes. They bet on the games, and Christy is not only in demand to be on a team, she often ends up with a few extra bucks. Nice, since she's between jobs.

Fancy laughs as she thinks of her friend supplementing her income playing horseshoes with the cowboys. Not too bad for a debutant from a fashionable California family. You go Christy! Never can tell about people.

The Saddest Day

Tug is sick. Fancy knows it's only a matter of time, he's close to thirteen and the vet says he has a brain tumor. Can't operate on him, nothing to do but give steroid shots to shrink the swelling and she's not sure it's the humane thing to do. Vet has told her it's time. Her heart cries in pain.

Poor guy has trouble moving his hind legs. Fancy jury rigs a sling out of an old tee-shirt, puts it around his belly to take the pressure off the back legs, he moves them off the ground, walks on his front paws as they go outside so he can do his business while she holds him up. He's a real gentleman and she sees he's upset when he messes in the house. Not his fault, but hard to explain to a dog. The sling works for a while, but Fancy knows she has to face the inevitable.

The morning she finds him lying in a pool of urine and excrement, it's clear what she has to do. His eyes look up at her. She sees his pain and sorrow. She holds his head, ruffles the fur around his ears the way he likes and knows the day has come. Picking him up, she takes him outside, holds him while he does his business and then washes him off. The sun is out, she spreads a towel on the grass, puts him on it to dry in the warm air. Time to call the vet. She puts it off until after she cleans the pantry where he's been sleeping. Goes out and helps him off the blanket for another pee. Her beautiful blonde buddy is rail thin, shaking and in pain. She knows the last kind thing she can do for him is to let him take his final sleep. The delay is her fault, she doesn't want to let him go.

The vet says to bring him in. She puts his bed in the back of the Suburban and lifts him onto it. Tears begin as she closes the back hatch. Inevitable. But not easy.

She holds his head as the first tranquilizer shot takes effect, strokes him and tells him he was the best dog ever. Does he know? Can he understand? He puts a paw out on her knee where his head rests. Goodbye Tug, I love you, she thinks as his body grows still.

The vet will have his remains cremated and returned to her in a small box. No way will her dear friend be dumped in with garbage. Respect. Fancy believes it's due to the animals who bring love and joy to a human life.

The ranch is quiet without Tug. Fancy feels like she echoes in the house without him. Myrtle the goat sits on the front porch and seems to be mourning too. No one to run around the ranch with, snooze next to in the office. They were always together. Even the guys are upset when they come to play horseshoes. He was their protector.

Fancy's not ready to go to the humane society like all her friends tell her. "Get another dog. There are plenty of them around who need a good home."

"You'll be doing a good deed for an animal in need."

Maybe later, just not right now. The pain of loss is too raw.

Would it be a sign of disrespect? How can you replace love so easily? Animals are close companions, not fungible substances like a chair or a car—one pretty much as good as another. Love isn't like that, whether it's a dog or a person, needs to be the right chemistry.

Four-footed Company

A friend from Europe knows Fancy likes dogs. Found out she had to put her beloved Soft Coated Wheaton down. A month later, she has a call from TWA. Two Jack Russell Terriers have arrived for her. She only wanted one. Life is like that. Sometimes you get more than you bargain for, sometimes less.

The two Jacks are like jumping beans when they arrive. Seventeen hours in a crate had not helped their active dispositions. The friend who sent them told her to keep the one she liked and give the other away. The family had too many pups and were looking for a sucker to fob them off on. Fancy was happy to oblige.

When she picks them up, the clerk at the freight desk asks, "What's in the crate?"

"Puppies." She answers.

"Oh yeah, the puppies from hell!" is his response.

The first time she looks at the little male, she knows he's going to be her new pal. The beautiful symmetrical brown, white and black markings on his face included two brown commas over his eyes that make him always look like he's worried. Irresistible. Tommy is his name, and he moves into her heart.

The little female does not like her brother and bites him at every opportunity. The poor guy hides from her, but she hunts him out for the next fight. Fancy finds her a good home. Discord is unacceptable on Fancy's ranch.

A while later, with all the livestock around, she thinks an

Australian shepherd might be just the ticket. Help her move the stock from one pasture to another.

Also, she likes the idea of a big dog, a real truck dog to park in front of the Mustang.

A friend who works at the local humane society calls her.

"Hi Fancy, got your dog."

"What dog?"

"Aussie mix off the Res. Typical. You know, midnight strangers passing through."

"Great, shall I come down and get it."

"Not yet, she's only two or three weeks old. Got the litter just before it was drowned. One of our workers grabbed a burlap sack with eleven pups in it. Can you imagine?"

Fancy's heartbroken. She hates the idea of drowning puppies, but it's common. Hard to make some people spay or neuter, easier they think to kill the pups when they come.

Her friend continues. "I found yours, just perfect."

"Can't I come and see them? Pick out my own?"

"Nope, just relax. You'll like her, I promise."

A week later, Fancy gets another call from the humane society, this time it's her friend's boss. "This Fancy?"

"Yes."

"Ever raise a litter of pups?"

"Yes."

"What ja'feed 'em?"

"Pablum, powdered milk and infant formula, added some powdered baby vitamins. Shots at four and six weeks. Should be weaned and on softened puppy kibble by five, six weeks."

"Yep, you got it right. Come pick up your pup. Momma can't feed them all and we have to get some gone."

Fancy stops at the store for baby doll bottles and supplies, heads to the humane society where she signs papers, makes a donation and is handed a small ball of fur—black, grey, white and tan, long tail but the rest looks like Australian shepherd. One ear is up, the other down. Fancy asks to see the momma. She looks like

43

Benji, but tired. Real tired. Must have been had by every one of those midnight strangers on the res, each pup around her looks different.

Fancy holds the tiny bundle of fur close to her chest and it snuggles into her warmth. "Ethel. That's going to be your name. Like Ethel from 'The Honeymooners'." The pup just snuggles closer.

Ethel lives in the office during the day and the ranch house at night. She and Tom take to each other from the start, always together. Myrtle, the goat, following along behind. Ethel puts up with the dirty tricks Tom plays on her. She has a good disposition, smart as a whip, stubborn as a mule.

Ethel has her own ideas about life. They go like this:

Baths are bad, make a dog smell strange. Every time Fancy grabs her, hoses her down, scrubs her clean with good-for-the-skin-makes-fur-shine shampoo, Ethel heads for the pastures and rolls in cow shit. Fancy hoses her off again, ties her to the porch in the sun to dry. Ethel chews through the rope to head for the pastures. Exasperated, Fancy puts her in a large kennel crate until she dries, takes her for a walk around the ranch on a leash so she can do her business. Then locks her in the house for the night, hoping by the morning, Ethel will forget about the indignity of the bath she's been made to suffer through.

Every male who arrives at the ranch belongs to Ethel, especially if they are good looking cowboys—the younger the better. Ethel can spot them a mile off, runs to greet them, and will sit with her long muzzle on their leg, warm brown eyes telegraphing eternal love, until they give up and caress her soft coat. That is, unless she's made one of her usual runs to cow pie heaven and her coat is caked with sticky cow shit. Damn dog!

She throws up on every trip in the car or truck. Motion sickness. Some truck dog! Friend Clara gets the idea to put motion sickness wristbands on her. Puts them on her front paws and wraps them until the little button presses a pressure point on her paw. Unbelievable. It works! Fancy keeps the wristbands in

44

the back of the Suburban and puts them on Ethel every time she heads into Los Angeles with her menagerie.

Fancy's friend Jane likes dogs and doesn't have any. She takes care of Ethel more often than not when a long car trip is in the offing. Why torture the dog? Fancy could give her a few reasons but refrains.

Jane gets the point one night at Fancy's when a bunch of local friends show up—young good looking cowboys as part of the crew. Ethel won't even look at Jane, who has been treating her with leftovers, back rubs and ear scratches for months. Fickle bitch! All Jane got when she called Ethel was a talk-to-the-tail sashay as the dog ran off to follow the cutest guy around the ranch.

Ethel has a favorite toy, a shearling covered gingerbread man shape with a squeaker, called "Bite The Man." They're only available at Restoration Hardware and Fancy buys them whenever she finds them. Ethel has six in her collection and loves each and every one. At night, she arranges her 'men' in a semi-circle, one paw on each end, her long muzzle planted in the middle. Guarding her herd. As soon as she falls asleep, Tom snatches the 'men' one at a time and hides them from her. The next day she spends hours searching so she can have all her 'men' together again for bedtime.

Fancy watches this game with fascination. If Ethel can't find one of her 'men' she's frantic, looking under cushions and beds, digging in the dirty clothes basket, all the while Tom sits on his favorite ottoman, paws crossed, with what Fancy is sure is a dog smirk. Ethel won't give up until she finds the last 'man'. As she arranges them again for the night, Tom watches. Waits. Fancy wonders if this is a game they play or is Tom actually torturing Ethel?...and enjoying the heck out of it! Another question never to be answered.

Ethel is a terrible watch dog! Strangers come to the ranch and she ignores them. Unless they are cowboys, then she flirts. It makes Tom, watchdog extraordinaire, furious. He wants his pack to put up a united front to repel invaders. Ethel couldn't care less. Tom is wily, he has his ways. As soon as he spots a stranger, he runs to wherever Ethel is sleeping, bites her on the rump, hard, until she snaps to attention and joins him in barking his warning. Her heart is never in it, Fancy can see her tail wagging, hopeful the stranger might turn out to be the FedEx man with a biscuit, or, better still, a very good looking guy.

Myrtle the goat is a much better ally for Tom. She follows him around the ranch and is always ready to back him up.

Fancy's asleep when a loud row outside wakes her. Fierce and panicked barking from Tom. Not good. She sleeps with a baseball bat next to her bed. Just in case. Grabs the bat, into her slippers and out to see about the ruckus. Tom's snarling and barking at a mangy coyote. The coyote's holding its ground just in front of the porch. Must have slipped onto the ranch looking for some water and easy pickings. Summer drought makes food and water hard to come by in the mountains.

Tom's tough, but not a match for the much bigger animal. Fancy's frantic he'll be hurt or killed. Coyotes hunt in packs, send one out as a decoy to draw the prey out and then they all attack. Terriers never give up and the coyote's not backing down, daring Tom to follow. Fancy has to keep him from chasing the coyote or he's meat for dinner.

Ethel slinks along so close to Fancy she can feel the dog tremble. Not going to be any use in this fight, Fancy thinks as she runs to Tom's defense, shouting, waving her arms, brandishing the bat. Never fought a coyote before, but she's willing to do anything to save her pal.

The coyote turns, some sound caught his ear. Myrtle pounds up the lawn and before Fancy even realizes what happens, she lowers her head, butts the coyote full speed. Broadside. Hard. The critter flies into the air. Tom and Fancy watch wide eyed. Ethel runs to cower behind a porch chair. As soon as the critter lands, it takes off whimpering, tail between its legs. Decision made: this is not a ranch with easy pickings. Tom snaps at its hind legs, Myrtle runs next to him, head lowered, primed for another charge.

46

Fancy yells for them to come back. They stop at the fence line, watching as the coyote slithers under the bottom rail to safety.

By now, Ethel has already slunk back to her bed. Fancy, with Tom at her side, sits with Myrtle for a few minutes, telling her what a good goat she is. Getting a bright idea, she goes into the house, finds a box of crackers, lays them in front of Myrtle. Every heroine needs a good reward. Her other treat is to let her sleep on the porch love seat. Fancy even forgives the occasional nibble on the wicker furniture. It'd take more than routing a coyote to have her forgive Myrtle's rose depredations...but she did save Tom. Maybe someday...

The next day, she orders a new sign for the front gate: "Warning – Attack Goat "

Ranch Managers

Ranch owners, at least new and inexperienced ones, have no clue how much work it takes to maintain a ranch. After a few months of rude awakenings and more rain, Fancy figures it out. Mostly.

Fred, her cowboy, gives her pointers about taking care of things, but he's too busy with his own ranch to help much. He suggests she needs someone full time, living on the ranch. Why not trade a place to live for keeping the place up? She thinks it's an excellent idea.

Her first is a real flop, much too friendly. See's Fancy lives alone most of the time, and thinks he might be just what she needs. What she needs is him gone.

Next one is even worse. Good recommendations. Studied animal training. She puts him in the apartment. Wrong move. Turns out he's a junkie and an alcoholic. The second time she bails him out of jail for starting a fight at the Mustang, he's history.

After she fires him, she goes to the apartment to make sure the place is cleaned out. As she opens the door, a feral smell hits her and she gags. The scent of an animal living there and no one's bothered to clean its cage.

She throws everything out, furniture, wall to wall carpeting, beds, kitchen pots and pans. Takes a month to get the stench out, even with a new paint job and a couple gallons of Kilz. From then on her pretty guest cottage will be reserved for visiting friends.

Plan A didn't work too well. Fancy goes for Plan B. Buys several used trailers, one for a rental, other for a ranch manager. The new deal is: one of the trailers rent free in exchange for keeping the ranch in good shape. Feeding the animals when she travels. Take care of Tom, Myrtle and Ethel. Needs someone she can trust. So she can come and go as she pleases, and she pleases often. Fred asks around, helps her find someone responsible.

Her new manager, Donald, a tall cowboy, came to Santa Isabella a few years past. Best butt in the Valley, and always in tight Wranglers, nice shirt, big hat and broad shoulders. Fabulous body, well worth a second look, bright carrot-orange hair, bit plain in the face but no way coyote-ugly. Exactly the opposite of what Fancy likes. Perfect!

Ethel falls in love with Don at first sight. She follows him around all day long, adoration shining in her soft brown eyes. Sleeps under his trailer at night. Fancy, who bottle fed her, stayed up nights with her, trained her with love, is forgotten in her passion for Don. And Ethel is not the only one.

Don does odd jobs at other ranches. Fancy doesn't pay him, he just pays her rent with twenty hours a week of work. He's got a list of chores. Does them on his own time. Got free electric in the trailer, just needs to earn eating and entertainment money elsewhere.

Fancy notices a lot more local women have taken to calling on her, tap on her office door, invite themselves for a chat. Not her stellar personality, she's sure.

They come to stare at Don, jeans taut as he bends over to trim the roses, muscles flexing under his shirt as he tosses hay to the livestock. Best views are on hot days when he takes his shirt off. Fancy smiles to herself. Seems her ranch has become more interesting than Chippendale's.

Mornings, as she drinks her coffee on the porch, enjoying the mountain air carrying the fresh grass and rose smell of the ranch, she often sees cars slip out the gate. Even expensive quiet motors give their approach away, no matter how silently they arrive, stealthy park in the shadows below Don's trailer. Not big ranch trucks, no way. Don's visitors drive the finest—Beemers, Mercedes, a Porsche or two.

Wives, left on ranches, trophies of husbands hard at work in Los Angeles, get bored sometimes. Training horses and riding is fine during the day, works up a good sweat, but all the bouncing between their thighs also works up a need. Tough on young women with no husband around to satisfy it.

And one thing she's been noticing. Don's wardrobe. Been a big change since he's moved to the ranch. New Wranglers, pressed and clean. Pair of Ropers, heels not worn and shiny black for line dancing or Sunday evening when husbands head back to Los Angeles for early Monday morning meetings. New tack for his horse, hand tooled and trimmed with silver Conchos. Leather jacket, button up the front with western style yokes. Fancy touches it one day. Soft. Buttery leather probably Italian made. Cost a ransom she computes.

Fancy doesn't mind. Long as no one gets shot by a jealous man...or woman. But good things often end. Don makes a few silly mistakes. Couple of outstanding warrants earns him three months in the hoosegow. Out in two for good behavior. But he has plenty of visitors. All his 'lady friends' set up a schedule so they don't collide. The BMW on Monday, Mercedes on Tuesday, Porsches Wednesday and Thursday. Damn if Fancy knows who comes the rest of the week, but she knows for sure Ethel would have liked to have her day too. Dog spent most of the two months mooning around Don's empty trailer with a soulful look. Fancy has no pity, faithless creature gave up the one who saved and nurtured her for another. Not like Fancy's jealous or anything.

Something must have happened to let the cat out of the bag while Don was away. Gossip in the Mustang maybe? Those who live all week long in the Valley know everyone's secrets. The ones who work in the city and come for the weekends aren't generally part of the local grapevine. Maybe one of the trophy owners spent a week at his ranch, fishing in the lake, drinking beer in the

Mustang, and got tuned in. Or maybe one got wise and came home early. Fancy doesn't know who spilled the beans, or cat, or whatever. But once Don was back at the ranch, the old steady stream of cars dwindled to an occasional one now and then. Ethel is clearly happy to have him to herself and even manages to worm her way into sleeping with him inside the trailer most nights. On the floor, he tells Fancy. Not to mess up the nice upholstery on the couches.

Don's mellow. Doesn't seem to mind the loss of his old celebrity. He's much like Fancy. Keeps to himself, once in a while joins her for a cup of morning coffee on the porch or a glass of wine before dinner. They're companionable at arm's length. Suits both just fine until a Cadillac starts showing up on a regular basis. Seems a real estate lady from the Valley has taken a liking to that fine butt. And she's single.

Fancy figures it's only a matter of time before she has to find a new manager. She's learned nothing lasts forever. But still...drat!

Snake Dancer

Pat drives up from Los Angeles to stay for a long weekend. He's Fancy's dearest and best friend. Well over six feet tall and generously described as portly, an elegant silver beard frames his handsome face. Someone once described him as being the neatest fat man they had ever seen.

Pat is gay, no bones about it. They've been best friends for over twenty years and sexual predilections are not an issue of concern to either of them. They worked in New York at the same time, and Fancy was thrilled when Pat's job was transferred to L.A. at the same time she moved. They're bridge partners, drinking buddies and friends who tell each other secrets they wouldn't dare relate to another soul.

As soon as he settles into his room at the ranch, they head out for cocktails, dinner and a nightcap or two. Back in their New York City drinking days, life was easy, all they had to do was call a cab to bring them home. Now Fancy is the designated driver so she's careful, slows down and finishes up with diet Cokes, no rum. Pat is free to do as he likes.

Pat is normally the picture of charming masculinity until he gets a few too many of his beloved Tanqueray martinis under his belt. After the first four or five doubles, restraint flies away as the "queen" inside spreads her wings. Once that happens, stories flow, his favorite is how much he's in demand by the 'chubbie chasers.'

They have their cocktails, dinner and stop at the Mustang for a nightcap before heading home. She opens the garage door for easy house entry, and as she gets out of the car, hears a tell-tale rattle. Rattlers come down from the mountains in the summer dry spells to find water and easy pickings of mice, moles and small cats. Fancy hops back in the car and puts her brights on. She wears boots, but still doesn't want to step on a rattler.

Pat spots it first. "Look, over to your left on the lawn. Big son-of-a-bitch." Words a bit slurred, not his usual vocabulary. It's the gin.

She looks and there it is, coiled with head and rattle up. Pat's right about the size.

Before she can say a word, Pat is out of the car on the opposite side from the rattler and into the garage. Fancy thinks to herself, sure, leave me in the damn car on the side with the snake. She's trying to figure out how to crawl over to the passenger side when Pat emerges from the garage, long tined pitchfork in one hand, spade in the other. What in hell? What's he up to?

In the blink of an eye, this quite drunk, very large, urban man is dancing ballet on the lawn with his weapons held high over his head. First he does a pirouette or two, shaking the garden implements as he turns. The snake seems interested, rattling in time to some unheard music.

Hardly taking aim, Pat throws the pitchfork. Accurate. He's pined the snake's head to the lawn between the tines. The rattles are louder and faster as the tail thrashes about. Two more pirouettes and another swift movement launches the hoe with the other hand, neatly severing the rattlers head from its body. All done in the blink of an eye and with the grace, style and surety of a three hundred and fifty pound Nureyev.

For once in her life, Fancy's speechless, totally impressed! The speed and confidence of his movements caught her completely off-guard.

New respect for her friend blooms like one of her fence roses. A side of Pat she had never imagined. And not only drunk out of his socks, but well into his queenie phase no less!

53

He leaves the snake on the lawn—both pieces of it. Stows his weaponry neatly back in the garage, and sashays into the house without a word. Serene smile on his face, a wobble to his walk.

The next morning when Fancy lets the dogs out, the snake is gone. Figures the neighborhood cats, owls, or a passing coyote had a good meal.

Late morning, Pat strolls out for breakfast when the aroma of coffee wafts into his room. Fancy thinks he looks only slightly worse for wear, all things considered.

"Here's coffee for my hero."

He gives her a blank and somewhat bleary stare.

"The snake disappeared over night. Must have been eaten by a hungry critter. I was afraid there might be more around but I looked before I let the dogs out.

He looks at her with confusion. "What snake? Who hero?"

"The snake you killed last night…you're my hero."

"Huhh?"

He doesn't remember a thing! No recollection of any snake nor does he remember killing it. When she recounts the story to him of his bravery and adroit snakes-man-ship in dispatching the monster, he looks at her in disbelief.

Fancy's sure he thinks she made the whole thing up just to kid him about drinking too many martinis. Every time she brings the subject up, he scoffs and laughs, telling her to stop, the joke is no longer funny. She has no dead snake as proof, even though the picture of his nimble snake dance is forever etched in her memory.

Could the ranch be magic? Brings out things in people they don't even know they had in them. Fancy wonders what it's been bringing out in her.

Horses Sneeze Too

Fancy's family is like most modern families, not so close. Mother and Sisters all live on the East Coast. Karen and Lars, her niece and nephew, keep in touch with Fancy, the rest of the family—no contact. The Sisters let years go by without a word. Until they want something. Always been the same. Karen and Lars visit, sometimes Lars stays, maybe a few months, maybe longer. Karen often takes vacations at the ranch. Once stayed as long as six months between jobs. Brought up in the suburbs, they're not much for ranch life, but they like the softer California winter weather.

In the thirty plus years Fancy's been a working professional, Mother has been to see where her only successful daughter works—never. Fancy flies East to see her at least twice, sometimes three times a year.

Big news arrives. Her mother is coming to visit. Karen will accompany her.

Fancy loves Karen. Mother—not so much. Fancy grew up to understand she'd been born solely to anchor her father, Pops, to his predatory secretary. Younger by years. Beautiful. On the prowl for a rich man to pay for her upkeep and her two daughters by a previous, and less affluent, marriage. Nevertheless, Mother was considered a trophy by Pops. The trophy already had children, but Fancy was security.

Fancy's childhood is mostly a blank. Mother spent it with the Sisters. Fancy always excluded. Busy with private secrets, they sucked attention from each other like vampires suck blood.

Books were Fancy's salvation. She learned to read early and devoured anything she could get her hands on.

When Fancy was old enough to understand the dynamic, she forgave Mother. Forgave the Sisters. Kept them all at a distance. No love lost. On either side. Fancy took over Pop's role as family provider. Whatever Mother wants, Fancy gave—televisions, new furnace, chandeliers, clothes for Sisters. Security. That's what she was. Always had been.

When Mother and Karen arrive, Fancy introduces them to Fred. He's cowboy po-lite, shakes hands, kisses their cheeks, "Pleased ta' meet you both. Fancy's told me a lot of nice things 'bout you." Hat off, he almost bows. Big smile. He's actually happy to meet them. Fancy's touched. His momma taught him manners.

Next night, Fancy invites Fred and his father, Hitch, for dinner. Both arrive with pressed Wranglers, polished rodeo buckles on their best belts, clean western shirts and the fresh scent of Ralph Lauren Chaps wafting off close shaved cheeks.

At dinner, Fancy takes note, Fred doesn't drink much with his father around. Hitch tells of moving herds across to Texas. Round-ups at a time when they still gathered several thousand head of cattle even in California. Mother's entranced. Her first real cowboy.

Karen, Fred and Fancy snag a smoke outside. They stand in an open doorway. Listen to Mother and Hitch chat. Friendly. Companionable.

Karen laughs.

"What's up?" Fancy asks.

"They're flirting." Karen giggles. Seems funny to someone in their twenties when the oldsters—both well into their eighties—can still flirt.

"How can you tell?" Fred is interested.

"They're comparing aches and illnesses."

Two days later, Fancy needs to catch up on some office work. Fred invites the women for lunch and a tour of the Valley. Growing up in the Valley he knows all the local secrets, who did what to who, remembers stories passed down by Hitch.

Mother wears a pant suit, hair perfectly coiffed, a cascade of white frills and ruffles peeking out of her jacket. Comfortable shoes. Fred studies her attire, nods.

Karen wears pristine white slacks, pink lace blouse, white high heeled sandals, lacy pink shawl. Carries a woven handbag. Fred doesn't nod, looks skeptical, says nothing. Piles them into his truck. Looks to Fancy like he swept it out. Ran a rag over the bench seat. Karen sits where the busted spring will poke her in the butt.

Several hours later, Mother seems all right as Fred hands her out of the truck.

Karen, a bit the worse for wear.

They thank him for lunch and the tour of the Valley.

"My pleasure. Not often I get to take two beautiful women out for lunch. Made my reputation for sure." Polite. Sober. He doffs his hat. Bends forward, almost bows. Fancy's pleased. Dust and exhaust trail the truck through the gate.

"Okay Karen, what's up?" Couldn't be too bad, Mother's trying not to laugh. "Fred do something to upset you?"

"Oh no. He was very nice. Drove us all around, told us about all the big ranches up in the hills, what their history was and which movie stars now owned them. We went to his ranch. To see Rosie." Karen seems to be suppressing a cringe.

"Gram stayed in the car. We walked to the corral." She looks down at her sandals. Not quite right for walking in dirt. At least it hadn't rained lately.

"He gave me an apple to feed Rosie. She let me pat her nose—it felt like velvet.

"So why are you making such a face?"

"She sneezed! Rosie sneezed! All over me. Horse snot! My blouse to my slacks! Horse snot"

Karen is one of those people who never gets mussed up or dirty. Everything always perfect: hair, nails, make-up. Clothes with never a wrinkle, even after a long plane trip.

Mother has her back turned. Fancy's sure she's holding back laughter. Positive. Her shoulders are shaking.

Karen continues. "Fred didn't think anything of it. He wasn't even concerned with the mess. I didn't know what to do. First I tried to rub it off with a Kleenex. No luck, it just smeared it all over. Then Fred handed me a rag he had in the truck. It was dirtier than my blouse. He didn't seem to understand, didn't get it. He handed me back in the truck and drove to the restaurant as if nothing happened." As she's talking, Karen unbuttons her shirt, delicately, two-fingered, trying not to touch it as it drops to the floor.

"Then, when we walked into the dining room, I was so embarrassed. You can't imagine! Had my shawl held in front of me the whole time. As soon as we sat down, I asked where the ladies room was—to wash my shirt and slacks."

Mother, red in the face, gave up trying not to laugh.

The disrobing maneuver has moved to formerly white slacks. Karen wriggles out of them as she continues.

"Can you imagine what he said to me? When I came back. He said 'You didn't have to worry. This is ranch country. Bet half the people in here have horse snot on 'em. Probably won't even notice.'" Huffing, Karen kicks the pile of clothes across the great room.

Within minutes, Fancy hears the washing machine beginning its cycle. By the time Karen is back on the porch, her hair's wet and she's wearing old jeans and the new Ropers she bought while on her adventure with Fred. Better ranch attire.

Fancy looks down at her own expensive ostrich Luccheses, now a bit worse for wear, even though she cleaned them in honor of Mother's visit. Wouldn't have bothered otherwise.

The next day, Fancy serves breakfast to Mother on the porch.

58

A typical Valley day is unfolding across the ranch. The willow branches sway in a light breeze and the brilliant blue sky whispers promises of perfection. Setting a tray, with coffee regular, a warm croissant with butter and jam, on the side table, Fancy heads into the kitchen for her coffee and Karen's.

She's planned a lovely day for them—a visit to several wineries, then lunch at her favorite restaurant overlooking the vineyards. Maybe even time to stop at a miniature horse ranch to see the adorable newborns, no bigger than a large dog and still wobbly on their spindly legs.

By the time she and Karen walk outside to join her, Mother is red faced and swatting flies from the food.

Mother starts. Petulant, "I don't know why you have to live here! Out here in the sticks... Why don't you come back to New York, get a decent place, a job in the City as an attorney?"

"Maybe because I like it here? Because I like the weather, the people—life on a ranch?"

"You had such a beautiful house in Beverly Hills. Why did you give it up? Now you have all those filthy animals around you...horses outside your kitchen window. Flies all over the place."

Karen looks shocked. "But Gram, this is like paradise. I've never seen anyplace so beautiful—the mountains, vineyards, the ranches. I'd live here in a second if I could afford it."

"What do you know? You'd want to live where you have horse snot on you all the time? I don't think so!" Her 'harrumph' is silent and understood.

Her voice smooth and comforting, Fancy's willing a diversion from the mercurial anger she grew up accustomed to. "Mother, it's a ranch. Horses live on a ranch. You grew up on a farm. Weren't there animals around? Flies?"

"Yes, but it was because we had to. You don't have to live with horses outside your kitchen window. You're rich. We were poor." Fancy hears an imaginary foot stomp. More than petulant.

"Sorry Mom, it's my life and my choice. I live here because I want to."

"Well, Miss High and Mighty, you can live like trash on a filthy ranch if you want, just don't ever expect me to come and visit here again." Mother pushes her breakfast tray aside and strides into the house.

All the color drained from Karen's face. She'd been looking forward to the day Fancy had planned and it seems it's not going to happen.

Fancy gives up. First of all, she's no longer rich, and fast becoming poorer every minute. And for pity's sake, of course there are horses outside her kitchen window. It's a ranch. Another ranch next door.

As she takes the untouched breakfast tray back inside, she finally gets it. No matter what she does, in her mother's eyes, it's never going to be right. Took a long time for Fancy to realize the misdirected anger at her success because Mother and Sisters are the ones who always benefited. But now she understands. Mother resents depending on her. She doesn't trust Fancy because she can't control her. Mother wants the Sisters to be the successful ones, the all-mighty providers of security. She has them under her thumb. The jealousy she holds on behalf of her other daughters is the poison that divides the family.

Success for the Sisters was never going to happen, especially at this late time in their lives. They have always been pilot fish, her mother the shark. Too late to change now.

She heads down to her office. Might as well get some work done since the tour seems to be cancelled. An hour or so later, Karen comes down to the office.

"What's up with Mother?" Fancy asks.

"I don't know what she's up to. She's in your bedroom on the telephone and I can't hear what or who she's talking to. I knocked on the door to see if she wanted anything and she told me to go away and leave her alone. So I did." Karen sighed. Fancy thinks she looks like a kid who was just told she couldn't go to the zoo when it had been promised.

60

"Come on, kiddo. Let's not let her spoil our day. How about we pick up some sandwiches at the deli and head to one of the wineries, get a nice bottle of Sauvignon Blanc and have a picnic under the trees. Sound like a plan?"

"Yeah! I'm up for that." Karen is almost out the door before she turns. "But what about Gram? Can we leave her alone in the house? Won't she be pissed off?"

"She's already pissed off. She told you to go away and leave her alone, right?"

"Well…yes."

"So, how much more pissed off can she get?"

When they come back to the ranch later in the day after a pleasant afternoon, her mother stands rigid in the doorway, hands on her hips, with an announcement. "I've changed our flights. Karen and I leave tomorrow instead of in three days. I don't want to spend another minute in this awful place. I know when I'm not welcome."

"Mother, you are always welcome. Just understand, I'm a grown woman, it's not your choice where I live, it's mine. And if you don't like it, I'm sorry, but that's the way it is. If you want to go home, okay. I'll take you to the airport tomorrow. What time's your flight? And why does Karen have to leave? She can stay and I'll take her to the airport for her original flight."

"No! She's coming with me too. I don't want to leave her here alone her with you." The spite and venom are unmistakable.

"Gram, I come to visit here all the time. What is your problem? I don't want to go."

"Well that's just too bad. I've already changed your reservation and paid for the difference. Looks like you're stuck with it." The smug smile of triumph that appeared on Mother's face took Fancy back to places she would rather not visit. She had learned years ago to keep her mouth shut.

Karen is obviously upset. She doesn't want to leave, but her choices are nil. If Mother can't control Fancy, she's going to make

61

sure Karen's her puppet and her pleasure in winning the battle is obvious as she yanks the strings.

Silence prevails on the trip to the airport. Karen tries to start a conversation but Fancy's too angry to participate.

Luggage on the curb, Fancy says "Bye, Mother. Have a safe trip home."

Her mother tries for a hug, "I only want what's best for you. You know that." Her voice is wheedling, like coaxing a child to take medicine she knows it won't like.

Fancy doesn't say a word, pulls away, palm up to stop any further words. "Okay Mother. Whatever."

As she hugs Karen, she whispers in her ear. "Don't worry baby, it's a long standing feud. Don't get involved; doesn't concern you. I love you and you know you're always welcome here."

"I know. Rest assured I'm never going to bring Gram along again."

"Good plan!"

As Fancy watches them board the plane, she's sorry to see Karen leave. But seeing her mother's back is another story.

Mending Fancies

Once back from the airport, Fancy realized how seldom she looked back to her childhood. She moved so fast she never took the time. Had to keep up with life as it sped by and she was good at racing. Never mourned her grandmother when she passed away—didn't even know she was gone until months afterwards. Typical— Mother never even bothered to tell her.

Is now the time to reflect? She's turned fifty. Without children to mark the passage of time, she doesn't even realize how old she is until she thinks of the half century behind her.

After years of suppressing memories, they now flow through her mind; a current liquid and twisting like a deep river determined to find its mouth. Her loud spoken answers to questions asked long ago wake her from dreams. Or perhaps the slight woofing of one of the dogs dreaming of bygone chases, breathing fast and paws twitching as they run through misty night meadows filled with twinkling fireflies and fleet ghost prey.

Fancy's father was sixty-two when he died. Fancy was thirteen. Will she live longer than he did? Sixty-two seems younger and younger to her. He left her at that awful time of life between child and woman when you need someone to set your mind straight about a lot of things—men and women, relationships, doing what's right. That was when he left her. Alone.

Pops had a massive stroke when Fancy was eleven. The entire right side of his body practically useless. He didn't take it well. He was only sixty, too young to become a cripple. Made up his mind a little thing like a stroke wasn't going to interfere with his life.

Every day for months, Pops went to work at his law office in midtown Manhattan. Sonny, his aide de camp, chauffeur, personal assistant and close buddy did the driving. After a while Pops tricked out his big Cadillac limo so he could drive, but only on short trips around the village.

When winter came, like the snowbirds, Mother packed up the family for an annual pilgrimage to Florida. Mother wanted sun. Pops went for the fishing. Pops insisted on taking the Cadillac, as usual. It was a harrowing ride with family protesting they wouldn't go unless Sonny and Mother did the driving. Pops stewed from New York down the Eastern coastline to mid Florida. He gave constant pointers and guff to whoever happened to be the unlucky driver.

Fancy's most vivid memory of him always stays close. Sometimes, when she is abruptly awakened, in that moment between sleep and alert, she smells the inland waterways of Florida, brine and fresh water blended with the soft decay of the vegetation surrounding them on the secret journeys she and her father took together.

It all started one day when Fancy was being her usual shitty pre-pubescent self.

Once settled into a rented cottage on the eastern side of the Everglades just outside Dania, Pops began disappearing. He'd push his lunch around on his plate, nibble at the few veggies, salad or pasta of his prescribed diet. Disgusted, he'd head out of the cottage with his lurching gait and cane, grab the car keys along the way, announce he was "going for a short ride" and would be "back in a little while." There was no stopping him.

Fancy was stuck listening to Mother's constant complaints to the Sisters. Mother had morbid images of Pops at his favorite dirt floored shacks teetering precariously at the edge of the banks of the inland waterways; stuffing himself with pork rinds and pickled pigs

64

feet, deviled eggs and fly droppings. Everything the doctor had forbidden.

This went on for several weeks. Sonny offered to go with him. Pops would have none of it.

Fancy was suffering through the terrible time when odd things began happening to her. Her body was blossoming in strange places. She had no idea why. She didn't know anything about sex, not a topic openly or easily discussed in her family.

A pretty widow lived next door. She lay in the sun in a mini bikini, not common those days. Sonny circled the woman like a vulture circled its prey. Pheromones were rampant and the damp heat of Florida didn't help. Fecundity permeated the air.

Nobody told Fancy anything. Mother and Sisters would be head to head deep in conversation. When Fancy appeared, the silence deafened her. Pops being sick worried her all the time, but, other than bitching and complaining about him, no one told her anything about his condition. Sheltered kids have no way of coping with mysterious hidden pressures except to act out. Depressed—angry and miserable—pouting is their best defense.

Fed up with both Pops taking off to unknown places and Fancy's pouting, Mother reached her breaking point. Making his get-away one afternoon, before he cleared the door, she grabbed Pops. "Oh no you don't," she snarled, "no sneaking out alone this time." She took Fancy's arm and thrust her at him. "You're taking *her* with you!"

While Mother usually wouldn't let Fancy get in the car when he was driving, maybe this time she was hoping they'd have an accident and not come back. Two annoyances gone—one fell swoop to an uncomplicated life. Mother didn't take stress well.

"You haven't paid any attention to your daughter, and she's bored to death. She's your problem today. I'm sick and tired of you running out on me and her lurking about with a nasty look on her face. Take some responsibility. She's yours too you know!" Mother's voice kept rising until it ended in a screech.

Pops' eyes went wide, color faded from his usually ruddy

cheeks. He heaved a great sigh. Fancy knew he loved her, but he'd seen her sullen behavior. Fobbed off on him—she'd spoil his plans for the afternoon. But…no choice.

"Okay, okay, stop the yelling. I'll take her." Just what Pops wanted—a grumpy kid with a pissed-off look.

Skulking over to the Caddy, Fancy slid onto the front seat, filling it with bad attitude.

His silver handlebar moustache tilted down at the ends reflecting Pop's mood. He pulled out of the driveway onto the country road; turned once to look at his unwilling passenger. Sighed and headed to the Everglades.

Fancy perked up. Maybe they were going to one of those fishing stores? Mother never let her play with the kids who lived in nearby trailers, insisting she'd get ringworm, nits, head lice, bedbugs, impetigo, the list was endless. Fancy smirked to herself, if she caught something nasty it'd serve Mother right!

Pulling into a ramshackle store at the side of road, Pops struggled out of the car. Fancy followed; hanging around the doorway, shoulders slumped so everyone who looked knew she was totally miserable.

Pops laboriously searched out items to put on the counter. The clerk, a fat woman with frowzy no-color hair, floral dress and red-veined face, filled brown paper sacks while Fancy watched. A six-pack of beer, four bottles of Mr. Pibs, a couple of pickled pigs feet, a dozen hard boiled eggs, a jar of Helman's mayo and a huge bag of potato chips. Pops bent down to a bottom shelf, held on to the counter and straightened up with a large bag of pork rinds. Absolutely forbidden food!

One narrowed look from his brilliant blue eyes and she hightailed it back into the car, after snatching the sacks of groceries. She put the purchases on the floor behind the front seat, wedged together so they wouldn't tip over, everything spill out. Maybe things were going to be more interesting than she had thought. Her mood lightened.

Pops slowed down to turn into a dirt track, hardly wide

enough to accommodate the Caddy. Leaves and branches brushed both sides and the top as they followed the track about a quarter of a mile into Everglades jungle and stopped in the middle of half-dozen beat-up cars and odd looking wooden trucks made from cut off cars. Fancy thought it looked scarier than the Gypsy encampments her mother told her never to set foot in.

Pops was a large man, but he was slow and crippled, no longer the protector Fancy once looked up to. She was a little frightened, but also thrilled. They were on an adventure together.

As soon as Pops' cane hit the dirt, a tall skinny black man in faded, torn coveralls came over and helped him out of the car. "Howdy, Larry, how ye doin' today?" he asked. A huge smile split his dark and seamed face.

"Great Leonard, good to see you. This is my youngest—Fancy Lady."

"How-dee-do, Fancy Lady? Yer father been tellin' us 'bout you." He stuck out a thin hand that looked as dry as the mummies in the roadside museums. As Fancy shook it she could feel every bone through paper thin skin. Leonard looked her up and down. "Yer daddy be right, ye be well named." Fancy's face flamed, she hated her name and was always embarrassed by it. He hit her sore spot.

Leonard turned to Pops, "Good ye could come. Sondralee over yonder, she done a special lunch fer ye today." This time a wink accompanied the wide smile.

A loud shout echoed out from the denseness of the jungle. "Larry, been waitin' on ye fer lunch, 'bout time you got here." It was a lilting woman's contralto.

Fancy had overheard Mother say she was suspicious Pops was having an affair…whatever that was. Fancy had gathered an 'affair' involved something with another woman. Oh my! She had visions of divorce, being in a home stuck with Mother and the Sisters. No Pops. Her depression returned with a thud. Her heart fluttered with fear.

Pops handed her one of the sacks, Leonard took the other.

She trudged along the well-worn path behind them. The dense jungle met overhead to form a leafy shaded tunnel, fragrant with leaves, moss and flowers; insects and small things hiding in the underbrush scurried into deeper cover as they passed. She didn't want to know what they were. Could be lizards? Rats? She shivered. The whole world surrounded Fancy—nature's cycle of life, death, and the decay needed to nurture new growth. At the end of the tunnel, the sun sparkled the surface of the inland waterway like sequins on Mother's party dresses. Pops reached behind to nudge her along, poking the crook of his cane on her tush. Thoughts of wildcats or snakes dropping down from the leafy vault above filled her with fear as they entered the passageway to the sun. Dutifully, she walked beside her father through the gauntlet of green.

Along the water's edge, several more black people waved to Pops, some seated on cut stumps, others on beach chairs. In the center of the group, but with a respectful space on each side, sat a monumental woman in a faded red and pink cotton dress. She must have weighted at least three hundred pounds, her face framed by a red bandanna tied like on the Aunt Jemima Pancake package. Fancy never saw a 'real' person with a bandanna tied on like that.

She was the most beautiful woman Fancy had ever seen. Her skin was flawless coffee-regular color, textured like rose petals, eyes a large almond shape with a slight upward tilt and long eyelashes curled like fringe. High cheekbones and an aquiline nose offset her smooth brow. Fancy couldn't take her eyes off the woman.

Like the queen with her court of admirers, she pointed imperiously to an empty folding chair. The only one close to her. Pops lowered himself into it after he indicated the sacks be given to her. His offering.

Then he presented Fancy. "This is my youngest daughter, Fancy Lady. Fancy Lady, this is Sondralee."

"Pleased ta meet ye, Fancy Lady. Yer daddy's been tellin' us all 'bout you…and yes, yer name suits." Somehow, when she said it, Fancy felt a compliment and wasn't embarrassed.

The hand Sondralee put out was striking—long, slender, well groomed soft fingers, nails filed and clear polish. Fancy shook it politely "Nice to meet you too m'am." The fresh scent of roses and lily of the valley wafted towards her.

Sondralee turned towards Pops, "How ye been doin' Larry—behaving yerself since I seen ye last?" The smile she gave him was tender and sweet. Fancy tried to figure out how old she was, anywhere between thirty and...there was no way to know. Her teeth were strong and white, she had all of them and her face was unlined... smooth.

Mom wasn't going to like this one bit if she found out. Fancy understood she was now the keeper of "The Secret." Pops hadn't told her not to tell, but she understood this was just between the two of them. She was her father's daughter—smart.

A bunch of kids played along the banks of the waterway, jumping in and out of the slow flowing current. They had nets for crabs and small fish. Fancy longed to join them. Mom never let her near strangers—impetigo and what all.

Sondralee caught her looking and shouted to the kids. "Y'all take care of Larry's daughter Fancy Lady, hear me! Make sure she don't fall in the water, and if she do, y'all gets her out! She commin' down to play."

Pops nodded towards the kids and Fancy took off at a run. Wow, kids, water, nets...all her favorite things!

The rest of the afternoon Fancy remembers as the best time she ever had. Ever!

Sondralee dragged over a big cardboard box filled with fragrant fried chicken and catfish. They ate the chicken and fish, potato salad, chips, deviled eggs dripping with mayonnaise fixed on the spot, fried hush puppies laced with bacon pieces and onion. The kids drank the Mr. Pibs while Pops and Sondralee knocked back the six-pack of beer.

After everyone ate their fill, Pops and Sondralee moved their chairs close to the bank, a respectful distance between the two of them and the rest of the fishermen. Sondralee handed Pops a long bamboo rod set up with drop line, bobber and piece of pork rind. They swung their lines into the water in unison. Occasionally they'd pull in a small fish, mostly sat in companionable silence.

There was sudden excitement and the kids ran along the bank to see. Sondralee pointed to a group of manatees making their way along the waterway. Their backs were streaked with deep cuts. "What's the matter with the manatees?" Fancy asked.

Pops replied, "Those cuts on their backs are made by propellers...boats fishing the waterways...progress...civilization. People not caring about the damage they do." Fancy saw his face turn sad in the middle of that afternoon of happiness.

Remembering the years when they too had put propellers in the water to fish, trolling for tarpon and big snook, she hoped with all her heart they never hurt a manatee, couldn't remember seeing one. A terrible sorrow for the big creatures engulfed her. How awful, how helpless they were, sharing their sanctuary with dangerous boats and propellers. No choice.

Back playing with the kids, and lifting small treasures out of the waterways with nets, she couldn't shake a feeling of regret for the manatees and how their peaceful life was threatened.

As the afternoon wore on, Sondralee pulled out a corncob pipe. She filled and lit it, drawing hard and inhaling smoke, then passing it to Pops when she was satisfied it was started. The two of them sat on the bank of the waterway as the sun set, passing the pipe back and forth, like two Indians at a pow-wow. Fancy had never seen her high powered lawyer father so relaxed, so contented. Happy.

When the sun lowered into the trees, Pops checked his watch and motioned it was time to go. He leaned over and kissed Sandralee on her smooth, plump cheek. She reached up and took his hand, squeezing it gently in both of hers. "See ye soon, Larry. Ye know I be here anytime for ye." Reaching up, she ran her hand slowly down the side of his face.

He poked Fancy again with his cane as they went back

through the leafy tunnel to the car. This time it didn't seem so fraught with danger.

As he turned the key in the engine, Pops leaned towards Fancy, about to say something. Then he was silent for a moment, frowning.

Fancy took his paralyzed hand, spoke first, "Pops, don't worry, we weren't here...just drove around...stopped at a couple of bait and tackle stores, talked fishing with owners."

His icy blue eyes pierced through her, started to say something, stopped, just nodded. Fancy sat looking straight ahead. She wouldn't ever breathe their secret.

As soon as they got back to the cabin and Mother, Fancy was dragged into the kitchen. "Where did you go with him?" Fancy was pissed off again. Couldn't her mother let him have a moments peace?

"Nowhere, just drove around...went to bait stores...asked about places to fish...not much...."

"Did he eat anything he shouldn't? You know, fried foods, fatty stuff?"

"No Mother...had a soda is all." Fancy yanked her arm away, frightened in the pit of her stomach for a moment. Could her conspiracy lead to Pops having another stroke? That night she lay in bed, frightened he wouldn't wake up the next morning and it would be her fault for keeping his secret— letting him eat food he wasn't supposed to have.

The rest of that trip, Pops took Fancy with him from time to time. Whenever possible, she made herself scarce when she thought he was going to make a get-away. She understood and gave him time to be alone with Sondralee.

No matter how hard Mother grilled her, like the Gestapo in the War, Fancy thought, she never told what they did, where they went. She knew Pops was proud of her for keeping their secret.

The next year, they went to the west coast of Florida, far from Sondralee and her wonderful fried chicken. Mother was adamant. No way was he going someplace where he could escape without her again. Still convinced the crippled old man had found himself another woman, she insisted, the Sisters backing her up. Pops caved in. Once again—no choice.

Everyday Sonny set up a chair in the sand and Pops slowly walked out to the beach. One-arm-casting his line out into sparkling waters of the Gulf of Mexico, he'd sit alone, watching the dolphins playing together companionably off-shore. Fancy sometimes sat with him, sure he was yearning for Sondralee and their friends, laughing in the Everglades on the other side of Florida.

Her family came back to New York in April that last year. In August, Pops passed away in his sleep.

It was a very, very long time ago.

Some nights, the memory of Pops sitting alone in his chair on the Gulf of Mexico haunts Fancy. Her tears flow as she mourns. But then she wipes them away, pulling together the other memory of him—sitting with Sondralee, laughing and fishing. Together on that bank in the Everglades.

Happy.

End of Fred

The office phone rings. No one else around so Fancy picks it up, says "Hello." Heavy breathing from the caller fills her ear. Ragged. Must be Fred. She arranges papers on her desk, leans over and pats a dog, checks her calendar. He'll say his piece when he's ready. Is he shy? Fancy has no idea.

Gravel voice, too much booze, too many cigarettes, finally begins, "'nother jackpot roping—ten steer a day for five days. This one's a Century. Leave tomorrow, settle in, sign up and go to an opening barbeque. Suit you?" His speech ends with a hum—sort of a low buzz that goes up at the end. A personal tic she's familiar with and pictures him smiling as the sound rises.

It suits her. "What time do we leave?"

Seven AM the next day she's waiting, suitcase packed, Tom ready too with his bed, food and leash. Called her secretary to watch the office. Monday's a holiday so she can close, Fancy'll be back to open Tuesday.

On the ride north, Fred explains this roping is called a Century— the age of both header and heeler add up to at least a hundred years. Many father and son teams enter, grandparents and grandkids, or partners like Fred and Arnie—same age, grew up together in the Valley. Since Arnie moved away, the Century is their annual chance to connect.

It's late September, weather cold. About sixty teams compete. Takes a long time, some nights not finished until three, four in the morning and back again at seven AM. Evening of the first day,

73

Fancy begins to feel bad, by the end of the second, she's feverish, coughing, has the shakes, and is wrapped in horse blankets, curled around Tom, lying across a wooden bench at the arena.

Arnie brings her hot tea, soup one time, a coffee laced with whisky, a couple of aspirin. Fred drops her off in the morning and picks her up in the evening when he's ready to go back to their room. No soup or whisky from him. Can be twenty hours between times she sees him. Sometimes, when the aspirin take hold and the fever subsides, she sits up and watches him across the arena talking to the other cowboys. Always has a beer in his hand.

Horses waiting along the railings draw her interest. After a day spent in hazy observation, Fancy realizes the horses have cliques. Four or five of them are always together, heads down in a circle as if they whisper secrets they don't want the other horses to hear. There are several similar groupings, and the cliques appear to be closed. If another horse comes over, tries to enter the circle, the clique may or may not let it in. If not, they whinny, move around to close any space where an interloper might try to push in. The insiders will bite or even kick the stranger. Occasionally a scuffle ensues and the cowboys come over to break up the fight. Don't want their roping horses kicked in the shins and out of commission. They take the troublemaker and tie it up at the other end of the arena.

She wonders if all of life and social interaction is the same. You go to a place, they accept you or not. If not, you become a spectator. If you're accepted, you become part of the group, an active participant. Does the acceptance of one horse and rejection of another have anything to do with the performance of the horses in the roping?

That night, when Fred picks her up, she asks him if some horses don't like each other and won't work together roping. He feels her forehead and hands her two aspirin and a bottle of water. Not a word.

The next day, she tries to concentrate on which horses are in which clique and if they rope together. She's remembered Fred

74

and his other partner's horses always wanting to be together on the same side of the trailer. Did they know they were partners?

Rosie is by herself at the rail. Arnie's horse is tied next to her, but they don't seem to interact much. Most of the time, Rosie has her head down, looking as morose as Fred.

Is the Valley like the microcosm of the horses? There are cliques of ranchers, celebrities, winemakers, the Mustang crowd, realtors, business people, merchants. Fancy hangs out at the Mustang, but is she really part of the clique, or just another spectator let in to study the quaint locals? She doesn't think of them that way—finds it arrogant and insulting to use the word quaint—but some of her visitors do.

To her, the Valley people are her friends. But she's no fool. Obviously, over the years, many of her visitors have behaved as if coming to the ranch was like being in a strange habitat where they can observe the customs of the natives. Like standing outside looking in on some obsolete tribal rituals.

Too much thinking makes her dizzy. Feverish.

The day is warm, only a hint of chill in the air. Fancy opens the blankets she's been wrapped in and lets the sun warm her body. She feels a little better. The sun sinking into her bones relieving some of the ache within.

Arnie comes over with a Coke. "Here, take this, didn't put any ice in it. Better without when you're sick." He reaches over and feels her forehead. Not so feverish. She smiles—someone cares if she's alive or dead.

Arnie's married, been so for a long time, kids grown with little ones of their own. She thinks he's probably been a good father. The way he is with her shows he's taken care of people before, knows how to look outside himself, tend to others' needs.

Fred was married once, no kids. Wife was a barrel racer, he rode bulls. Rodeo couple on the circuit. Never speaks of it.

By the time Fred drops her off at the ranch, Fancy is better, the flu receding, her body healing.

She nods 'bye' to him as she takes the dog bed and suitcase

75

out of the back of the truck, Tom beside her. That's it. Neither has said a word, but the understanding is clear. She and Fred are no longer an item. He's only able to love his booze. Self obsessed. Like all addicts. It took a while, but Fancy understands.

As his truck rounds the corner past the weeping willow, she shrugs and thinks—not his fault…and not my problem.

The Herb Garden

The ranch across the way from Fancy has been for sale since she moved in. A caretaker lives on the property, a cheerful cowboy named Jed who comes over to Fancy's for horseshoes and beers. Comes and talks with Donald, her manager, even joins her on the porch for coffee once in a while. Just to talk, hear another person's voice. A lot of space and a lot of dark on a ranch if you live alone.

The sight of moving vans, cars and activity one morning is a welcome sight. New neighbors maybe? It's a little isolated on the ranch, would be nice to have someone close by. On the way back from running errands in town, Fancy sees Jed talking to some moving men and decides to put her purchases away before going to check out the action.

"Hey, Jed, what's up?" She hails from the road.

Jed has a big grin on his face. "Durn! Can you believe it? Someone finally bought the place…moving in now, and keepin' me on as ranch manager too." He puffs his chest out a bit. She knows he likes living on the ranch, no rent, and a little jingle for caretaker wage, but he's a bit lonely.

"So, tell me everything. Have you met the new owners? Where're they from? Look like nice folks? What're they going to do? Retire? Ranch? Raise horses?"

"Whoa girl! Take a breath. Yes, I met 'em. Seem nice enough. From the East, like you. Don't know exactly where from, but you kin hear it in their voices. Man and woman, don't know if they're hitched or not. She's a little bit of a thing, he's a big guy, seems okay, real talkers, both of them." He motions her to a bench under a tree where he can keep a weather eye on the movers and still talk. "Said something about turning the place into a herb garden, grow stuff natural, no pesticides, need to get government certification. No one ever growed nothin' on this ranch before 'cept weeds, so it'll probably be easy, soil not contaminated and all. Don't really know much about them things."

"How old are they, do you think?"

"Aw, Fancy, I'm not good at ages. Mebbe forties—fifties?"

A new Cadillac Eldorado pulls into the driveway, banging it's way over the deep ruts in the driveway before stopping in front of the bench. Jed runs to open the passenger door for a tiny woman, blonde hair in a 1940's style page boy, svelt figure and big smile. "Howdy Miz Flavia, been talkin' with your neighbor, Fancy. She owns the spread just over yonder."

Fancy shakes a very small, delicate hand and surveys designer jeans and sequined western style shirt. Custom made boots. Pink snakeskin. "Hi, Flavia. I'm pleased to meet you. Welcome to the neighborhood. Nice to see people moving in here finally…place been on the market a while.

"Well, Fancy, nice to meet you too. And this is my boyfriend, Eric."

A large meaty hand engulfs Fancy's. The man is not only tall, well over six feet, he's also wide in the shoulders and chest, sporting a sizeable belly. Face round with dark stubble. Bald on top, fringed with long black hair, a bit greasy and pulled into a pony tail. Small black eyes, piggy looking and slitted. He doesn't say anything, just nods. Fancy thinks she might have heard a grunt.

"Pleased to meet you, Eric. Welcome."

He nods again, this time to Flavia, "I'm going to check to see how those morons are doing with the moving. I know you labeled all the cartons, but they didn't look like they knew the difference between a dining room and a bedroom…probably all sleep in one room hovels with dirt floors for all I know…don't even know how to read…" His voice fades off as he goes into the house.

Fancy looks at the moving men, Mexican or Native American, one black guy who seems to be in charge. Okay, well, she's now got a bigot moving in across the street.

Flavia watches him leave for a few seconds, her brow furrowed. Turns to Fancy, "So, what do you do on your ranch?"

"I have a few critters, but I'm not a rancher. I have my office there."

"Oh, what do you do?"

"Consulting work, television business, some sales."

A loud voice from the house, harsh, vibrates across the driveway. "Flavia, I need you to get in here right now. Make sure these idiots know where to put things. I'm not straining my back moving boxes because you didn't have them put in the right rooms. That's what we're paying them for. You make sure they're doing their job right." Fancy sees he's got a cooler, must have been in the Caddy. Reaches in and pops a beer open as he sits on a kitchen chair one of the movers left on the porch. Puts his feet on the railing.

Flavia turns pale. Her shoulders slump. "Yes, dear. I'll be right in."

Fancy pumps her hand, "Nice to meet you, I gotta run, don't want to get in your way…interfere…you have things to do. …need anything, I'm across the street." Rolling her eyes at Jed, she runs across to the safety of her ranch.

That night, on her porch, Fancy can hear a man yelling. New sound to the area, must come from the new people.

Two days later, as she's having her morning coffee on the porch, Flavia appears in the driveway, waves. Fancy waves back and hails. "Want some coffee?"

"Would love some."

"Black, regular or what?"

"Black with a little sugar?"

"Coming up."

The two women sit in the morning mist as the sun warms the valley. Fancy starts the conversation. "Jed tells me you're going to start an herb farm."

"Yes. Eric had the idea to grow organic herbs, dry and sell them. Cheaper to start an agri-business with herbs than wine or apples, turns money the first year. Eric's so smart and good about those things." Fancy watches as Flavia turns her left hand around, right hand holding and massaging the left wrist. Stiff? Old injury?·

"What did he do before you came here?"

"He worked in funeral parlors, casket sales. Eric's very talented, that man can do anything with his hands."

"Always good to have a man around who can fix anything. Were you in the same business too?"

"Oh no, I'm a software engineer. I held good positions in several of the big companies in Silicon Valley. When I was contacted by a head hunter for my last position, I got some great advice—insist on stock options. I did. When the company went public, I cashed out. After taxes the options were more than sufficient for the down payment on this ranch and then some. When Eric wanted to try herb gardening, I agreed to support him until he got the business running." She looked down for a moment, wringing the napkin next to her coffee. In that split second, Fancy thought she saw something like despair in Flavia's eyes. And then it was gone, the bright smile tightly back in place once again. "I think I have enough set aside to tide us over for the year it will take to get the business profitable."

"How nice. And he is an experienced gardener?"

"No, but a he's researched herb growing and has been reading books about it. He's convinced it will be successful."

"I see."

"I'm so lucky to have a man with such entrepreneurial vision. We're looking forward to an idyllic life here in the Valley."

Flavia stopped massaging her wrist and Fancy noticed a long scar down its side.

After twenty minutes of discussion about which beauty parlor was best, where to shop for groceries and did Fancy know of an available housekeeper; Eric appeared at the entrance to the ranch. "Come on Flavia, get your butt over here and stop talking. I can't do everything by myself. Now move it!"

Flavia hastily put her cup down. "He gets a little impatient sometimes. Don't pay any attention." In a matter of seconds, Fancy watched her new neighbor go from an animated, smiling woman to downcast eyes and hunched shoulders walking down the drive, her back receding into the morning mist.

A few days later, Fancy is at the Mustang with Polly when Eric comes in. No Flavia. He nods at Fancy. Brusque, his expression daring her to say anything. Takes a seat at the other end of the bar.

Polly serves him a beer and returns to Fancy. "You know that guy? Think he bought a ranch somewhere near yours."

"Yeah, I met him. He and his girlfriend bought the one across the street from me. She seems okay. Flavia. Nice enough woman, must be smart, is a software engineer. Him—jury's still out."

"The guy's got a short fuse. Got into it with one of the cowboys t'other night. Had to break it up—lucky some of the regulars were here, don't know what I'd a done if I was alone here—would 'a had to call the cops, I guess." Polly shook her head. For all the booze and testosterone in the Mustang, fights were generally few and far between. Most of the fighters had been long ago eighty-sixed, and any newbies who showed a tendency to disturb the tranquility were soon set straight.

A tentative knock at the kitchen door surprised Fancy one morning a few months later.

Flavia. "Hi Fancy, I wonder if I can impose on you? I need to go to town to buy a few things and…maybe…could hitch a ride with you the next time you're going?"

"Sure. No problem. I'm going in about an hour. To the market and the pharmacy. Where's your car?"

"Eric had an accident last night. Ran it into a tree on the way home from the Elks Lodge. He's working on repairing it now. I'm so blessed to have a man who can fix things the way he does."

Fancy left that alone—said only, "I'll come by and toot for you when I leave."

"Perfect. Thanks"

Three months pass, Fancy sees no visible movement to prepare the ground for farming. Eric has taken residence on their porch with a cooler full of beer by his side. His only movement seems to be leaning down to pop another brew. The car sits wrecked in the driveway and Fancy automatically asks Flavia if she wants to go to the market.

Polly says Eric has taken nighttime residence on the barstool at the end corner. "How does he get here?" Fancy's curious.

"Jed drops him off and leaves. Eric cadges a ride home from anyone he thinks might be driving in his direction."

Fancy has given up sitting on her porch in the evening. The usual ranch peace is disturbed by shouting from across the way whenever Eric is not at the Mustang.

Polly has the night off and comes for dinner, her man out of town for a few days. After dinner, they sit on the porch until the shouting begins from across the street.

"What in hell is that about?" Polly asks.

"Damned if I know. It's what I hear every night he's home."

"Let's go listen to what he's saying."

"No way am I going over there."

"Nah, me neither. I just thought a stroll along the road in the evening air might be nice—get a little exercise—digest our dinner."

"Okay, I'm up for that."

As soon as they cross the street, the voice becomes clear. Eric's strident shouts echo from their ranch. "It's all your fault, I'd fix the car if it wasn't for your putting all your shit in the barn. I need a place to work."

"But Eric, it's my office files, I have to store them somewhere. I told you I'd move them off to the side, and give you room to work on the car. But they're heavy... I can't move them myself." A sob interrupts before she continues with a catch in her voice. "You won't help me move them, and every time I ask Jed to help me, you have him take you to the Mustang instead."

"You stupid whore, this is your fault. You know I have a bad back and can't lift anything. ... and don't forget, it was your decision to move to this god-forsaken place." A crash echoes from the house followed by a yelp and crying. "Shut the fuck up or I'll give you something to cry about! I'm going out, anything to get away from you. I'm bored. What else do I have to do to entertain myself but go to that crap-house Mustang and sit with the stupid shit-kickers!" The door to their house slams. Eric's shout rips into the soft evening air. "Jed, get over here now, I need a ride!"

Fancy and Polly crouch down behind the bushes ringing the fence and pray he doesn't come out the gate. They creep up the road, as far away as they can from Flavia's sobbing and Eric's bellowing. Once out of sight around the bend, they cross over to Fancy's side of the road where they walk back, talking and laughing, loudly obvious in their enjoyment of an evening stroll as they turn into her gate.

Fancy sees Eric is back on his porch. Jed probably skipped out for the evening to get away before being grabbed for a ride someplace. Smart move, Fancy thinks as she watches Eric lean down to his cooler for yet another brew. Must have been empty because he yells towards the house, "You bitch, why didn't you buy more beer today when you and that other cunt from across the street went to the market? How do you expect me to fuck you rough the way you like it when I'm thirsty." He slams the cooler closed and stomps inside.

Both Polly and Fancy cringe as they enter the ranch. Eric had to have seen them on the road, obviously wanted Fancy to know exactly what he thought of her. They look at each other—shocked.

83

Quizzical. Fancy shrugs. "Least he's not my problem."

"Amen to that. Mine neither." Polly grabs her handbag, and keys in hand, runs for her pick-up. "But I'm getting the hell out of here before he decides to ask me for a ride."

About eight months after moving in, Flavia is once again at Fancy's door. "I'm sorry to bother you Fancy, but I need another favor. My computer is broken and I'd like to get on-line. I have some important work to do."

"Sure, no problem. Come into the office and I'll get you set up. What happened to your computer? I thought it was new."

"Yes, it was. Eric and I had a fight last night... he got so upset he threw it across the room." Flavia's eyes slid to the floor. "All my work files were on it. Hard drive and motherboard are both shot. Luckily, I saved them to my old company's cloud, so I didn't lose everything. Still...I need to try to reconstruct what wasn't backed up...big fee as long as I can still make my suspense date. It's going to be close..." Her face is red. Fancy can't miss the imprint of a large hand in shades of purple and yellow decorating her slender wrist, a bracelet of pain and self-inflicted shame.

Flavia follows Fancy's eyes and hides her wrist under the other arm

Fancy sets Flavia up with a computer. Left her in the office without another word.

Later that afternoon, Flavia comes over to Fancy's desk where she'd been working silently. "You know...his upset is all my fault. He came here with me and I promised I'd have enough money to see us through until the herb business got going. I've taken on these consulting jobs to tide us over, but I need my computer." She starts to sniffle. "Now we don't have the money for a new computer or to buy new seeds for the herb garden."

"I thought you had all the seeds already. Special types that weren't commonly found."

"I had a wonderful collection. Everything all set to plant. But

84

around Christmas, Eric got mad at me again. Usually, he breaks my grandmother's china, but this time he threw the cabinet, you know…. where all the seeds were catalogued. I couldn't stop him when he took it outside…threw it off the porch."

Fancy saw the despair in Flavia's eyes as she continued. "All the sections, broke into bits, everything scattered and mixed up in a big pile of glass, plexi-glass and seeds…all over the ground." Tears filled Flavia's eyes at the memory. "He was so sorry. He tried to clean it all up, save what he could, even though I know it was my fault for making him angry."

"I see. So now you have to replace all the seeds?" Trying to keep her voice even, to not display the shock and disgust at what she's hearing, Fancy can't look the other woman in the eye. All she can think is: how can any living person be so unaware of their own stupidity.

"Yes, and unfortunately they're expensive—not available just anywhere. I have to order them from Europe, to pay a broker to clear customs…a complicated process."

It's too much for Fancy. No way can she keep quiet. "Why doesn't he get a job? He's a big strong man. Bet he could find work in town, or on one of the ranches, just while you get the other business working."

"Oh no, he's got a bad back, he can't work."

"Flavia, has he ever worked at anything other than selling caskets?"

"Well, he's had his own businesses and been very successful."

And then, Fancy flashed back to her middle sister, Annette. Frail, dying of lung cancer at seventy-three, kept barely alive by a long trailing plastic hose attached to an oxygen concentrator.

Fancy came to visit the family several years ago. Annette and husband still living on Mother's buck. Fancy heard her brother-in-law screeching. "Annette! Get up here now! Right away…" Saw Annette gasping for breath as she started to run up two flights stairs, puffing oxygen as she went. Stopping Annette, Fancy said she'd see what he needed. When she got to their bedroom, he was sitting comfortably in a club chair with his feet on a hassock watching television.

"What's wrong? What do you want?" Fancy asked.

He looked startled at seeing Fancy rather than her sister. "Oh, I just wanted Annette to hand me that glass over there." He pointed to a water glass on the night table—a couple of feet away.

The explosion was quiet. Fancy had long passed her breaking point with the man. Voice smooth and silken, her eyes that deadly grey everyone who knew her well came to fear. "Oh. I. See. You couldn't get up out of that chair and walk two steps to get the glass. Instead, you screamed like a banshee in pain for your wife, who is dying and can't breathe without a machine, to run up two flights of stairs to come and hand it to you?"

He looked at her in shock. His face a puzzle. He shrugged. What was she so angry about? He was just behaving the way he always had for fifty years. What was *her* problem?

In the same deadly voice, and with icy calm, Fancy said. "Get the fuck off your fat fucking ass and get the glass yourself. Now. If. You. EVER…scream at her like that again, I promise you, one night you *will* find yourself sucking feathers from under a pillow I'll be holding over your face…and you know I can…and will…do it." Her smile showed teeth clenched between white lips. Silence. As her smile stretched further, she waited two beats. "Get it?"

His eyes went round.

"Answer me! Do…you…understand?"

"Yes." His voice was soft and breathy.

"Good." She slammed the bedroom door on her way out, trembling with rage. The urge to smash the old man had been so strong it had taken every ounce of will power to control the adrenalin coursing through her.

That night, at dinner with Mother, Fancy recounted the story. When Annette came in the room, Mother told her what Fancy had done. "He better behave from now on when she's around. She's not afraid of him. I've known for years she'd just as soon kill him as look at him." Mother couldn't suppress her smirk. Fancy knew there was no love lost between Mother and her son-in-law.

Later, Fancy remembered asking Annette, "Why don't you tell him to move the fuck off his ass and get his own glass or whatever he wants? You're not his slave." Annette looked shocked. "Oh, I couldn't do that. Then he wouldn't love me."

"It sure as shit doesn't look like he loves you now." Fancy's reply dripped acid in its dead-pan delivery.

"It just looks that way to you. You don't understand anything. I've always known when we were old, he'd be nice to me."

"What do you think you are now? Pre-pubescent?"

In disgust, Fancy turned away, unable to even look at her sister. Stupid cow. Married to a man like that for fifty years and still telling herself things would be better some day.

Since early adolescence, Annette provided Fancy with an excellent education of the likelihood of change in a bad marriage. Gambling, cheating, business failures, screaming abuse, were all Annette's fault and she willingly took the blame. Even the flashing memory of it, years later, brought the familiar twist to her stomach.

The ping of an e-mail coming to her computer brought Fancy back to the present. The pleading look on Flavia's face couldn't stop Fancy from going on. "Then why doesn't he start a new business, and while we're on the subject, what happened to the others that were so successful?"

"In one, his partners screwed him. In the other, he couldn't keep up with the cheaper competition."

"Then what did he do?"

"He went to stay with friends— borrowed money from his mother to live. It was a very upsetting time for him."

"Then did he go and get a job?"

"No."

"Why?"

"This is none of your concern."

"You're my friend, and you're depending on this man to set up a business to pay for the cost of your mortgage and living expenses?" Fancy shakes her head, reaches over and takes Flavia's hand in hers. "Don't you see you're being used and abused? But it doesn't have to continue. You're a respected professional with a career. You can easily make it on your own. This relationship you're in is toxic…almost textbook, and you're a classic enabler."

Flavia cries and snuffles. "You don't understand. He loves me. He's so good to me."

Fancy's eyebrows go up. "Seriously? Screaming at you, hitting you, breaking your things, is being good to you? You're better than this and deserve better than this. You need to get away from him and do it now…before he really hurts you. This pattern of abuse escalates." Fancy meets Flavia's eyes to see if she's listening. "…and it always ends badly!"

Flavia puts up her hand, palm out. "Stop! You don't know anything about us, or our relationship. Mind your own damned business! I love him and I am *never* going to leave him!" She stomps out of the office, her shoulders rigid.

All Fancy can think is, sure lady, yell at me. Whatever you have to do to ignore the truth. She shakes her head as the office door slams.

Silence. Fancy turns and leaves the office too. The air is stifling and she needs to get away. Flavia's reaction says it all— she's a victim and Fancy hopes she won't be around to see the last bitter act.

Six months pass. The Caddy rusts in the driveway, leaning over onto a flat tire. Eric has become a fixture on the porch with his cooler. Flavia comes over off and on to use Fancy's office for her consulting work. When she comes, their conversation is restricted to groceries, the weather and using the computer.

Several weeks later Fancy takes her favorite stool at the

middle of the bar and Polly leans in close. "Did 'ja hear? Eric, your charming neighbor, got eighty-sixed from here. Picked a fight with one of the cowboys again. This time a few of the guys took him outside and tuned him up a bit. Glad I was off that night and the owner was tending bar." A couple of customers came in, Polly stopped washing glasses and served a few drinks before coming back. "Eddie and Jim were here, told me about it. Said Eric picked the fight, like last time. Glad to see him out of here. Wanted fast service and tipped for shit…musta' figured he deserved being waited on hand and foot and didn't have to pay for it. He scared me…didn't like to be alone with him here at night. If it was only him and me, I'd call the owner and tell him I was going to close down." She slapped her bar rag down as if she was slapping him.

The next day, Fancy decides it's time to talk to Flavia again. She's still working on her business in Fancy's office, but there is little conversation between them. Fancy starts easy like, but she's determined to say her piece. "Heard last night Eric is banned from the Mustang. Did you know that?"

"Yes. He told me one of the cowboys started a fight with him and they took it outside."

"Funny, I heard from three friends who were there that it was the other way around—Eric was the lit fuse, started pushing one of the guys and shouting."

"Everyone always blames him for everything."

"I've been here quite a while and never heard of a fight at the Mustang until he arrived." Fancy held tight to the back of Flavia's chair, blocking her from getting up or leaving. "I also hear him shouting and screaming at you all the time. I see how you behave when that happens. I hear you crying, your arms are bruised and if you think make-up covers black eyes, you're sadly mistaken. His fist and hand marks are always all over you. How can you stay with him?"

"You don't understand. I love him. I owe him. He's been

with me through so much. He came here with me. I wanted to come, to change my life. Move to a ranch. He gave up everything to be with me."

"Exactly what did he give up? A job, a career?"

"No, but his family is back East."

"And who had the idea to start an herb farm?"

"He did. Heard it was a good business."

"Okay, so when is he going to start planting it?"

"He can't, he has a bad back."

"Then who's going to do the work?"

"I was, but I have to get this consulting job done to get the money to buy the equipment and seeds to do the cultivation."

"Why doesn't he get a job while you do that?"

"We don't have a car for him to use to commute."

"He was the one who wrecked your car— I thought he was going to fix it."

"He needs special tools and parts we can't afford."

Fancy shakes her head. "Why don't you just put on your big girl panties, kick his ass to the curb and get on with your life. The guy is a loser!"

Flavia's face turns red as a beet as she begins to tremble and cry. "I don't want to live alone, have a little life like you do. I want a big life—have a wonderful man next to me, and...I love him."

"You mean living on a ranch with a man who screams at you constantly, hits you, wrecks your car, sits on his ass drinking all day, and blames you for everything wrong in his life—is your idea of a big life?"

She screamed, "He can't help it. He had a terrible childhood. But he loves me and he sure knows how to show it when he wants."

"Oh, I see. So the sex is great and you'll rescue him?"

"He does so many things for me, takes care of me. I told you, I owe him."

"How exactly do you owe him?"

"It's none of your fucking business what I owe him," Flavia

90

screeches. "I just do, and that's that! Just because no man wants you doesn't give you the right to butt into my life." She stomps her foot and makes a fist at Fancy. "Or maybe you're a lesbian...that's it, you're a fucking man hating lesbian. That's why you don't like Eric! I hate you! Mind your own business and leave us the fuck alone!"

Fancy puts up her hands in surrender, then breaks into one of those uncontrollable laughs, the kind that come at funerals, or weddings–places and times you know you shouldn't laugh, but can't help yourself . The more Fancy tries to stop, the more she laughs, tears running down her cheeks, hiccoughing and bent over double.

"What's so funny, bitch? You're the joke. Can't have a relationship of your own and trying to break mine up? Go ahead, laugh all you want, but stay out of my life and tend to your own. Eric's right, you're nothing but a nosy, interfering bitch! "

Fancy is the office door slammer this time. Once outside, she's not sure if her tears are from laughter or sorrow.

Flavia still comes over to work in the office. Keeps to herself...silent...unapproachable. While Fancy feels sorry for her, she knows she can't help her and stays as far away as possible. Because of the tension Flavia brings with her, Fancy wants to kick her out of the office, tell her to find another place to work and stay away, but she knows the other woman has nowhere else to go and can't bring herself to cut her only life line and close her out of her only refuge.

Summer passes. The tension grows. Everyone who used to stop by and visit during the day, keeps away. Fancy's bookkeeper now takes the books and files home with her to work on there.

When Fancy had complained to Polly that she didn't like going to her own office because of the cloud Flavia had brought there, Polly pointed out that she was now enabling Flavia to put up with Eric by giving her a safe place to hide.

She's come to a decision and won't put it off any longer—

time to tell Flavia to find a new place to work.

Soon as Fancy walks into the Mustang, Polly motions her over. "Did 'cha hear? Eric was arrested last night. Jed called the cops on him. So much yelling and banging, Flavia screaming and crying so loud he was afraid Eric was killing her. No way a guy Jed's size could stop him, and he doesn't own a gun."

It scares Fancy to imagine the small man trying to wrestle a bear like Eric. Even with a gun...unless he had a BIG gun. Shotgun maybe? Sawed off, like hers.

Polly continues. "Police drug Eric out of the house, found Flavia on the floor behind the couch, beat to shit...nose twisted 'cross her face...broken arm. Took her to the hospital...still there I think. Eric's in jail 's far as I know." She makes a loud "tsck" sound as she wipes the bar down. "Talk about creeps, that guy is one and gives them to me!"

Phil, a local sheriff, comes into the bar. He's a Mustang regular and hardly gets through the door before Polly starts working him over. "Hey, Phil. Hear anything about what happened to Eric? You know, the shit who lives across from Fancy...brought in last night for domestic abuse?"

He eases himself onto the bar stool next to Fancy. "Yeah. Bastard's already out. His woman won't press charges. She keeps saying she tripped and fell off the porch." He shakes his head. Serious. "Living across the street from that asshole, Fancy, I'd keep my doors locked and my gun loaded. Checked him out—got a record. This guy likes beating people up, 'specially women, and they don't have to be his wife or lady friend. So far he's managed to escape real jail time, but guys like him escalate. He won't be able to get away with it forever."

Phil put his hand on her arm. "Now you listen good, if he sets foot on your ranch, you call me. Ya' hear?"

"Okay Phil. Thanks for the warning. Wow! I knew he was bad news, but—" Fancy just shakes her head without finishing."

When she gets home, she makes sure no one's hiding in the

shadows. The dogs come out to greet her, tails wagging. Nothing out of the ordinary. Inside, she locks everything up tight, takes the dogs into the bedroom with her, sawed-off shotgun next to her bed. Loaded. Both barrels.

For a week, Flavia's nowhere to be seen. Fancy doesn't go looking for but can't help worrying about her neighbor. Fancy assumes she's embarrassed and avoiding the possible 'I told you so' or stooping to a lying explanation she knows no one will believe. She knows there is nothing she can do to help other than keep her mouth shut and be around to pick up the pieces if Flavia asks her to. Still, Donald has changed the locks on the office doors. If Flavia wants to come into the office to work, now she can ask each time.

Key in the lock to open the office on Monday morning, Fancy sees an envelope sticking out from under the door. Flavia's now useless office key inside and a note. "Thanks for everything. You've been a good friend. Flavia."

As she puts the note down, Jed runs up, breathless. "Fancy, you have to come see this…won't believe it otherwise." He grabs her arm, drags her from the door, "…can't hardly believe it myself."

As they walk across to Eric and Flavia's house, Fancy sees the Cadillac is gone, the tool shed door is open and it's empty. The porch is missing Eric's chair and, to Fancy's horror, the front door, once a beautifully designed Mexican carved rustic slab of wood, is gone along with the frame it was set in. "Oh my, what happened here? A home invasion?...fight? Are they all right?"

"Seems so. They flew the coop."

"What? Who?"

"Eric and Flavia. Bank foreclosed. Guess she couldn't keep up with the payments, what with him not doing a thing but drinking and hollering."

Expecting blood, Fancy walks inside the house. No blood, but she can't believe what she's seeing. Broken glass and garbage

93

litters the floor. Every light fixture, stick of furniture, crown molding, curtains and rods, light switch covers, all gone. In the kitchen, no appliances, cabinets ripped off the walls, ones that didn't come easily smashed to bits, sink and faucets, microwave over the stove—taken. Everywhere they look throughout the house they find wanton destruction—or cannibalization. Sinks, toilets, towel racks, toilet paper holders, removed or broken. Shutters, blinds, cabinet knobs, built in drawers, either pulped or taken helter-skelter. In one bathroom the toilet is shattered, water running over and leaking past the tile bathroom to the custom hardwood flooring covering the rest of the house.

Jed leans over and tries to turn the water off, but the handle had been bent open. He stuffs an old towel to try and stem the flow. As they leave one area of carnage, another one greets them. In what had been the living room, Fancy sees a patch that looks like urine streaking down one wall, a pile of human feces beneath. Eric's last fond 'goodbye.'

The rage soaked walls scream madness and hate so loud, Fancy can't wait to get outside into the air. Suffocating and stunned by what she saw, she begins to cry. Jed sees the tears course down her cheeks, and puts his arms around her, patting her on the back like he would a small child. "There, there, now Fancy, sorry to upset you so. Let's go back to your place …sit down, catch your breath and I'll fill you in."

"Sorry for the tears…but I saw…awful fury. Too many emotions…pain… sorrow…desperation. You know?"

"Yes. I do know. Felt pretty much the same m'self."

Back in her office, Jed brews a fresh pot of coffee while she wipes her tears away and blows her nose. As she looks around her office, Fancy is grateful to see all her computers still there—including the one Flavia worked on. Everything intact in Fancy's world.

After a while, holding the steaming cup in her hands, Fancy wants to hear the whole story.

Jed, himself still shaken, begins. "I imagine the attorneys give them plenty of notice, telling them exactly when they had to get out, the date when the bank would take over the property. That Eric, he had the whole thing planned like a bank robbery get-away. Gotta' give him that. U-Haul truck and five guys come up around ten PM last night." He refills their cups and sits back down as cleansing sunlight filters into the office. Fancy looks at the motes floating in the rays, wondering if they were free of the stresses of the human condition.

"I'd been hiding out in my place for a week, not leaving without a tire iron in my hand. Truth be, I was scared what that bastard might do to me after I called the cops on him for beating Flavia."

He shakes his head, looking down at his hands for a second. "I heard what was going on inside there for months and did nothing. Probably should 'a spoken up sooner, but I like to mind my own business, you know?" Fancy nods. She does know.

"This time was much worse...couldn't let him kill the woman, even though she's dumb enough to stay with him. Still...

"Then, last night, I heard the truck pull into the drive, strange voices, and snuck over to see what was going on in case the shithead was up to no good again. Got close enough to hear Eric give instructions—to not leave a thing in the house that could be unscrewed or ripped off, take everything and pack it into the truck. Then it was like a war zone, drills, hammers. Surprised you didn't hear it."

She shook her head. "Funny, something was disturbing me, couldn't figure out what but don't recall anything out of the ordinary other than feeling creepy. Spent most of the evening watching science fiction movies, TV must have drowned out the noise...fell asleep in a recliner with one dog on my lap, others next to me. Didn't wake until the morning sun came up, television still blaring. Left it on for the news when I let the dogs out, fed them, showered. Never heard a thing."

Jed continued. "When I saw what was going on, I made myself scarce. Hid in the bushes and watched for a while. Heard him bellowing at Flavia, 'I'll show that fucking bank! Foreclose on me will they? When I'm finished with this place there won't be shit left for them to sell.' All the while she's crying, trying to calm him down, saying 'It's my credit you're ruining, the house is in my name and I'll be responsible for any damage. Please, please stop this. I'll lose everything.' He shoves her away, takes up a hammer, I'm afraid he's going after her again, but instead he starts breaking all the windows on the ground floor, all the while screaming filthy names at her.

"That's when I decide to keep my distance. I hid out back behind the house, nothing much out there for them to take. At one point, I hear him calling my name. I don't come. Then he starts calling me every name in the book and screaming again at Flavia for being soft hearted and keeping me on the place. I crept around to make sure my cabin was locked tight and went to ground again. Funny thing was, he never did try to go into my place to look for me or do any damage."

All Fancy can do is shake her head in disbelief. She had heard about similar destruction when people were angry about foreclosures, but never so close to home. Or people she knew. Or anything so violent.

"Once the truck was filled with everything they could squeeze in, they both left in it, towing the dead Caddy behind. Gone by five AM, just as the sun's coming up." Jed shakes his head. "Never saw anything like that in my life."

"But what about the ranch? How can they just leave? I thought Flavia bought it?"

"She did, but seems the bank foreclosed when she quit makin' payments. Bank's now the new owners."

"So soon? They hadn't been here more than a year and a half, two at most?"

"Two men from the bank showed up—eight AM sharp, local sheriff with them, waving papers to evict Flavia…put the place up for auction. Sure were shocked when they saw the shape the house was in."

"Oh my. Did you hear any mention of where Eric and Flavia were going?"

"I didn't. Honestly Fancy, I watched the whole thing from as far as possible. Wasn't about to get in the middle of that or become partly responsible for what they done. Owed me back wages too but once I saw the goings on, I'd already kissed them goodbye. So no, I have no idea where they're off to." Rummaging around in his pockets, he hands her another envelope like the one she found earlier in her office. "Here. This is all's I know. Go on, you can open it."

Inside is a folded paper with something stuffed inside. As she takes it out, she sees hundred dollar bills—a decent number of them. The note is short. Flavia's handwriting. "Jed, thanks so much for all you've done, I know it wasn't always easy. I hope this tides you over until you find another place. Ask the bank, they might hire you as caretaker again. Fondly, Flavia."

"So that's it. All she said?"

"Yep, left the note tucked under the door to my cabin. But I took her suggestion. Talked to the men from the bank, and they're keeping me on as caretaker. Want me to repair the inside best I can. Send them an estimate to replace all the stuff Eric took and I can stay until the place is sold."

"That won't be any time soon in this market. Nothing is selling around here, or anywhere for that matter."

Jed smiles back at her. "I think we're back to peace and quiet again."

That night, Fancy takes a glass of red wine out to the porch and sits with her feet up on the rail. She looks at the weeping willow through the V her boots make and lets out a sigh she hadn't realized until now had been pent up for months. Her shoulders relax and she rolls her head around to release the tension in her neck. After a while, Jed walks over to her gate and she motions him to join her.

"Still can't believe she left with that monster." He says.

"I tried several times to talk to her. Hoped I might get some sense…beautiful woman…intelligent too. But she kept saying how much she loved him—owed him." Fancy shakes her head and shrugs.

"No accounting for taste, I guess."

They sit silent for a time, looking out across the lawn, towards the mountains in the distance, watching the last pinks and roses of the sunset fading slowly into the darkening sky.

"Sure is nice and quiet tonight. I bet I'll hear the screech owls a little later." Fancy says.

"…and look, the hawk is back." Jed points to the silent sentinel on his perch. "All's right with the world again."

"At least it is here. I'm not so sure about every place else." Fancy takes a sip of wine, along with a deep draft of the fresh moist night air. She can still make out the weeping willow, outlined dark against the fading light.

Not one hole ever dug to plant one herb in two years.

No one ever did hear where they went. Fancy and Polly figured Flavia was still with Eric—her ticket to the big life.

Jed stays on, paid by the bank to take care of the place. They often have morning coffee together, Donald comes up to join them now and then. All of them shaking their heads at the peculiar life decisions people make for themselves.

Fancy takes her morning coffee and her evening wine to the porch again. Good to enjoy watching sunrise and sunset in the tranquility and peace of her little life.

Here Comes The Judge

Saturday afternoon Fancy is in the office—catching up on paperwork for clients while she waits for friends to arrive for a few days stay. The open sliding door she's facing entices a warm breeze to filter around her desk. Ethel and Tom snooze at her feet alongside Myrtle, her red hide and white polka dots shining after a good brushing, which she loves. Critters are Fancy's company in the office—keep tabs on her—make sure she sticks to business.

The quiet shatters as hoof beats pound across the driveway. Five very large brown and white streaks thunder past the open door. Oh damn! Cattle are loose. The past few days a fire raged in the mountains ringing the valley and friends brought stock down from the hills to graze in Fancy's pastures. Keep them safe, well away from the blaze. Now they're running around the ranch. Double damn! She'd left the entrance gate to the ranch open in expectation of guests visiting from New York City. Not so safe.

Visions of cattle running amok in and out of cars on the four lane just over the rise has Fancy out of the office and quick behind the cows, dog and goat entourage hard on her heels. Luckily, the cattle head left up the hill towards the house. Fancy veers off to the right and slams the gate before the siren call of freedom and the highway beckon the runaways.

Once the gate's secure she takes inventory. Three head are in her garden making a leisurely meal of the giant zucchini she'd forgotten to cut back. Good, at least someone wants them.

Myrtle found some roses to trim and is ignoring the crisis. Fancy shoos her away in Act Thirty of the War Over The Roses.

The other two cows head up the hill and round the corner of the ranch house. Must have discovered the satellite dish and fruit trees. There are apples on the ground, a few apricots still rotting, plenty to amuse for the moment. Fancy knows her favorite persimmons will be next. Must rescue them.

Ever try to herd five cows with one person on foot? Dogs can help, but only if they know what they're doing. Her dogs have no clue.

Fancy's dressed ranch-elegant to greet friends. Long full western skirt, clean cowboy boots, embroidered western shirt and hat. Not typical round-up garb. Any available man shouting distance from the ranch is gone for the day, off fishing, playing golf, or just playing.

A car's tooting at the gate. A Cadillac. Of course. Her friends from NYC, an attorney and a Criminal Court Judge. Both ladies. Friends from the old days when Fancy practiced law in Manhattan. A while ago. She'd been wondering what to do to amuse them. Hmmm.

She opens the gate. Tells them to quick get the car inside so she can shut the gate behind them.

"Why quickly?" the judge asks.

"Just drive inside, I'll explain later." Lady lawyers, they never do anything you ask unless the reason is given first. She should know, she's one herself.

The Cadillac pulls inside. "Sure glad you ladies arrived just now." Fancy says.

The Judge and friend Lisa look at her with tilted heads in question.

"Got some livestock loose and need help getting them back into the pastures." No hello, no nothing, not a welcome. Just a plea for help. Okay, so much for manners, Fancy thinks as she tries to catch her breath.

"Ummm, eh, how can we help?" Lisa's wearing Gucci flat-heel loafers, designer black jeans with gold stitching and her long curly hair is tied back on her neck with an elegant black velvet ribbon. Chic. Manhattan to the max.

"You ladies have any hats or scarves in the car?"

"Well yeah, she has a baseball cap," the Judge says, pointing at Lisa, "with sequins...I've got a sun hat." The Judge is wearing what look like L.L. Bean jeans, a white mock turtleneck with a new looking flannel shirt overtop. Neat. Nice. Preppy. She's even wearing Topsiders, no socks. Very East Coast casual. Short hair too. Cap cut. Thin face, looks in charge. Well, after all—a judge.

"Okay, that'll work. You can help herd them back to their pasture. Cows don't move if they don't have to, and the best way to get them going is to scare them a little, make noise, flap stuff about. They get disconcerted. Enough flapping and yelling— they'll move."

The women look at Fancy. Dubious. Like maybe she lost her mind? Been too long on a ranch? Time to come back to NYC? Probably never did much flapping and yelling before. Lisa steps up. "So, we get them moving, then what?"

"The trick is to spread out—funnel them through the open gate over there—back into the pasture." Fancy points. "If one gets away, the others will follow, so we try to herd them together first, then direct them."

Fancy holds up her hand. "Hold it a sec, let me get some things—might help." She ducks into the office and emerges with a medium size Confederate flag on a pole and a tennis racket. Hands the flag to the Judge, the racket to Lisa. "Wave the heck out of these and yell like mad."

"Yell? What do we yell?"

"Who knows, yell anything, just so long as you make a lot of noise. The object is to scare, not sing them to sleep." Tenderfeet. What will they ask next, Fancy thinks.

"Where do you want us? And where should we end up?" The Judge is back in control.

"First, we have to get all the cows to gather. I'll go to the garden and move the three there into the center of the lawn. If you two can go up behind the house, over to that side," she points to the opposite side of the house from the garden, "and move the two cows around to the front, maybe they'll herd together."

Everyone goes to their assigned spot, the dogs follow Fancy. Myrtle scoots off to keep the ladies company. She probably thought they might be more interesting. They might even have something to eat.

"Now on my signal, wave, run and shout." Fancy calls over her shoulder. The other women nod.

The grass is slippery. Damn sprinklers had been working. Fancy's skirt is wet and dragging along the hem, her best boots are showing wet marks at the toes, likely to ruin them in the bargain.

She's madder than a pit viper with boils at whichever fool left the gate open, and ready to smack the first cow that comes near her. The three cows in the garden are unsuspecting as she assaults them with loud yells. Just to be more impressive, she grabs both ends of her skirt. Vivid flowers bounce like large angry birds as she jumps up and down flapping like mad. The cows take off at a decent trot.

Just as they make the middle of the big lawn, Fancy sees the Judge in hot pursuit of a cow, both chased by the goat. The Judge's yelling instructions to Lisa to move her cow along, "Keep up, don't let that Bossy lag behind, we have to keep these two together.

Lisa looks tired already, her once neat hair has come undone and is a mass of straggly curls falling in her eyes. She looks unhappy. Very unhappy.

The Judge, on the other hand, seems to be enjoying herself. She can't stop laughing. Fancy didn't think her face could look so joyous.

After five minutes of yelling, flapping and swatting, the five cows are more or less in a herd around the trunk of the weeping willow. Lisa's panting, Fancy's beginning to see the humor of the situation and the Judge sports an ear to ear smile.

Fancy splits them up, she'll take the back of the tree, Lisa on one side, Judge on the other, on a count of three they all start to yell, flap, swat and run. The dogs get into the act; they're barking and yodeling like mad. Myrtle ignores the melee, she's munching a lovely rose bush. Fancy throws her a death look but can't do anything at the moment. Myrtle throws back a look that would be a smirk if she wasn't a goat.

The Judge is swatting any cow within reach with the Confederate flag, Lisa is pounding after the cow on her side as she brandishes the tennis racket and Fancy takes up the rear flapping her skirt in the air like angry dragon's wings. She's howling yippeeee-yi-yee-ky-oh-ky oh, thinking it sounds close to something she heard once in an old Roy Rogers movie...maybe Gene Autry? The other women must have liked the sound because they take it up. The ranch is the stage for three howling, yipping and ki-yay-yay-ying, cow-whacking, flapping, swatting, running, leaping, hat-waving women with tennis rackets and flags. At first, the cows are dumbstruck. They won't move. Fancy thinks she can read cows thoughts—what the heck is all this about and who are these odd creatures cavorting and yelling?

The first close brush with the Confederate flag changes the lead cow's mind, it bucks and flies to the safety of its home pasture just as Lisa leans way forward, tennis racket raised in anticipation of whacking it on the flank. The darn animal gallops before the whack lands but Lisa's still in forward motion. Her feet slip on the wet grass. Face plant into the dirt. The other cows follow, docile now, carefully avoiding the floundering female. One tries to get away, but Fancy's too quick. A howl and a flourish of skirt and the last cow heads into the pasture. The Judge, standing guard at the gate, slams it shut, banging the latch home with a secure and satisfying 'thunk!'

"Gotcha!" She's exalted.

Fancy skids over to help Lisa up, the grass like a skating rink as her smooth leather soled boots go out from under her in a rooster tail of mud spattering up into her new skirt. As the ground comes up to meet her, Fancy catches the image of the Judge, wide-eyed, hand over her mouth. Lisa panics for a second, fearing Fancy's about to dog pile-her. Safe, the panic morphs to laughter. What else can Fancy do but laugh too. There they are, three New York City lady lawyers, covered with mud and laughing like fools. But the cows are safely locked in their pasture. A day's chore well done.

Several hours later, everyone showered, smelling good in fresh jeans or sweats, they lounge on the front porch watching tri-tip sizzle on the bar-b-q next to corn on the cob and garlic bread. Salad with ranch dressing rests on the table by potato salad and several bottles of good Andrew Murray merlot, open and breathing. Neighbors arrive, tie their horses to the fence in time for dinner. While the tri-tip cooks, it's time for salami, cheese, crackers and home-cured olives. Everyone laughing as the ladies recount the day's action. Poking fun at the city slickers pretending to be cowgirls for the afternoon. Big plates fill with mounds of juicy red meat, salads and garlic bread take the sting out of both lingering pains and barbed jibes. Laughter cures the hurts as do friendly dog noses nudging for ear scratches and treats of anything that might be left on plates. Garth Brooks filters out into the soft night air as heads nod with too much excitement, wine, food and laughter.

As the guests untie their horses or start up their trucks to leave, Fancy glances over at the pasture where the cows happily munch hay. Myrtle, next to the gate, begins to nibble on the rope used to pull the latch open. The mystery of the open gate—solved. Just as the latch is about to open again, Fancy's on the run with loud whoops and several expletives requiring immediate deletion. Myrtle turns. The expression on her goat face is clear. "What?" Fancy even hears it in her mind as if it had a New York accent.

First things first. Before the dinner clean up, the rope is replaced with a length of chain and a padlock.

At bedtime, before turning in, the Judge comes over and hugs Fancy, "That was the most fun I've had in at least the…the last quarter century! …not always easy to get my job out of my mind and really relax. Thank you!"

Fancy hugs her back. Playing cowgirl for an afternoon can sure be more fun than any day as a Criminal Court Judge in Midtown Manhattan.

Maybe Myrtle saved the day after all.

Damned goat!

Hitch

Fancy's at the new coffee shop in town, outside table, enjoying a cappuccino. Reading the local paper. Not much news to excite in a small town. Stock auction, coupons for restaurants. Sale at the tack store.

She looks up as a car nosily pulls into the spot next to the Suburban. Hitch. Fancy smiles at him, waves at him to come sit with her. He smiles back. Old Hitch took a shine to Fancy the first time Fred brought her around. Feeling was mutual.

Two hours later, sun's moved in the sky but they're still at the table. They've missed each other and are catching up.

"Goin' to the rodeo in Salinas next week?" Hitch asks.

"Didn't have any plans to." She looks at him a minute, thinks about her words before asking, "Want to go? I'll drive if we can get rooms."

"I got a buddy who manages the Red Roof Inn just outside a' town…could give him a call and see if they got two rooms left."

"Okay, let's do it."

They both like to travel, prefer to do it with company rather than alone.   With no further discussion, they take to hanging out together.

He's in his late eighties, close to forty years between them. An old-fashioned gentleman, Hitch opens doors to usher Fancy inside, asks what she would like and then orders for her when they go out to eat. He knows how to treat a lady. Courtly.

Hitch is an old cowboy; even says so on his California

Driver's License under "profession." When he was a young hand, he was a heavy drinker and smoker, just like his son. One day he decided he'd had enough and stopped. Just like that.

His wife was a patient woman who passed away some years back, leaving him alone in the big ranch house. He does what he likes, cooks for himself, makes treats for friends. Come olive season, friends and neighbors deliver empty jars and grocery bags filled with ripe olives. Hitch gifts those he loves with jars he's filled with plump, delicious, cured olives.

Beef jerky is Hitch's specialty. It's reputed to be the best jerky in at least five counties. He passes it out like cigarette samples. Especially at rodeos.

Apples for his pies come from the gnarly tree out back of his ranch, and some from Fancy's gala trees.

Around the end of September, Hitch stops by. "'Bout time to get the apples, starting to dead fall, squirrels having at 'em. Come on."

She grabs a couple of L.L.Bean. canvas bags, dumps a ragged pair of cotton gloves into one, pushes a straw hat on without a look at her hair. "Let's check my trees before we go." He's out of the car, stretches his back and takes the bags from her.

Ten minutes and a half a bag full of galas, they're off to his ranch, she follows in her car.

They have the routine down pat by now, he shakes the branches with a long rake and she picks up the apples as they fall. Both bags are filled by the time they stop, and Fancy's back has had far more bending than it needs.

Companionable in the kitchen, they sit across a table harking from the 1930s, rectangular white enamel with slight raised rim, thin line of gray. They peel and core the apples. Next step is to pile them in a chuck-wagon size stew pot, squeeze lemon juice on top, shake and leave for slicing later. "Lemon keeps 'em from turnin' brown." Hitch intones as he wipes the lemon off his hands on a dish towel that saw better days at least a decade or two ago.

An hour later, the pot overflows with thin sliced apples,

lemon juice and sugar laced with cinnamon. Hitch makes the pie crust while Fancy goes home to read her messages, close up the office, feed her critters, check their water. Maybe have a little something to eat.

Soon as Hitch takes the first pie out of the oven he calls Fancy. "Come and sample. Gotta' see if they're any good."

They sit together on the patio in the late afternoon into dusk. The sun turns the mountains special high desert shades of oranges, pinks and lavenders while they eat warm pie with the vanilla ice cream Fancy picked up to go with.

Hitch has made ten pies, two at a time into the oven. Fancy times them but Hitch has final say about when they are done. "Crust has to be just right, don't much like soggy bottoms." He let's go his familiar cackle at the double entendre. "When the crust turns a good firm brown, time to take 'em out to cool." He's the expert. She listens and learns.

Hitch talks about old times in the Valley. "Ain't been in the Mustang but a time or two since I give up drinking. Not so much fun to sit and drink Coke. 'Member when it was full 'a cowboys, horses tied ta' the front rail. Couple a pick-ups. Spur tracks carved the front porch pretty good back then."

He looks off at the lengthening shadows, shivers a bit. The fog has begun to roll in from the sea and the temperature drop is evident. "Yep, plenty 'a men with fingers missing in those days." He examines his own fingers, hands brown, still calloused, fingers now bent. "Some fellers never did learn not to wrap them ropes too tight 'round the horn at roping or brandings." The cackle again. "Nowadays they pick up the finger, put it on ice and run ta' the hospital ta' see if it can be sewed on again. Sometimes it can. Old days we just threwed it away and took the branding iron to seal the stump." He shook his head and looked out from the hill over his ranch. Twenty-five prime acres of good ranch land. They both know the value has changed from that of a working ranch to a piece to be eventually cut into five and ten-acre movie star and rich people make believe ranches. Like Fancy's.

She goes in, checks the pies, brings one out for him to approve, then takes the other out of the oven, puts the last batch in. He won't cook them all, has already put six in the big coffin freezer. "When the temperature drops, we'll have good pie come January."

"How'd you get your name, Hitch?" she asks after their first piece of pie is gone and the coffee is still warm.

Face creased like a puckered apple, his eyes twinkle with mischief. "When we was kids, didn't have no new clothes, not like the new generation. I was the young'un and wore all the hand-me-downs. My brothers were bigger 'n me and had to tie a rope 'round my middle to keep my pants up. Kids always teased me, got up from sittin' 'n hitched my pants up, then had a hitch in my walk too. Earned the name Hitch and it stuck."

Fancy can't help laughing. She pictures the little guy with the baggy pants, and the old guy who still has the hitch in his step. Still pulls up his too-big pants. He's a little challenged in the hip and butt department.

"Name was par-tic-u-lar good for me too. Pa come from England…settled down and stayed in Chicago a while, but didn't care much for the cold. Moved west. Heard it was warmer. He never was one to stay anyplace too long anyways, wanted to travel, see the world. Always movin' someplace, see what's on t'other side of the mountain."

He serves them each another small sliver of pie, she plops more ice cream on top and puts the rest in the freezer.

"When Pa left Chicago, he headed south west, hoping for warmer weather. 'Stead, he ended up in Oklahoma—middle of a blizzard. Braves from a village 'a the Potawatomi tribe found him—horse dead alongside, most frozen to death. Lucky 'twas the Pots found him, and friendly ones too. Took him to the village and he spend the rest of the winter there. When he left, more'n a year or so later, he had a passenger and a half: my ma, full blooded Pot, and my oldest brother inside her." He looks away at the remembered image of his mother. Fancy had seen the only

109

photograph of her, dark hair and eyes. Somber. Solid. Posing motionless for the photographer as they did in those far away days. Beautiful strong bone structure she passed along to both son and grandson.

"She was the best thing my Pa ever did, he knew she was a good woman, put up with him and his wanderlust, went right along with him, kept him on the straight and narrow. He was such a rollin' stone his friends called him 'Itch'—always itchin' to see what was next. There you have it, natural to have Itch with his little sidekick Hitch. We was always together, my Pa and me. Ma finally made him settle down when I come along. He'd sneak off once in a while, but once we hit California and the sun, he knew he'd struck his own kind of gold."

As the story unravels, Fancy wonders about her own roots. Her grandfather's family had been early settlers in New England, could there be a little Mohawk or Iroquois in her blood too? Her grandfather had blue eyes and red hair, but a typical Mohawk nose and cheekbones. Could a pretty red-haired English lass have been hanging laundry outside a settlers cabin when a handsome brave passed by and found his own kind of gold? Could have been. She likes the idea so much she might just add it to her personal history.

Travelling Partners

Loading their bags into the candy apple red Suburban, a dog or two if allowed where they're heading, Hitch and Fancy hit the road. Often. Winters they head to Las Vegas—every December for the National Finals Rodeo, at least one other time just to gamble, and then again for her business conventions.

Weekends they spend at rodeos up and down the Central California Coast in the summer, up to Salinas, Oakdale, down to Santa Barbara, Ventura, over to Turlock for a team roping. One year they even drive as far as Winnemucca, Nevada to cheer on friends at a team roping. A bull riding competition in Santa Maria catches their eye. Anything with gambling, cowboys, bulls, steers and dirt is just their style.

They don't care too much where they go, as long as there's a good restaurant, horses, cowboys and a clean motel with two rooms that allows dogs. They're amiable company for each other and neither gets on the other's nerves. Suits them both just fine.

By six AM every morning, they're in the stands, seated at the railings watching warm-ups. They like to catch the morning heats to see which cowboys compete in the afternoon or evening rodeo. Hitch's been a fixture at the rodeos for more than sixty years and knows just about everybody. At least they know him, and he's still pretty good at remembering who's who.

Fancy loves the amount of testosterone flowing around her, finds it thrilling. She watches broad shoulders, tight butts in tighter

111

jeans and is only slightly put off by the Skol or Copenhagen chewing tobacco spit in the dirt or worse, in cups carried around filled with nasty brown sputum.

She was in love with Roy Rogers when she was seven, even has a picture with him to prove it. Her oldest sister took Fancy to her first rodeo in New York City when the National Finals were held there. Since then, she's been fascinated by tall muscular men with narrow hips, high-heeled boots, western hats and fancy shirts.

There is something inherently appealing about cowboys. They sit with straight backs, expensive western shirts, bib front or V-shaped yokes, stylish embroidery, Wranglers cleaned and pressed with creases, boots shined and hats dust-free and ready for the performance. Don't forget those tight jeans. They don't go in for the old-time movie western shirts with flowers embroidered on the yokes like they used to sell at Nudies in Burbank. The new style is more conservative, but equally elegant, fashionable clothing lines sporting names of Country singers like Garth Brooks.

Hitch brings her up to date on western lore. "See Fancy, the real prize is the buckle. Belt buckles, like to be medals of honor…worn with the same pride. Rodeo winners git both prize money and a buckle. Might be silver, bronze or brass, depends on how big the rodeo is, how big the crowd, important, or cheap. Each rodeo has it's own distinctive design, then the city if it's different, and the year. That buckle, it's the real prize—money gits spent and gone, but that buckle there, it carries the memory of the win for life."

Fancy takes to studying buckles on the sly, doesn't want to give the wrong signals. Some are so large they must be a problem to wear if a guy has a little paunch, and downright painful if the paunch includes a hang-over belly. Still they wear them, suffer the discomfort. Better to be a slim cowboy with a neat waist if you want to wear a big buckle. It doesn't matter, whatever the shape or size, a rodeo cowboy wears his prize.

Most cowboys even start out the mornings smelling good. Polo. Stetson. Old Spice. As they ride around the arena to warm up their horses, their cologne or after-shave wafts through the early morning aromas of horse, manure and hay. Clean manly man smell. Irresistible.

These are truly American men, Fancy thinks. Probably the last ones left in our heritage. Except for Native Americans dress, cowboys wear the only real national costume of the country. Fancy likes to take part in this tradition, even just as a spectator.

Rodeo horses are equally spiffed up, shined, curried, tails and manes braided. Tricked out saddles polished and tack is clean and on display. When the men walk, their spurs clink and jingle. One morning, Hitch pokes her in the arm, leans over to her. "Look at that jackass over there." He points to a tall man in a fancy shirt, clean western hat and shiny boots. Everything looks new. "Look at his spurs." She does, extended from the heel, shiny, round, looks like a pie crust cutter, serrated. "Kick the flank too hard with 'em on, cut the side of your horse. Don't need that if ya' know what yer doin'. Shakes his head. "No need for the likes of those if the horse is properly trained…or the rider." Hitch turns, spits in the dirt, mumbles something under his breath. Fancy never saw him do that before, he doesn't chew or spit. Sharp spurs must have really pissed him off. She will not ask what he mumbled.

Later, she notices the good riders have spurs like a softly rounded finger extending from their boots. She remembered Fred wore the same.

At the first rodeo Fancy's goes to with him, when Hitch gets out of the car, he looks like he's gained a considerable amount of weight. She doesn't want to say anything to embarrass him so she keeps quiet. Once in their seats, she understands.

Almost every rider passing by during warm-up stops to say hello to Hitch, who then pulls out a zip-lock sandwich baggie of jerky and hands it over the rail. He's managed to stuff several dozen baggies into his ancient oversized canvas Carheart coat. By the time they head on home, he's back to his usual size, the jacket hanging loose around his wiry frame. If he runs out, the last cowboys to visit with him are sorely disappointed. "Next time," he assures them.

Fancy might be a good deal younger, but Hitch always takes her elbow to help her up the stairs. Opens doors for her. Even buys her presents of silver and turquoise jewelry for her birthdays and holidays. She buys him gifts of soft flannel shirts and the warm sweaters he likes that zip up the front.

A born storyteller, not at all like his overly taciturn son, Hitch recounts events from the old days on the ranches in the areas. They're on one of their rambles and he points at a gate. "That ranch there, the triple G, good ranch, used to run two…three hundred head of cattle most years, sometimes more, always prime stock. Good place to work, too. Always paid wages on time, right to the penny."

Another time he scowled as he jerked his head in the direction of a long newly painted fence line. "That spread was owned by one a' those movie star pretend cowboys. Absent most a' the time. His foreman was a real piece a' work. Charged every hand on the ranch a percent a' his pay just to keep his job. Hard times in those days. Pretty near everyone out a' work so they paid the son of a gun." Out of the corner of her eye, Fancy saw him looking down, almost as morose as his son. A bad memory.

Hitch managed a few ranches in his day. Hung out with the other cowboys in the area, some of his friends going south to Hollywood to work as extras in the westerns. He did a turn or two in a couple of films when they used the Valley as a location. Didn't want to go to L.A. when they asked him to be in a few more.

One brilliant morning, signs of spring in fresh cut grass, buds and birdsong, he drives around the circular driveway on Fancy's ranch and toots the horn. Tells her there's a branding down the road. "Come on, let's go."

It's six AM. She puts on the coffee, runs to throw on clothes, brush teeth and hair, put on Stetson and boots. Pours coffee in go-cups and they're off. This first time, she has no idea what she's in for, but what the heck, never been to a branding. Always good to have a first time. She expects a few cowboys in the dirt with a couple head of cattle being branded.

In fact, it's a major event. The local tradition is for the cowboys and ranchers in the area get together, bring in the grazing stock from the hills in preparation for the spring stock auctions. In the old days, each ranch had a foreman and full time hands, all lived on the property. Hitch explained, "Ranches too small nowadays, don't pay ta' keep a big staff, maybe a ranch manager....part-time wranglers when needed."

At brandings, people from neighboring ranches flock together to do the work. In the weeks that follow they move from one ranch to another. The costs is kept down and also gives an excuse for a party. All the volunteer workers and their families are fed, and a decent spread or they'll not show up next branding season.

Hitch and Fancy are ushered over to a couple of benches set out around one of the corrals. She's fascinated. The corral is filled with a dozen or more men and women in jeans, boots, hats, gloves, working in assembly line fashion. Everyone knows exactly what to do and they mesh like a well-oiled machine.

Hitch explains "Calves born in the past year are sorted into male or female. Then the males are further sorted into breeding stock—bulls—or steers." That's been done already and the calves are milling around in separate pens.

As they watch, one at a time the calves are let out into the crowded central arena. Cowboys on horseback rope the frightened animals and cowboys on the ground grab them, turn them over onto their side, quickly tying three legs to keep them still. Others rush up to castrate those destined to become steers, slather antiseptic on the wound. It's done so fast the critter hardly knows what's happened. Shots are injected by someone else and then their horns might be removed, the stumps sealed with tar before a brand is burned on their flank. The rope binding legs is untied and

115

the confused calf is herded by the cowboys on horses and cow dogs into other pens where they wait for their ultimate fate—back on the range, the feed lots, or the stock auctions. There are several groups working so fast it takes a while to figure out what's actually happening.

The sun is relentless and Fancy was warned by Hitch to wear a big brimmed western hat. Hers is lightweight straw, new and clean. No dust. Plenty of sun block. She's branded as a newbie. Doesn't matter. She's with Hitch.

The rhythmical and precise way everyone attends to their jobs is mesmerizing. Each animal is processed like a part in the choreography in a western ballet. Out of the pen, roped, three legs tied, slash cut made, testicles in pail, paint brush into coffee can, slather antiseptic, shots – one-two-three, horns, brand, untie rope and herd to pen. Next.

Soon, the holding pens are filled with critters howling for mothers who have already been checked by the vet, doctored and moved back to the pastures. These babies now face life on their own. Their cries bring a harsh reality to what Fancy's been watching in the sun and swirling dust. Unfolding before her eyes is the origin of the sport of rodeo. She got it. Traditions centuries old of contests between different ranches, towns. Ancient work transmogrifying into modern entertainment.

Looking off to the foothills and up to the mountains that enfold the Santa Isabella Valley in their golden arms, she wonders how long these traditions will continue. Feels Hitch next to her on the bench, laughing with old friends at some long ago foible. Smells the heavy odor of seared fur and burned horn. Every so often a whiff of antiseptic makes its way through the cigarette smoke from the Camels or Lucky Strikes most of the cowboys still smoke. Hardly any Marlboros. Smells mixed with dust. No cologne or after shave at a branding. Ranch life. She begins to understand the culture so far apart from what she's lived in the past, it's almost like being on another planet.

The other side of this well choreographed ballet she's been

116

watching is the theatre of life and death for the animals. Will destiny pick them for meat on the table or a life as well fed breeding stock? She's sure her thoughts are the musings of a tenderfoot but they put a new slant on her carnivore leanings.

After the branding is complete, the last calf out of the pens, the party starts. Long tables and chairs spread out near a barbeque the size of a small SUV.

Someone has brought a fiddle, a guitar makes its appearance and music fills the air, drowning out the plaints of the new steers. Several men get up and sing along to "Home On The Range," "Red River Valley," "Ghost Riders in the Sky," and "Git Along Little Doggie." Fancy hears a gravel growl next to her—Hitch singing along. She turns just in time to see him wipe a tear away. Memories of the old days, rodeos and roundups past. Brandings when the cowboys coming to help numbered close to a hundred. Sad times now—lucky to get a dozen visiting helpers with families. Music brings the old times back. Some good, others bad, some too painful to bear. She turns away. Leaves him to his privacy.

The traditional meal is served—tri-tip seasoned with a mixture of herbs, salt, pepper and garlic spread out on the barbeque over smoldering oak logs. A salad with Ranch dressing, garlic bread, and beans—dishes brought by friends and neighbors: casseroles, cookies, pies, sausages—all homemade! Cheeses from local goats. Wines from Valley vineyards, and a keg of beer next to a tub filled with ice and sodas. A Santa Isabella Valley feast.

Hard to keep her mind from running the short distance between the tri-tip on the barbeque and the calves crying for their mothers. Fancy's not happy to see her food live and in distress. But after a half-hour of inhaling the fragrant meat cooking in the traditional seasoning, she's so hungry she'd knock the horns off the steer and run it across the barbeque herself, ready to bite it on the hoof.

Hitch is led to the place of honor, head of the table, amid all the food, still handing out baggies of jerky. He's a rock star in the

117

ranch circuit and treated accordingly. Everyone comes to pay their respects. Ask if they can bring him something. He is, after all, the real McCoy. One of the last of the real cowboys of this area now filling up with gentrified ranches. Gentlemen ranchers. Fancy feels like she's sitting with royalty. In fact, she is.

The owner of the spread comes over with a small brown grocery bag and plops it on the table in front of Hitch. He bends over, and in courtly fashion thanks Hitch for coming. Fancy imagines him doffing his ten-gallon hat, sweeping his cape aside and bowing as he makes the offering.

The rancher leaves. She pokes the bag. It's squishy.

"Hitch, what's that in the bag?"

"Oysters."

She's horrified. Oysters should not be out of their shells in the sun. She comes from East Coast oyster country. "Shouldn't they be refrigerated right away?"

"Naw, they're probably still warm."

"Why are they warm? Oysters should be kept cold." She's totally confused.

"They're prairie oysters… you know…Rocky Mountain oysters." His smirk turns into the familiar cackle. This is a joke of some kind. Then she gets it.

"Balls? They're the balls?"

"Testicles ud'be nicer put." His smile is full blown. "They make good eatin'. I'm gonna make ya' some."

She's not sure this is an offer she's keen to take him up on. "How do you cook them?"

"Slice them inta' small slabs, dredge 'em in flour or bread crumbs, better if you wet 'em first with beaten egg. Fry 'em in oil or butter…butter's better. Delicious."

She actually tried them the next day while he stood by to instruct her in the proper preparation. They were good. If Hitch went to a branding without her, or a friend brought some 'oysters' to him as a gift, he'd drive to her ranch, around the circular driveway to cozy up to the front door and sling a bag of them up on the porch. Hopefully someone would be home to get them into the refrigerator before they went bad in the sun.

One night Fancy served 'oysters' to Lars and one of his friends. Didn't say anything. One of the boys said, "What is this I'm eating? Tastes good."

"Oysters, prairie oysters."

"Are these those squishy things Hitch tosses up on the porch?" Lars asks.

"…ummm, yeah."

"Are they…testicles?"

"…ummm, yeah."

He pushed them to the side of his plate. "No thanks. And… thanks a lot for serving them Aunt Fancy." He's pissed.

"Listen, we live on a ranch, and these are considered a delicacy. Live on a ranch, eat like a rancher. Didn't you like the taste before you knew what they were?"

"Okay, I did. But it's a guy thing. I just can't do it."

"All the cowboys like them."

"They grew up eating them. I can't get my mind around it."

"Then finish your veggies."

At first, she thinks not to mention this to Hitch—doesn't want to offend him. One second later, she decides to tell him— and already hears his raspy gravel cackle in her mind.

Last Rodeo

Fancy and Hitch sit in the stands at the Santa Flora Rodeo. They're close to the arena, third row up.

Fancy is pensive, thinking over her life, where she is now, and how she and the rodeo participants are closely allied in their lives. They love what they do, but their time is always limited and not of their own doing. Bones and tendons give way without permission, some can be mended, some not. If the body gives out, the cowboy is out of luck. Could be one bull ride too many, maybe a shadowed arena and a hidden hole to stumble a horse. Companies bought and sold, new management bringing in their own clique to work with. Happens every day. Then what? Do we mend and sign up again for the next ride, or look for something else to do? Hard to say.

The loudspeaker blares into her thoughts, the announcer calling for the bull riders, and she thinks about the rodeo clown, Vince, who strides into the arena with his dogs. Can't get him out of her mind. She's met him a few times—he and Hitch go way back. Probably too old to do what he does.

Her mind takes over as she watches him waving to the crowd, and thinks about what she knows of his life. Is it an allegory for her own?

Vince was a bull rider before he became a rodeo clown. Hitch let on this is supposed to be his last rodeo. Afterward— retirement. She wonders, does he get to fulfill his dreams? ...and what would they be? Maybe raising and training cow dogs?

Squinting against sun beating down with unforgiving summer heat, she watches him cross the swirling dust clouds of the arena, his name and face unknown to the crowd. His partners—Art, Australian Cattle Dog, and Vanilla, Corgi mixed with something else—at his side.

Time to leave old cowboys and pals behind, Hitch has said. Vince complained his bones ache, too much mending, broke near all that could be broken. Been thirty years or more, 'goin' down the road' to every cow town along the Interstates. San Luis Obisbo. Salinas. Oakdale. Visalia. Chowchilla. Temecula. Turlock.

Dogs, bag full of costume rags, all piled into a third-hand truck, so old he jokes someday he'll "shoot it to put it out of its misery."

The dogs sleep with him in the truck-bed in good weather; in the cab, curled comfortable and warm around him in cold or rain. No money for hotel rooms for clowns. An empty gun rack holds his least grimy shirts. His baritone voice and a six-pack accompany eight-track versions of Waylon, Willy, Loretta and Kristofferson. Sometimes late into the night.

Never got to Vegas for the National Finals.

Today's his last ride on the power of a drug he can't kick.

Wind blows, bringing the sweet sweat-smell of man and animal, mixing it with popcorn and cotton candy. The snorts and whinnies of horses sing their songs on the wind accompanied by dogs howling out back by the stables.

Inside the ring, Fancy sees a bull riding cowboy tossed to ground one second short of the magic eight to glory. Arena sand chokes his mouth, blinds his eyes. A quarter-ton of mean wants to stomp him. Vince's turn now.

Crowd tense, silent but for sibilant intake of breath, waiting in expectation of death while they watch the ragged scarecrow and two dogs sprint to the rescue. A clown to save the hero?

Art and Vanilla bark and pivot as trained, drawing the attention of the bull. Vince's torn and patched pants, neon orange wig, red suspenders, face painted in mocking joy and solitary teardrop, all mark him the fool.

He nears the broken cowboy and begins his work, signals the dogs to scatter the attention of death. His job is to distract.

Men with a stretcher will save the cowboys life.

The bull turns to see him, another victim in its sights. Horns lower, hooves paw the ground. Muscles bunch in raging power. Vince holds. He must stay the time it takes to move the cowboy onto the stretcher and behind the barrier to safety. The hero to be saved.

He's only a clown— no magic eight seconds for him.

Fancy watches as his motley blows in the wind, flapping. No one sees the tape and bandages beneath holding his broken body together.

Ready yet? His eyes slide sideways to the men and stretcher. Almost safe. Two seconds more. Miniature twisters swirl behind the yapping and dancing dogs.

Red striped stockings cover ropey muscled legs as he prances, jumps up and down, shouts, feints, and waves ratty red rags. Attract the beast. It launches towards him. His eyes gauge distance.

Does he live one more day?

Like the toreadors, he faces death in the afternoon. But Vince's garb is no elegant suit of lights, he has no sword, no cape to swirl, no picadors with lances, no novice frightened bull.

It ain't this bull's first rodeo. He's cagey and wise to the tricks of wily clowns like Vince.

The smell of fear mixes with hay and beer as he times his action. Too soon or too late, either way can bring horns, through the groin, the abdomen, the neck. The heart.

Just one last time to feel the surge, adrenalin rushing—the high he craves.

The bull takes his mark, charges. Vince leaps. Clean. Grabs the horns and vaults to his second of triumph on the back of the bull, standing tall, arms raised in victory to the cheers of the crowd. Runs down the back to hurdle over the tail and off, like the ancient bull leapers of Minos. He's survived. Once more.

Vince and dogs pause at arena's edge. Art and Vanilla wag their tails in ecstatic frenzy. Vince bows. Dogs twirl. From the bleachers, roars of approval fill his ears.

The bull stands alone, snorting over a missed target. Another time will come.

Later, scarecrow hat replaced by battered black Stetson, outsized tattered jeans traded for well worn Wranglers, Fancy sees Vince leaning against a stable door post, smoking unfiltered Camels, a Coors in bent and crooked fingers. Talking with other clowns and old cowboys.

Once more, he's earned the beers they buy for him.

Art and Vanilla sleep tired beneath a bench.

And as he looks around, sun still bright in his eyes, Fancy knows exactly what he's thinking: maybe—just one more rodeo.

Never Volunteer!

The dog days of summer bring quiet to the office. Clients vacation with families. Martha's Vineyard, St. Tropez, The Cape, Newport Beach. Business is slow.

Evelyn, friend who worked on several productions with Fancy, calls. She's producing a short western film as a promo for Dusty Trail Productions, or DTP, a company that supplies historically correct western clothing, artifacts, horses, riders and tack, for period western films.

DTP has a group of riders who arrive on set complete with costumes, horses and experience. Western film producers get the whole package. The cowboys are not actors, in real life are lawyers, accountants, businessmen and a few horse trainers. They love playing hooky from reality to be historical re-enactors at fairs or in western films. The gang includes a passel of typical cowboys and ranch hands, a Mexican vaquero complete with sombrero and silver studded saddle, a boss rancher, townspeople, a Comanche, Apache, and a Sioux or two. When the shoot or gig is finished, the last desperado dead in the dust, off comes the western regalia— back to their normal lives.

Evelyn is freaked. "Damn, the shoot's planned for Texas, and I found catering services at a reasonable price. Now it's here in California— because everyone's shooting pilots and new series no one will give me a break on catering…the whole shoot's only three days." The phone's quiet until, "Damn again! I've promised the crew food since they're all working for free…can't let them down."

124

Fancy thinks about it for a moment. "Listen Evelyn, will there be a place to cook at the location? How many people will there be?"

"The cast and crew is about twenty-five, we'll have some extras and family on the set so probably thirty to thirty-five, depending on the time of day. One of the guys is bringing a large barbeque and we can use the kitchen at the location."

Shows how nuts a person can be. Fancy thinks it might be fun. She knows her way around a barbeque. A few days on the range with cowboys…why not?

"If I do it, will I have a place to stay, like a motel—no trailer or tent? If you promise two slaves to clean pots and help out…maybe I'll do it."

"The catering crew's supposed to stay in the house at the location. Family will be there too."

"Nah, I like to have my own room and not stay in someone's home. Good luck in finding your caterer." Fancy dismisses the whole thing. She likes her privacy and sharing a bathroom with an unknown family— not her idea of a good time.

An hour later Evelyn calls. "Two more quotes just came in for catering and craft service. The price is worse than expected, everyone is adding a premium for high season. How about if I get you a motel room and guarantee two slaves?"

Insanity takes over. Fancy says she'll call back in a few minutes. She calls her buddy, Christy. "Hey Christy, want to take a vacation? A short western feature set in the desert at Lake something or other out beyond Palmdale. Needs a caterer. Evelyn's project. Lots of cowboys camping with horses and trailers. Only a three day shoot and we'll have a motel room and two slaves. Want to come and help? I'll be cooking three meals a day for cast and crew."

Fancy knows for sure Christy's crazy too. Insane woman, she agrees on the spot.

Plan is to meet the day before the shoot, stock up groceries at Costco, check out the cooking facilities—get organized. The barbeque to be set up before they arrive.

The location house is main hub and office, horses stabled out back, kitchen and refrigerator for meal prep.

Cowboy cooking is a snap for Fancy. She didn't waste a thought on feeding the masses on an unfamiliar outdoor barbeque. Where she lives, local ranches are party central, each taking one holiday—hers is Labor Day. Cooking for over a hundred guests—no problem.

Christy and Fancy head out to the desert east of Los Angeles, the candy apple Suburban filled with huge pots and pans, knives, cooking implements, tee-shirts, jeans, baseball hats, dog food and bowls, cases of diet coke and Dr. Pepper, beer, large plastic glasses, a huge cooler; Tom and Ethyl barricaded in a corner.

Ethyl still hasn't seen a handsome young man she didn't like, especially cowboys—must be the smell. Everyone on the ranch refers to her as "the slut" because she sashays her rump and wags her tail while lovingly turning soft brown eyes to the best looking male in the place. She *really* likes cowboys. Eau de Cow Shit? This adventure will be like a five star banquet for her.

Fancy plans the menu like she'd plan a battle. Every night starts out with an appetizer, Kielbasa sausage first night, bacon wrapped chicken livers next and Italian sausage the last. The first night main course—barbeque chicken marinated in olive oil, lime juice, herbs de Provence and garlic, Greek salad, fettuccini Alfredo. The next night— tri-tip Santa Maria style with beans, potato and baby greens salad. The last night—lasagna with antipasto salad. Garlic bread standard.

Since cowboys like pie and ice cream—different warm pie with vanilla ice cream every night.

Lunch on the run—sandwiches, tacos, or hamburgers and hot dogs, depending on the day. Cookies and fruit for snacks.

Breakfast hearty—croissants, scrambled eggs and sausage, breakfast burritos or pancakes and eggs with bacon. Doughnuts and muffins. No one will go hungry.

Craft service providing sodas, water, fruit, cookies all day long on location.

One of the cowboys comes over in the midst of planning. When he sees the menus, he tells Fancy it's better than a twenty million dollar shoot he just worked on. Evelyn's happy since everyone's working for free. Good food is a great bonus.

The shoot's to begin at first good light, about seven AM. Breakfast finished by six-thirty, saddle up and ride to the location.

Fancy sets up her huge coffee maker the night before and one of the slaves is to turn it on by five AM. She has a forty-five minute drive from the motel to the set. It will give her an extra few minutes of sleep and keep the crew satisfied until breakfast is served.

They load up the food in the Suburban, two small station wagons and a Lincoln Continental, all packed to the roof. No one imagined they might need a truck for all the groceries.

Fancy and Christy had tucked two large bottles each of rum and vodka into a separate cart to hold aside, pay for themselves. Evelyn saw the bottles and grabbed them. "That is the least the production can do for you."

The ranch they'll work out of consists of a good sized house on two acres. A large dirt backyard, barn, stable, corals filled with horses, mules, dogs, trailers, kids, cowboys and trucks. In the driveway in front sits a sad looking beat-up six foot long barbeque. Looks like it's seen a few too many rodeos. Dejected. In the broiling sun. Picnic tables and benches for at least forty fill the space to the road. How many people are they expecting? Fancy's having second thoughts.

A tent covers the tables, but the barbeque and cooking area stand exposed in the relentless desert sun. What in hell are they thinking? Fancy envisioned a more serviceable back yard set-up with some grass and trees. Shade for chrissakes! As far as the eye can see are barren rocks and dry desert. No a speck of green other than the small cactus garden set in the dirt front yard.

The whole area is the back of beyond. Tract houses thrown up during one of California's many housing booms now either vacant or broken into, a few lived in by people who figure broken down rusted vehicles and machinery are proper lawn décor. The boom had long bust. Tricked out newer trucks decorate driveways of homes in sad need of repair. Fancy has found herself the heart of rednecksville.

Christy snickers aside to Fancy as she looks around, "The person who named this area Lake Whatever Run-a-Mucca was either joking or stoned. Wouldn't mind a toke of what they were smoking." Not a vestige of a lake nor a drop of water to be seen for miles. The landscape reminds Fancy of pictures of the moon—stone, dirt, dust. The only formerly live things—tumbleweeds floating and rolling over everything. Fancy has landed on "Dune." Planet Arakis laid out before her.

The president of DTP, Dennis, is both star and director. He gathers up the producer, the cast and anyone else with a horse who wants to ride. Off they go into the desert to scope out the locations one more time.

Fancy and Christy head into the house to check out the kitchen. Crap! They're speechless. To say the kitchen is filthy is an undeserved compliment. Fancy retches. Christy gags. The oven is caked with cooked-on filth. Christy opens the refrigerator. It looks like a science experiment growing "The Thing" inside. The smell is overwhelming.

"Shit, this is the dirtiest place I've ever seen. And this is where I'm supposed to prepare and cook?" Fancy is ready to walk out the door and forget the whole mess.

"We gotta clean this place, but not before I get into a hazmat suit with a hammer and chisel." Christy's looking around. Wild-eyed. Maids they are not, they need more than slaves—maybe a team of them? With heavy duty tools? Pressure hose? Boots?

Some god of mindless fools had guided Fancy's hand to buy Costco-sized anti-bacterial kitchen cleansers and sprays. First they throw every furry science experiment out of the refrigerator. Next step—scrape off dried multi-colored gook coating every surface.

And where the fuck are the slaves? Evelyn is nowhere in sight. Probably hiding. The lady of the house obviously never cleaned a surface. Never!

The lady of the house, however, is in evidence. She's looking on with hands on hips, tapping her boot. Watching. Probably thinks Christy and Fancy are finicky.

The kitchen has an L-shaped tiled counter doubling as breakfast bar facing sliding glass doors to the dirt corrals and old barn. Nice design, filthy tiles.

Christy finds a tire cleaning brush in the back of the Suburban and goes to town on the bar. Turns out the grout is not dark brown, but white. Once the counter is clean Fancy notices something sprinkling more debris on their sparkling work.

Evelyn distracts them, checking off her list of chores for the production.

"Evelyn, where are our slaves? Remember, you promised us two...?"

"...due any minute. We have two wannabees, film school students, to help you. Don't worry about it. Got it covered!" She makes another check mark on her list on her way out.

Okay, Fancy decides worry isn't going to help as she and Christy clean the filthy kitchen—slave work for sure. Two extra pairs of hands would be appreciated. Damn, the bar counter is dirty—again!

And then Fancy sees it. A parrot cage, complete with parrot, hung above eye level over the breakfast bar. Parrot poop and seeds cover the once clean counter. She was so busy looking down at the filth she hadn't looked up to notice the birdcage. The parrot and Fancy eye each other. One of them has to go. Fancy is damn well sure which one is out.

The lady of the house is shifting her boots on the scruffy beige carpet smirking and taking in the action.

"Ma'am, please put the parrot somewhere else in the house." Fancy is polite and businesslike as thoughts of psittacosis spread over her cooking space.

"The parrot stays in the kitchen. ...been there for years...that place is his home!" The woman digs her heels in.

Fancy sidles up to her, scratches her chin for a moment, looks outside, turns her head up to the ceiling and sighs. "Lady, the parrot goes or I do. You can do the cooking when I leave. I'm not havin' parrot shit all over my cooking. Now!"

She throws a furious look at Fancy and stomps out the sliding doors into the dirt. Christy looks at Fancy. They didn't know whether to flee or giggle. Maybe fleeing is better?

Back into the house storms the woman, now followed by her husband, a huge foot-shuffling cowboy sporting a mammoth beer belly hanging over an equally large silver belt buckle. My god, was all Fancy can think, that must really hurt when he sits down.

"Please, the parrot has to go elsewhere. I can't cook food for all these people in unsanitary conditions." Fancy decides to try her best behavior and gives her sparkling publicity smile. It's totally lost on him. Couldn't give a hoot.

"I don't see what's unsanitary. We been cooking here for years. I say the parrot stays." He gives Fancy his flintiest look. She hears an imaginary booted foot stomp.

It just happens Fancy has a forked meat turner in her hand. Forgetting exactly what her implement is, she aims it at him and waves it under his nose. "Now look here, the parrot is going. Now! If you don't remove it, I will...or we're out the door and you can explain to everyone why there's no food to eat." Fancy's eyes narrow and turn from their usual cheerful blue to a flinty gray. It's a slight movement but one that puts the fear of the Devil into anyone who ever worked for her in her other corporate life. "And you might not like my choice of bird disposal." The fork points in the direction of the hapless parrot.

Keeping eye contact with the big lug, and waving the fork, she starts toward the cage. Hubby grabs the cage first, and in one swift motion he and the bird are gone.

Later, Christy finds the poor bird in the bathtub where it

languishes for the duration, glumly sitting on its perch in the cage watching everyone go to the john. Looking carefully at the family, they didn't seem to use the tub much and it was as good a use for it as any. Eyeballing the bathroom and the strange grayish fuzz taking over the base of the walls and inching up the side of the tub, Fancy gives a sigh of relief she held out for a motel. She'd seen bad motels, but never one as raunchy as this ranch.

Just as the bird situation is straightened out, a big commotion hits the yard, everyone running around screaming. Evelyn, standing in the dust, looks stricken.

They rush out to add to the confusion and finally find someone coherent enough to explain. There had been an accident. While the guys were checking the locations, they had raced around on horseback. Coming around a sharp corner, Dennis had not seen a large cactus arm reaching out over the trail. It hurled him off his horse onto the rocky terrain, lying lifeless, a scarecrow...no pole to hold it up.

The cowboys quick off their horses run to help. One, seeing him motionless face down turns him over, the movement starts Dennis breathing again. Another grabs a cell phone, calls emergency. A helicopter arrives within minutes and Dennis is taken to the hospital. By the time Evelyn is aware of the accident, Dennis is already in the air.

Snatches of news drift in all afternoon and night. He has a major concussion, he's in a coma and unresponsive, broken ribs and collarbone; not moving. He's in Intensive Care with twenty-four hour monitoring.

Christy and Fancy mentally pack up to go home. Dennis was the director and star, how can the film go on?

Dennis' partner, Allen, the guy with the cash for the production, has other ideas. He's already spent a goodly amount of cash for food, sets, accommodations, script, film, camera rental. Allen's a seasoned producer of porno films, and the show must go on. One of the other cowboys with acting experience will be the lead, Allen is now the director. Evelyn's in the hospital to keep an eye on Dennis. No slaves in sight.

In the twitch of a steers ear, Christy and Fancy realize they've lost status: from high dollar executive friends doing the catering as a favor to Evelyn, down the pecking order to the very bottom: location "cooks and kitchen help." Without pay. Crap!

The crew, demoralized by the accident, still have to be fed. Evelyn, the only link to Fancy and Christy's real lives— gone for the duration. The scullery jobs are reality rather than play, slaves available or not. Trapped. Or, they can run for the Suburban and split...fast.

Fancy skulks out to the driveway and surveys the mournful barbeque. She stacks wood and charcoal in its belly and gets the fire going. When the coals are grey fringed, she packs twenty large chickens she's been marinating on the grill and gets dinner going. Hopefully, a good meal will cheer everyone up and get them ready for the next day. Fancy may be many things, but she's not a quitter.

Christy heads back into the kitchen for more prep and cleaning. Later, Fancy's rooting around in the now clean refrigerator and hears a strange whirring sound. She has no idea where it's coming from. Scans the kitchen.

Christy smirks. "Looking for something?"

"Yeah, I keep hearing a whirring sound and I don't know what it is."

Fancy's facing the refrigerator. Christy points up. Fancy looks. There, on the top is a small wire mesh cage with a little rat running like mad on his wheel. One look at Fancy and Christy can't stop laughing.

"You knew about this?"

"Yep."

"You weren't going to tell me about this rodent?"

"Nope."

Christy is rarely if ever monosyllabic. A new art she's perfecting?

"Figured if I didn't say anything it wouldn't bother you. Didn't either 'till you saw it."

Fancy, shaking her head, takes the little cage and gently sets it in the bathtub next to the parrot. Friends. Keep each other company.

Cooking twenty chickens on a grill takes a long time and constant turning. After the first hour, Fancy has a lot of respect for the guys at El Pollo Loco. Now she knows who's crazy—not the chicken!

Interspersed with the chicken is the Kielbasa, cut up and stabbed with toothpicks. A snack for the starving before dinner. They need to be turned on the grill too.

The flies make their entrance about five PM. Dormant during the heat of the day, the scent of cooking chicken brings them around. One of the kids deputizes himself official fly swatter and makes a pile of them on a picnic table. Christy hands him a red cup to use as a mortuary. A giant pot is hauled out of the Suburban for the fettuccini. Fancy notices the dogs are covered with dirt, horse shit and grease. Dog heaven! Ick!

The sun sets in the west lighting up the driveway, the barbeque and frying the cook. Christy watches as the sweat pouring off Fancy's face marinates the chicken with yet another concoction. Between the hot summer sun and the heat from the barbeque, Christy's afraid Fancy's going to keel over as she ministers to the chickens, turning them regularly to cook evenly. She breaks out the rum and diet coke for Fancy and the vodka and grapefruit for herself. That's enough to hold Fancy for the moment, but more is needed.

Christy takes action. Finding the producer, she goes into vamp-flirt mode. Arches her back a bit to show a well-endowed chest, a little hair tossing accompanied by smoldering eyes. Success. A tent arrives. The producer directs it set up over where

Fancy stands.   Christy hands her a giant red plastic cup—her remedy to keep Fancy going—diet coke librally laced with rum—and plenty of ice.

Soon Fancy doesn't care she's hot and dirty. She's not much of a drinker usually, but this is an exception. She's both dehydrated and pissed off—more than usual. Fancy gives a sigh of relief—shade is paradise, the drink—bliss! After a few rum and cokes, she thinks the grunge covering her is the beginnings of a suntan. She keeps that idea until later when the shower washed it off.

By the time dinner's ready, the ranks have swelled considerably. From a group of about twenty-five to thirty, at least fifty hungry people are watching the chickens anxiously, as if afraid the birds might fly off the grill. Without telling anyone, Allen invited the neighbors to dine. He thought it would ease any discomfort the traffic a film shoot might cause. Somehow, seems he just forgot to tell Fancy.

The neighbors are delighted. They arrive with children, dogs, husbands and wives, grandparents, aunts and uncles, former lovers, friends, probably even a second-cousins best friend's step-sister for all she knows. Luckily, Fancy has no idea about portions. If she errs at all in her cooking, it is on the side of "too much is better."

When everyone is served and seated, Christy counts almost seventy people. They all have full plates. Then they come back and have some more, and then some come back a third time. The chicken and the Kielbasa are long gone and someone is scraping the bottom of the pan for the last strand of fettuccini.

When the pies appear on the top rack of the grill to warm, Fancy imagines she's witnessing a collective orgasm. Least it sounds that way. Christy scoops great dollops of vanilla ice cream over the big slices of warm apple pie Fancy hands to her and the tension level drops with a thud. At least no one is going to go hungry.

No slaves appear. One of the cowboys takes pity on the slaveless cooks and makes the rounds with a black leaf bag to pick up the plastic plates and cutlery. The last piece of pie is sufficient bribery to commandeer a kid to wipe off the tables.

One of the neighbors sidles up to Fancy. He's at least six foot four and must weigh a good three hundred pounds, all muscle except for the start of a serious beer belly. "How long you going to be here?" he whispers anxiously in her ear.

"This is a three-day shoot."

"Will you be cooking every night?"

"Yep, breakfast, lunch and dinner tomorrow and the next day—just breakfast the last."

"Oh, thank you, thank you! What time is breakfast?" He hugs her so hard he lifts her off her feet.

They've created a monster. Now the whole neighborhood is an enthusiastic audience as well as the crew.

The giant pots have to be cleaned. No sink big enough. Christy flirts with one of the cowboys. He takes the nasty pots to an outdoor spigot and scrubs them clean. It pays to have a coquette with you, especially one with sexy eyes to twinkle, long hair to toss—a lesson Fancy learns that night. She's so tired and annoyed, she's snarling at everyone. Grandma was right, she thinks, you do catch more flies with honey.

Christy and Fancy crawl into their motel room. Fancy dirtiest and first into the shower. Covered with grease and smoke, she smells fowl. When the water hits, she groans. Sweat, dirt and melted chicken fat roll off sunburned skin. Never in her life did she remember water and soap feeling so good!

When she exits, towel wrapped and pink from vigorous scrubbing, Christy pokes her head into the tiny bathroom.

"What are you doing?" Fancy asks.

"I wanted to make sure you were in there alone. You were making such loud moaning sounds I thought you snuck in one of the cowboys. The dogs sat outside the door and looked like they were keeping watch."

Once again clean and in pajamas, they refill their drinks and sit outside to relax in the cooling desert air. Soon they're joined by crew and some of the actors, everyone staying at the same motel. Cold drinks and quiet conversation go a long way to release the tension of the day.

Up at five AM next morning, teeth brushed, hair finger combed and out the door in fifteen minutes. No point in make-up or fussing. By noon everything will be covered in dirt, grease and food anyway. Fancy put on her uniform for the duration—tee shirt with sleeves rolled up, tank top underneath for when the day warmed up, baggy jeans, rolled up bandanna around her forehead to catch at least some of the sweat before it drips into the food.

She looks in the mirror for a moment before leaving. Sure a far cry from custom monogrammed shirts and Parisian designer business suits. Mock shooting her cuffs, she laughs at her image in the mirror and realizes she's having more fun than she deserves. Law degrees and executive positions be damned!

The dogs don't want to get up. Has to push them outside to do their business so early it was hardly light. Rest of the time they're happy because the crews' dogs come to sniff their intriguing odors—close to the cooking.

Breakfast goes off without a hitch but the kid assigned to put the coffee on did not plug the pot in. The cowboys start complaining about no java at five-thirty. Fancy makes plans, she'll hunt the kid down. Kill him. Painfully.

Dennis is out of Intensive Care and now breathing on his own. He had a collapsed lung. Everyone perks up a bit with the news. At least he's alive.

By nine AM Christy hands Fancy her first rum and coke. Never in her life had a drink that early before, but Fancy doesn't refuse. Seems like a real good idea. The day appears to be well over the yardarm by then, but might just have been wishful thinking. Sure went down cool and smooth. Lots'a ice, a bit sweet. Caffeine to keep her going. Nice.

That night when Fancy stokes up the barbeque for the seasoned tri-tip; she spots the kid who was supposed to plug in the

136

coffee. Ambling over, she grabs him by the arm. Big smile on her face, "What's your name, son?"

"Andy, Andy Wallman."

"What'cha doing here on the set? Family to someone?"

He yanks his arm away from her. "I'm a film student here to assist." Arrogant. "Who are you?" Hostile.

"I'm the one who feeds you. Why didn't you plug the coffee pot in at five AM like you were told?" Voice quiet.

"I'm not getting up so early to do your job. You plug it in! I'm the assistant to the assistant director and I have my own work to do. You can't tell me what to do—you're just the cook!...and I need my sleep."

Cocky little bastard wiggles his shoulders at her and stands his skinny ass up as straight as it goes. Just about right to be kicked, Fancy thinks.

Kid picked the wrong person to be snotty to. Fancy Lady didn't get her name for nothing. She learned long ago not to take shit from anyone. Picking up a large wooden mixing spoon she backs the kid up against a table. No place to run as she waves it at him. Christy's checking the action, expectant look on her face. One dog on either side of the kid, both growling low in their throats. Look like they might like a bite or two of ankle. They knew when their mistress is angry, feel the vibes, ready to help her out.

"Now listen to me you little pissant, all you have to do is roll out of bed to plug that fucking pot in. I have to drive forty-five minutes to do it. So here's how it goes—that coffee is plugged in tomorrow like you were told or you'll have this plugged into your ass when I arrive. The cowboys want their coffee on time." The spoon is pointing between his eyes and hers are mean as a pit viper's with boils. "You get me?"

Christy's in hysterics as the kid flees. "Where did you get 'pissant' from? I thought that was classy." The two of them laugh.

Fancy's still mad. "Little shit head. I'll make sure the producer knows his name all right. Got'ta remember to take this spoon with me from now on. Sure comes in handy." She holds it up, turns it around, looks at it lovingly.

Two kids hang around the cook tent swatting flies. No one knows who they belong to, maybe crews' kids, maybe neighbors'. Both nice kids, boy and a girl 'bout eight or nine, asking to help. They fill up two giant sized red plastic cups with fly carcasses and haven't even begun to make a dent in the fly population. Help to put out the paper plates, forks and knives rolled into napkins. Polite kids, ready to do anything that's asked.

Fancy has some suspicions about the neighborhood though. One of the kids asks if his mom can have dinner tonight. She's coming home later that day, he says and Fancy thinks the mom isn't just coming home from work, sounds like a longer time.

Fancy has no problem. "Sure, why not, everyone else comes for dinner. How long has she been gone? Did she take a vacation?" She's just friendly and making conversation with the kid. He likes hanging around, helping, talking.

"She been gone two year, she been in jail and we been livin' with our aunt."

Okay, there's a jailbird neighbor. It could happen anywhere. But still…

Just after the kid leaves, a police car pulls up and one of the officers comes into the cook tent, now laughingly referred to as Fancy's "office." He studies the tri-tips for a moment, assessing her culinary skills.

"How long you been cookin' out here?" he asks.

"Two days, but it seems like a month." She says as sweat drips down her face.

"Have you seen anyone go into the house next door?"

"Not that I noticed, but I haven't really been paying attention."

"Well, here's my card, if you see anyone, call me." He hands Fancy his card with embossed badge symbol in gold.

"Who do you expect?" she asks. "Anyone special I should look out for?"

"Could be. Lookin' for a male, late twenties, or a woman, older, his mother. He beat her up badly few months ago and split, but I hear he's back in the area again. He has a history of violence and she protects him no matter what he does. We think he's dealing again too. Could be dangerous."

That convinces Fancy. If she sees anyone go into the house next door, she, Christy, and the dogs are history. She'll leave all the people hungry…not getting into the middle of any gunfight. Back at the grill, she studiously avoids looking at the house.

Two hundred and fifty chicken livers wrapped in bacon last less than the blink of an eye and those who are late for diner are out of luck.

When Fancy stands at her cutting board serving the thirty tri-tips she cooked, she notices the ranks of diners has swelled. Christy counts over eighty; it's hard to be accurate as they keep moving around to get up for seconds and thirds. Fancy slices the meat thinner. Lucky for her the tri tips are big.

The kid volunteer shyly comes up to her with a very large, tough looking woman. "Here's my momma. I wanted you to meet her. Momma, this is Fancy, she been cooking for us for days and I been helping."

A beautiful smile changes the stern scary face into a sweet mother. "Thank you for being nice to my boy. I know it's been hard on him. He been talking 'bout how nice you been to him." She's suddenly soft and warm and her voice is light and gentle. Fancy feels guilty for thinking of her as a jailbird. After all, she has no idea what the woman had done.

"It was my pleasure. You got yourself a real nice young man...polite...sweet boy." Fancy means every word. Without thought, the women lean toward each other in a gentle hug. The boy looks on, pleasure obvious.

The tri-tips gone, the garlic bread devoured, a few sad shreds of lettuce wilted in ranch dressing all that is left; again a collective moan of pleasure goes up as blueberry pies are carried out to warm on the barbeque. Everyone keeps a weather eye on the pies as the dinner debris is cleared away and vanilla ice cream begins to soften.

As Fancy clears up the last of the mess and scrubs down the grill on the barbeque, her friend of the night before once more sidles up. "What's for dinner tomorrow?" He whispers in her ear.

"Italian sausage, lasagna, garlic bread, salad with salami, cheese and pepperoncinis, but I'm not going to tell you what pie. That's a surprise."

Her friend is almost salivating. She can see him planning how to get off work early so as not to miss out on the sausages. He looks misty eyed.

"You married?" she asks.

"Yes, and I have two kids." She remembers seeing him with a stout woman and two equally stout little boys.

"Doesn't your wife cook for you?"

"She doesn't know how, we go to MacDonald's every night for dinner. Once in a while we go to Family Buffet, but not very often, it's too expensive. I haven't had a home cooked meal in years. Family is in Ohio so we don't get back there very often." A wistful look creeps over his face. "Sure is nice to have home cookin' again."

Fancy gets another gentle hug and he's off.

By now the dogs are beyond filthy. Ethyl has successfully seduced several cowboys into feeding her sausage or bits of meat under the table. Her soft brown eyes fill with love while she rubs against their legs, leaving a residue of fur, grease and shit on their chaps or jeans.

That night Christy hits the shower first. It's only fair, her flirting conned one of the cowboys into doing pots again. Still no slaves.

As she leaves the shower, Fancy admonishes her. Christy moans too.

Back in the shower, Fancy moans to her heart's content. Nothing, not even sex, can feel as good as a shower after fifteen hours of desert sun and barbeque grease. Her feet have sunburned

Birkenstock sandal straps etched in white. Filthy water swirls down the drain. She remembers the old adage, 'Never Volunteer.' That's one she'll certainly never forget.

Clean again, they sit outside with cocktails, the evening cool and conversation usual to a location shoot. Camaraderie and stories of other shoots, other times, fill the air. They bring out rum and vodka and pass the bottles around. The soda machine at the motel has a busy night. The dogs are so exhausted they pass out next to Fancy's feet, content to listen to the talk and banter rather than sniff around at desert critters in the motel courtyard.

The next morning coffee is made on time, the cowboys are happy. They are even happier when warm croissants, strawberry jam and butter accompanies scrambled eggs and sausage. Still not a slave in sight. Fancy has almost given up, but Christy's still hopeful. No sign of the pissant. Maybe Fancy scared him off?

Midday they're in the kitchen preparing sandwiches for the crew. Fancy's working an assembly line on the counter. A breeze blows in from the open sliding doors. It's almost pleasant. Christy's checking out the storage closet for chips and sodas. Rooting around for mustard and pickles in the refrigerator, Fancy hears a snuffling scuffling sound behind her. A mule is at the counter scarfing up the sandwiches, lassoing them into his mouth with his long tongue. Fancy whacks him on snout with a spatula and chases him outside.

One of the kids of the house is laughing. "He come in all the time; nothin' safe once he learned ta' open slidin' doors with his nose."

She rescues as many of the sandwiches as she can, figuring at this point no one cares about a mule nibble or two missing, cleans the counter yet again and makes the rest, about seventy-five in all. After two days of cooking in the dirt and the heat, she's resigned— semi-clean is okay. Sanitary conditions aren't a requirement as long as the food is good. At this point, she probably wouldn't look twice at the parrot and the rat.

141

It's the last night. Fancy cheated; the lasagna is Costco frozen. Giant pans cooking in the oven then set out to warm on the grill next to fragrant garlic bread and Italian sausage. The salad is finished. Fancy has consumed almost the entire large bottle of rum, with a little help from the cast and crew at the motel, Christy already well into her second bottle of vodka.

The crowd has grown once again. The picnic tables can't hold all the diners and the overflow sit on truck tailgates, folding beach chairs, nearby rocks. Fancy doesn't care, it will soon be over and she can go home.

The Stockholm Syndrome has set in. Christy and Fancy start to like their captors, even identify with them. They know they're in deep trouble when the whole adventure is almost becoming fun. Time to get the hell out of Dodge…run Fancy, run like the wind!

Ten pounds of sausage gone. Six giant trays of lasagna licked clean by dragging remnants of garlic bread over the remaining sauce. Then the *piece de resistance*—peach pies, warm and dripping with ice cream. A loud swoon from the direction of the tables, unheard by Fancy. She's watching the little boy and his momma sitting together, talking and smiling; her huge friend and his family stuffing themselves; the cowboys, in from the range, or location as it were, chatting, and for once, not pushing Skoal into their cheeks or spitting in their ever present cups.

Dennis is recovering nicely and moved his feet for the first time, which seems to be important.

Since slaves are nowhere in evidence, the neighbors pitch in to help clean up the mess, taking the garbage bags around and bussing the tables. A community feeling fills the air. Someone brings out a guitar and a banjo player sits next to him. The night is pleasant, not yet high desert cold. No one wants to leave. A couple of bottles of schnapps are passed around, Fancy makes another big pot of coffee, sets out milk and sugar. Everyone begins to sing campfire songs interspersed with old familiar hits. The Beatle, Stones, Three Dog Night and Credence Clearwater tunes. Fancy and Christy are used to the hard days and aren't so tired. Familiar songs fill the cooling desert air as the sun gifts them with the daily spectacle of its colorful exit over the mountains.

As the happy diners drift away, Fancy's big friend comes over. He bends down to whisper in her ear, "I'm really going to miss you. Do you think you'll ever come back again?"

"I don't think so. We wrap up tomorrow and I'll be leaving after breakfast. They have pizza coming in for lunch so I won't stay."

"Well, I just want you to know how much I appreciated it...loved your cooking."

He bends over and gives her a tender bear hug and a sweet kiss on her sweaty greasy cheek. There is the hint of a glisten in his eye as he shambles off to collect his family for home.

The next morning they pack up and head back to the ranch. Before going home, the dogs need washing...need it bad! They are walking toxic waste sites. Fancy managed to wall them off into a tiny spot in the back of the SUV, squelching the wish she had crates to tie them to the top luggage rack. Desperate, she finds a one hour dog wash. Fancy and Christy have a not-cooked-by-them meal at IHOP while waiting for the dogs to undergo the indignity of decontamination.

Relaxed by the luxury of being fed and served by someone else, the dogs once again fluffy and degreased, Dennis recovering, the film in the can, Christy sits quiet with her calculator. "Did you know we served over 700 meals in three days?"

"Holy crap! That many?" Fancy can't believe it.

"Yep, I tried to keep track every meal."

Fancy pulls the Suburban in front of Christy's home. As she gets out, she looks at Fancy with a huge grin. "Some vacation! Thanks a lot...by the way, what have you planned for us next summer— a chain gang?"

Timmy

Timmy hangs out at the Mustang Saloon. Most people leave him alone. Try to steer clear. Some of the cowboys, especially the ones off the Res, tease him, not mean, friendly, make him feel like one of the guys. He seems to enjoy the recognition, happy when they speak to him.

Timmy's not quite right, just a little slow. Overweight. By a lot. Probably hard on his heart to have such a big belly. He wears baggy jeans, crotch slipping nearby his knees, large tent-like plaid shirts. Dark curly hair covers his head, arms and mats into the v-neck of his shirt. His deep black eyes convey little beyond sadness to anyone who cares to look. Few do. His neck sports a galaxy of moles and warts.

Fancy thinks he probably likes the local girls, but they all shy away from him. She understands. He makes her uncomfortable too. She would speak to him, offer a modicum of friendship, but with the intuition of women, she knows he might misinterpret any small sign of friendship. She keeps her distance.

Polly is tending bar one cold winter night, temperature sinking into the 20's. Sure to be frost on the windshields in the morning. Fancy is bored, alone at home, nothing on television to interest her. Only seven-thirty and black as pitch outside, she bundles herself into her shearling jacket, drives to the Mustang to gab with Polly. Better than an empty house. Polly shoves Fancy's usual, a diet Coke with Bacardi dark back, in front of her. That way Fancy uses a half shot with a large glass of Coke and gets a free soda refill for

144

the second half of the shot. No DUI on the way home.

Timmy sits on the short arm of the bar, head turned and looking out the window. The rest of the place is empty.

Polly and Fancy sit across from each other in the middle of the long part of the bar. Gossiping. A cold wind blows in as the door slams open, bangs against a nearby table. A short blonde huffs inside, looks around fast, casing the joint, and plops herself down right next to Timmy, carefully ignoring the other twelve empty barstools.

The blonde doesn't look like a local. Face not familiar. She's wearing a crisp white blouse under a short dark mink jacket, black gabardine dress slacks and elegant black boots. Not cowboy boots—but Italian or Spanish, expensive from the look of them. Leather soft and smooth. Fancy knows boots. Couple a hundred bucks for low. No ranch dirt. Gold earrings, bracelet and watch. Gold Movado. Classy. Visitor...or guest at a ranch maybe?

Polly asks what she wants and, with a long look towards Timmy and a pause as she licks her bottom lip, the blonde says, "I'll have a Slippery Nipple. Please."

Polly does her one eyebrow raised thing at Fancy who looks down into her rum and coke. Timmy sits up straight, eyes popped wide open.

Drink served, Fancy and Polly go back to their conversation, leaving the two at the other side of the bar to their own devices. A half hour later, their attention is caught by scuffling sounds. Timmy and the woman have moved to a table in the corner. Close to each other. The blonde is pretty, a bit windblown, strongly built and country-healthy despite the expensive city clothes. Picture a serving wench in a Medieval story. She's leaning into Timmy, her hand tracing across his chest under his shirtfront.

Polly and Fancy blink a few times and look away. Fast. This is something neither one is interested in seeing. Too much unwanted information. Was the chick stoned or drunk when she came in? Don't know. Didn't look that way at first glance. They shrug at each other and go back to their conversation, unmindful of the muffled sounds.

Fancy looks over again, a particularly loud moan drawing her attention. The blonde is almost climbing Timmy. One leg stretches across the lower part of his belly, his hand under her bottom holding her in place. Both her arms circle his neck, one hand caresses his moles, tracing circles around them, the other running through his hair.

Fancy slaps a fiver on the bar and looks at Polly. "Well, girl friend, I'm outta here." She studiously ignores the kafuffle to her right.

Polly has none of it. "Don't you dare leave me alone with that!" Her head points in the direction of the two. "If you walk out that door I'll never speak to you again!" Her face is turning a little red. Fancy almost believes her.

"Shut the place for the night. No one's around. You won't miss any business."

They both glance into the far corner. The woman is licking the warts on Timmy's neck.

Polly looks at the clock over the bar. It's close to ten o'clock. Fancy's right, the town's shut down for the night. "Yeah, okay, but how do I get the lovebirds out of the place?"

"Hand her a tab. Say you're closing down for the night and would she please settle up. Then start putting everything away. If you want, I'll stay with you until they leave."

Polly nods and prepares the bill. The woman pays. No problem. As she climbs off Timmy, they see his shirt open all down the front. Black curly hair forming a soft-looking mat covers the mountain of his belly and chest. Fancy looks away, she doesn't want to see anything else open. Definitely much more information then she wants!

The woman gets up, adjusts her blouse and shakes out her hair; bends over and takes Timmy's hand. He looks a question at her with his black empty eyes and she motions with her head to follow as she pulls him up. When they walk out, the light shines on her. Fancy sees the blonde's not early twenties as she first thought, probably late thirties, maybe even early forties. Still.

The door opens, cold air rushes in once again and the porch lights glitter on the hood of the new black Cadillac limousine parked by the steps. The woman opens the passenger door for Timmy and shuts it with a soft thud once he's inside. She's already in the driver's side before Polly has the bar door locked, cutting out the action and the cold winds.

Timmy left his jacket on the table next to the door, a black lump gone unnoticed. Fancy moves to pick it up, try and catch them, but Polly puts her hand out. "Don't bother, I don't think he's going to need it tonight. I'll make sure he gets it tomorrow." Fancy looks down, unquiet about the evening events, but doesn't say anything.

They close up the place together. As Polly runs a rag down the length of the bar, Fancy voices what's been bothering her. "Do you think he's going to be all right? I mean, that was really strange. That woman was…after all?…what did she want with him?"

"Don't worry about Timmy. He's a big strong guy, he can take care of himself."

"Still…do you think we should call his family? …someone? Let them know where he is?"

"We don't know where he is. He lives on the Reservation with his mother, he's well over thirty and should be able to take care of himself. Let's just close the place and go home. Please."

Polly turns off the lights, puts on the alarm and locks the door. Fancy sees a few flakes of snow in the street lights overhead as she pulls away from the parking lot. The scene is tranquil, like Christmas. Unusual for California, it reminds her of her home on the other side of the country and she feels disoriented, as if being someplace unknown.

When she arrives back home, the ranch house feels cold and damp…empty. Instead of lighting a fire to kill the chill, she goes to bed, patting the covers to invite the dogs to sleep on top, wanting the sounds of their breathing for comfort. Still, all night she tosses and turns. Conflicted. She keeps dreaming about Timmy with the blonde. Different scenes, different places.

At first she sees them in the woods; the woman on her knees in front of him, her face buried in a thatch of black fur at his groin, his belly bouncing up and down over her head. He's standing against a tree, his arms twisted back, tied around the trunk. Fancy understands he's screaming but no sound comes from him.

Then they're in a dank, shadowed place like a movie set castle dungeon, the woman on top riding him like a Brahma bull, flicking a whip across his arms and her own buttocks as she urges him on.

Next, he's in a room, dark, seedy, paint peeling off the wall like a cheap motel. His life slips away into a dark pool from a wound across his throat, the woman in shadows, her face partially hidden; watching as his life stains the grubby sheets and drips to the floor while her hand furiously works her pubic region.

Fancy wakes up with a start, sweat drying on her own neck. Goes to the bathroom. Splashes water on her face. Opens the door to let the dogs outside for a quick pee and admonishes Tom, "Don't play with any skunks, I'm not in the mood to deal with you tonight." The little Jack Russell gives her what she thinks of as a 'dirty doggie look' and trots off into the shadows, returning with a flick of his rump.

She goes back to bed, still anxious, acid burning her stomach as two Tums melt in her mouth. As soon as she falls asleep, the strange dreams flicker once more across her subconscious, moving from sensual to bloody—some only a flash of light into a pit of darkness. They carry with them a sense of unknowing, a probing into something deep inside that doesn't want uncovering. The places where unquiet lives.

As she drinks her coffee the next morning, she realizes she's exhausted. Probably been up off and on the entire night, she thinks.

Too many questions won't let go. Had the woman taken

Timmy's virginity? What did she want from him? Fancy knew nothing about the sex lives of men like him. Would the guys on the Res have fixed him up as a joke? ...as a gift? She's heard stories about such things. There always seemed something innocent about the big man. He sat on the outside of life, a spectator, never part of the action. What had he thought about? Could the woman have wanted his innocence? Taken advantage of him? There was certainly nothing sexually appealing about him from Fancy's point of view. But who knows what other people look for? Had she and Polly left him in the clutches of a succubus?

Shivering, she remembers when the woman entered. Walked directly to Timmy without looking elsewhere. An immediate target—straight trajectory. Fancy shakes herself. Heebie-jeebies. It had been a dark night, cold. Spooky. She pushes the thoughts from her mind and tries to get on with her day.

Polly calls her early afternoon. Her shift started at noon, and by the time she arrived at the bar, the owner, who opens at six AM for the early drinkers, told her Timmy stopped by early to pick up his jacket. Fancy is relieved. He's all right. She immediately forgets the incident.

A few days later, Timmy's mother calls the bar looking for him. No one has seen him and she's worried. It's not like him to go someplace without telling her. Fancy hears the story from Polly as they chat like always across an empty bar.

"Do you think he could have run off with that woman?" Polly asks.

Fancy is puzzled. "I still can't see a nice looking woman in a limo stealing Timmy. Can you?"

Polly laughs. "He sure wouldn't be my first choice if I was wealthy enough to afford that car. I'd find me some hottie with a nice six-pack!"

Fancy laughs at the image. Polly has been living with the same man for years and Fancy can't ever remember seeing her even look twice at any of the guys who came into the bar.

Days pass. Neither one mentions to anyone their strange night at the Mustang. Once Polly wonders aloud to Fancy, questioning who the woman was. She never saw her again. They admit to each other they're reluctant to tell the story, ask around to see if anyone knows who she is.

Fancy wakes with cold sweats a few more times. Queasy, apprehensive, her stomach always full of acid and dread, in fear of the thing with no name, sleeping in all of us, waiting, watching…

Finally chalks it up as one of those odd mysteries life leaves unsolved to rattle around in your brain at night. Leaves you unquiet.

***

Some kids laying a trap line in the mountains eventually find Timmy, or what's left of him. Sitting propped against a tree, his shotgun next to him, pointing at what was left of his face. The scene didn't add up. Suspicious, said the local gossip.

Odd placement for the shotgun if he'd shot himself.

Police ruled it suicide. Didn't much bother about some Indian from the Res who did himself in. Plenty of that goin' round, especially a fat guy without all his marbles. End of story.

By the time Timmy's in the ground, even the gossip has gone as cold as he was.

Intrepid Hunters

The denizens of Santa Isabella can't wait for hunting season to begin. Off season they talk about hunting and hang out at the gun clubs. Not too much game locally, so every fall a bunch of the guys fill up their camper shells with shotguns, rifles, ammo, camo and booze and head to Wyoming or Montana.

There is generally a detour to the 'Bunny Ranches' in Nevada for a little sex-creation on the way back and forth. No one is supposed to know, but the secret isn't well kept, especially after Eddie brings one of the ladies back with him as a live-in.

Aside from the 'bunnies', elk is the preferred target, female if possible, next come deer—venison steaks and liver are always in demand. Hunting tags are purchased the minute the season opens and the guys hunt for as long as they can, some even working as guides.

After the kill, the critters are bled out and taken to a slaughterhouse to be butchered, trimmed and packed in white freezer paper, contents marked and frozen. By the time they get back to Santa Isabella, the beautiful animals are reduced to neatly packaged meat with magic marker labels.

Fancy has her own thoughts on hunting. She understands herds must be trimmed or the animals will die of starvation. She's against hunting as a sport, but if the meat is eaten, actually put to use, she can live with it. When she hears of hunters going to Alaska or Russia for bear or for trophy elk, it makes her blood boil.

151

When the hunters return, barbeques spring up every weekend, venison liver or steak, elk tacos, elk spaghetti sauce, or just plain elk burgers. The first time elk was served to her, Fancy was hesitant. Then she became a fervent supporter of the elk hunt. Delicious. Since most of her friends and horseshoe players are hunters, her big freezer is always well stocked with the nice neat white packages from Wyoming butchers.

But off season, the hunters are bored. Santa Isabella has a short hunting season and the local deer are smart. On the way into town, acre upon acres of tender grass and hay fill with grazing deer. Overlooking his herd, a huge stag with a splendid rack stands silent watch. Local hunters know of him and drool. But the wily giant knows his territory.

As soon as hunting season is announced, every deer on the entire mountain range gravitates down to this particular spread. Along the roadside, men with shotguns stand every couple of hundred yards to protect the herd from any fool dumb enough to try his luck at thinning it. Off limits. While locals know the drill, strangers learn soon enough.

One morning a volley of shots resound across Fancy's ranch. She leaps out of bed, grabs her baseball bat. Tom doesn't like loud noises, quivering, he heads under the bed. Ethel couldn't care less, nothing disturbs her beauty rest.

The clock reads four-thirty AM. What the hell? Fancy opens the blinds to see what's up. Has Santa Isabella been invaded? Under attack by aliens in spaceships? She doesn't think so as she drags on jeans, tee shirt and runs her fingers through her hair. Keeps the dogs inside and goes out to the porch, no boots, bat in hand.

Every tree in the yard has a guy hunkered down behind. Shotgun in the air, poised for attack. She's not sure if she's up for laughing or yelling. Goes for yelling. "What in the name of whatever god allowed fools do you think you all are doing?"

From behind one of the trees a voice calls back, "The

152

Canadian geese are here, thought we'd bag a few...to keep the shit on your lawn to a minimum."

The geese are a pain. For some inbred reason, every year when they make their flights south or north, Fancy's ranch is a preferred stop. They stay for a day or two and leave behind mounds of poop. The dogs give chase, run in the poop, track it all through the house, cottage and office, not to mention the trailers. But it's against the law to shoot within the town limits—which the ranch is. Fancy imagines the constabulary arriving en masse.

"Listen, you guys. Get the hell off my ranch with your guns. This is private property and I don't want trouble with the police." Just as she's about to get enough breath to continue, a volley of shots ring out. Seems another flock of geese came in for a landing. Couple of bodies flop to the ground.

"Ah come on Fancy, we don't mean no harm, that is, except to the geese. Leave us have a little fun." Jim's come from behind his tree. Several other hunters show themselves. At least they have the good grace to look a little sheepish. Speaking of sheep, hers are cowering in a corner of their pasture making plaintive baaahs. The steer is pawing the ground. For a moment she has the idea of letting him out, he'd sure run the guys off. But they might decide to shoot him too. Bad idea.

"Listen guys, this isn't going to happen. Next shot I hear I go inside and call the cops. But, if you stow your armaments in your trucks, I'll make a big pot of coffee and some pancakes and eggs. May not be as much fun as hunting, but it's the best deal I can offer."

She hears a little grumbling but the guys come out from the trees and stow their artillery. Three of them have dead geese in their hands, happy retrievers at their heels. "Hey Fancy, want goose for dinner tonight?" One of them yells.

"Not a chance, but thanks for the thought...and please— don't clean them until you get home." The idea of picking shotgun pellets out of her dinner is not appealing, and she has no use for dogs running around with feathers sticking out of their mouth and goose shit on their paws.

Her mother always said you catch more flies with honey than with salt. Might be right too, even though Mother was generally more liberal with the salt she poured on the wounds Fancy's sisters were quick to make. Never could remember any honey from Mother. Sometimes it takes a bit of teeth gritting to put the old homilies to use.

But this time, pancakes and coffee did the trick.

What Lies Beneath

Having a ranch brings certain responsibilities. One of which is hosting annual holiday parties. Fancy's holiday is Labor Day. And not just the day, the entire weekend.

In the Valley, holidays are celebrated with vigor. And a lot of people. Fancy figures a hundred and twenty or so friends and neighbors will be visiting.

When the day arrives, she's set out six sacks of tri-tips, a full keg of beer, plastic plates, knives, forks and napkins. A plastic bowl the size of a washtub overflows with a gigantic salad, those package ones with iceberg lettuce and shaved carrots, completed with sliced onions, tomatoes and cucumbers. A huge bottle of ranch dressing joins an array of olive oils, salad dressings and balsamic vinegars.

Neighbor Jim arrives towing a barbeque he's made—big enough cook half a steer at once. Or two dozen racks of ribs. Big.

Fancy finishes slathering baguettes with a mixture of olive oil, butter, chopped parsley and crushed garlic for garlic bread and pats Sniders seasoning on the tri tips while Jim fills the barbeque with dried oak logs. The oak gives the meat a special flavor and he hunts the mountains for downed trees and branches. He likes to do the cooking, cold beer in hand, prominent smile under a luxuriant gray handlebar moustache. Blue eyes twinkling, receding hair hides under a black 4X Resistol with a Quarterhorse crease. The hat's pushed back a bit and in between beers he hooks one finger under his belt and surveys the fire until it meets with his approval. The smoke is a harbinger of great food to come. Valley people like their tri tip with a good dollop of oak smoke, mesquite is for the tourists. The locals know better.

Guests start to arrive around noon, everyone bringing something to add to the feast. Salads, cakes, more beer, soda, casseroles, pies, chips, still more salads of all description join their companions to tempt any palate. Makeshift tables groan, but manage to hold it all. Trucks of every size, vintage and description, many hauling trailers or filled with camping gear, jockey with good-natured courtesy for a place on or around the ranch.

Valley parties are two days long. No one wants a DUI so guests bring their own sleeping accommodations. Fancy will serve breakfast the next morning, cooked on the barbeque, of course. Pancakes, eggs, bacon and sausage. Coffee. Lots of coffee.

Tables and chairs borrowed from the village are set up around the willow, a net strung across the upper lawn. Badminton or volleyball, take your choice.

The keg is tapped, red plastic cups fill with cold beer. Fancy hears bits of conversation as she rushes around doing last minute set-up.

"Want to set up horseshoes behind the barn?"

"Maybe we should dig a fire pit first."

"Look at the damn dogs, already sniffing at the food." One of the men breaks away from the red plastic cup toting group and shoos a couple of curious dogs away. He waves his big hat at the dogs, "Git, you critters or I'll lock you up." The dogs hunch down. Caught. Ears flatten as they scurry away. They'll be back. Everyone brings their dog with them to parties. They get along with each other same as the folks who brought them.

Another of the men sees Fancy hauling a cooler and goes to help. They dump in two bags of ice, then add soda cans and a few bottles of local white wine, Sauvignon Blanc is the favorite. Red wines open on the food table breathe in the fresh air.

A truck arrives with friends from the Reservation. They pile out carrying large disposable pans, one filled with creamy potato salad, another overflows with tamales and the last has layers of beans, rice, cheese topped with guacamole and sour cream. Bags of tortilla chips to scoop out the layers. More beer. Lots of laughing kids who immediately chase the dogs. Then the dogs chase them. Screaming, laughing and barking. Quite a ruckus.

Fancy grabs Tom and locks him in her bedroom. Tom doesn't like kids, especially screaming ones. Fancy does not need a law suit over a bite. No way. The rest of the critters are fine. Ethel has already snuggled up to one of the little boys and is content to sit forever while he rubs her ears. Later in the day, Fancy sees the same kid and Ethel spooning together, both sound asleep on a blanket under one of the fruit trees. Kid has his arm around Ethel, she's put a paw over his hand.

Myrtle's hot on the trail after a few of the screamers. Little kids always drop food and she's hopeful. Goats are smart. Screaming doesn't bother her.

One of the little boys is Fancy's favorite. His father is full blooded Native American. The boy has long braids trailing down his back and is so beautiful people think he's a girl. His father sets them straight, "Not squaw, he Heap Big Warrior." The boy giggles and stands up straighter at his father's fake movie Indian line and delivery. Fancy resists the urge to grab and snuggle him. Not the right thing to do to a Heap Big Warrior. She knows not to embarrass him.

Neighbors arrive with croquet and set up the game on the lower lawn near the pastures. Fancy stops for a minute to look at the players. Cowboy hats, long braids with feathers. Fringed vests. Big buckle belts, boots. Nicely pressed western yoked shirts. Something inside her swells with pleasure to see the English gentry's game played by this generation of cowboys and Indians. Very cool!

Someone arrives with a guitar and the porch is his stage as he sits with feet dangling over the edge and sings into a Karaoke machine mike.

A BMW arrives with an English actor and his wife. They have

a ranch close by. Following close behind is another Beemer. Brought along some of their friends visiting from L.A.. Everyone is welcome, five more make no difference.

The kids begin a raucous game of badminton.

Three horses trot through the gate with dogs barking behind. The young women riding them slide off, walk them to the first pasture, remove saddles and tack and don't have to slap rumps to encourage their horses to run through the open gate. Cowgirls. Tall, slender. Beautiful.

Next arrival, a van from the local seminary. Fancy smiles as they pile out. Young, handsome novitiates. She's not religious— actually anti-religious. She blames religion as the curse of civilization, thinks it divides mankind. But she does like the seminary crowd. Any kind of respectful group—from AA to Zen Buddhists—can use it as a retreat. The brothers are cool, never press her to convert, honoring a long established, courteous and companionable truce. Friends volunteer at the seminary, and she does too, selling shaved ice cones at festivals. The brothers always come to her parties, bring the novitiates and bags of fruit. Most guests are used to the friendly men in their long brown habits and know many of the Brothers by name.

The novitiates head for the games, trying their hands at croquet first, then over to what has turned into a volleyball competition. As soon as the young men begin playing, the three cowgirls decide to play too.

Some of the guests begin to drift to the barbeque. Aromas of tri tip, onions mixed with peppers, and garlic bread are enough to draw a crowd. Jim has set a gigantic pot on one end of the barbeque and fresh picked corn is steaming. Fancy's favorite. She's good for at least two ears and hopes there is enough to go around. Before forgetting, she runs up to the house returns with two paper plates filled with bars of butter, salt and pepper shakers stuffed in her jeans pockets. Corn's not the same without.

Fancy is sure she hears the low roll of stomachs growling as she passes through the hungry gang. She smiles to herself as she catches whiffs of fresh cut grass, cow pies, the sizzling meat on the barbeque, apple pies cooling, after shave and garlic bread. If she closes her eyes she can almost follow her nose to the direction she wants to go.

Luke, a neighbor, is busy setting up chicken races over by the guest house. He's jury rigged a racecourse out of old fencing, a small pen at one the end with a board to keep the chickens penned for the start of the race. At the other end, a mound of chicken feed. Each chicken is given a number and he's already making book on the racers—even figured a tote board with ten races and the numbers of each racer.

Each race has two winners; first place gets two thirds of the betting pool for that race, and the runner up gets a third. The chickens are in cages on the back of his truck squawking so loud they drown out everything else. The races won't begin until after the food is served and Fancy wonders if the chickens will ever settle down. Luke must have heard her thoughts. He moves his truck to the other side of the cottage. Almost out of earshot, but not quite. Certainly better.

The space in front of the stable fills with trucks, they crowd up to the house and around the driveway. Some are parked along the verge of the road outside the fence. Fancy calculates about sixty, seventy vehicles. Most folks have arrived by now.

Just as she's calculating and trying to match vehicle with face, Jim motions her over. "Tri tip ready, got 'em sliced and garlic bread cut. Let's go."

Fancy begins to shout, "Come and get it. Food's out and ready. Don't let the meat over...." She's almost trampled by the rush.

An hour or so later, Fancy and some of the kids haul black plastic bags around the tables to collect the garbage. They rescue any leftover meat for the dogs, cans for recycling, everything else into the trash. Seems the sound level has gone down many decibels. Most of the cowboys have retreated to the horseshoe pit.

She can hear the rumble of man-laughter and jokes and an occasional 'thunk' as a horseshoe soundly hits its mark. Christy has come up for the weekend to help with the food and to party. Fancy hears her laughter coming from the horseshoe game.

She sees the porch is full, every chair taken, some on the steps, others with feet dangling off the edge as guitar strains fill the soft summer air. September is one of the warmest months in the Valley and the locals know it's best not to exert yourself too much after a big meal.

A group of the older locals gather in the shade in front of the stable. She sees Hitch holding court with a gang of his cronies, his ever-present cup of coffee in hand. She can hear them in her mind, talking about hunting, old rodeos, friends gone. His cackle rings above the guitar and she's happy he's having a good time. This is his kind of gathering, he likes being with people, talking with old friends. A perfect day.

By the guest house, a crowd cheers for the chicken races. As soon as a race begins, the shouting starts, everyone urging their pick on to the finish line. Then it's quiet for a few minutes until Luke sets up the next race. Fancy leaves them to it. She needs to get the place clean before the critters get to the remains. Myrtle loves paper plates with food leavings on them and Fancy worries about the goat's digestive tract handling the amount of trash left behind.

The table that held all the food is a shambles. Most everything gone and scraped clean except a few things no one seemed to like. A Jello fruit salad is almost full, some creation with broccoli looks untouched. The bean casseroles are empty, like someone mopped up the last bite.

Her musing on local gourmet tastes is interrupted by shouting from the volleyball court. One of the novitiates is on the ground, rolling down the slight incline. Everyone is laughing, including the young man. One of the cowgirls offers a hand up. He stands, a bit red-faced and dusts himself off as the game resumes. Fancy goes back to her cleanup.

160

A few minutes later, the shouting and laughter start again. This time it's another of the novitiates on the ground and another cowgirl is pulling him up. The third time it happens, Fancy walks up to the game to watch for a while. Seems there's a plot unveiling itself under the guise of volleyball. The cowgirls are bouncing into the novitiates, knocking them down like tenpins.

Finally, one of the guys picks himself up and, instead of going back to the game, stands firm, hands on hips and looks at the girls. "Okay!" he says, "I get it. Want to see what's beneath the habit? Well here goes!" He bends down and grabs the hem of the long garment. The ranch has suddenly gone quiet. Fancy is horrified. The cowgirls are interested. He pulls the habit up, first displaying sneakers and socks, then bright plaid madras Bermuda shorts and a flaming orange golf shirt. He looks around at the girls, "Now are you satisfied? Can we get back to the game?" The habit flows back down to its usual coverage.

The cowgirls at least have the good grace to look slightly embarrassed as everyone in earshot laughs at them.

As the sun slides over the mountains, the horseshoe players dig a pit in Fancy's lawn. She expects it. No problem. Soon large boulders ring the pit, and behind them, chairs. The guitar player ambles over and sets up out of the smoke when the fire is lit. The chairs are filled, front row first so booted feet can warm while perching on the boulders. The rest of the party slowly filters over with, chairs, blankets, anything to sit or stretch out on.

When the sun goes down in the high desert climate, it cools off. The temperature can drop as much as thirty degrees in an hour or two. The cooling night air is good for the grapes she's been told, not so good for sitting around at night without a fire to warm.

Someone hauls out a giant bag of marshmallows. The kids run off to find sticks, chocolate bars and graham crackers. Fancy likes her marshmallows plain—lightly toasted and gooey in the middle. She foregoes the s'mores.

Luke has given up on the chicken races and arrives with peppermint schnapps, a large thermos of steaming hot chocolate, and paper coffee cups.

The light evening fog is redolent with the sweet smell of cooking marshmallows, hot chocolate, mint and s'mores as it fights with the smoke for supremacy.

The dogs have given up the battle to snag whatever tidbits hit the ground. Tired from racing around the ranch, they move toward the fire and curl in any available space, providing their backs as additional foot-warmers. After a while, the guitar player is accompanied by snores. Cool nights also make excellent sleeping weather.

Fancy looks at those gathered around the fire, out across the ranch to the campers and trailers with their inside lights glowing like gold coins in the dark. A dome tent housing a family is suddenly lit from inside by a lantern and provides a shadow dance of mother getting two kids ready for bed.

Her boots propped on a warm rock, Fancy remembers a night in Monte Carlo at the Hotel de Paris. Dinner with clients. Evening clothes, black ties, minks, diamonds. Art Noveau gilded rooftop sliding open to glittering Mediterranean stars. Elegant silver and porcelain service atop fine linens. Candles wavering in the slight air movement from the open roof.

On her way to dinner, she enters the crowded antique wrought iron elevator. Looks at a handsome man, breast to breast with her, recognizes the movie star. He likes her too as they eye-fuck during the slow crawl to the top. When the elevator jerks to a halt, they head in opposite directions. Off to what they're there for—business. They stop at the same time and look back. He shrugs his shoulders, tilts his head. She discretely waves her fingers. Regrets?

As she glides across her reverie, a small hand takes one of hers. It's Heap Big Chief and he looks tired. Small voice, "Daddy said to say good night and thank you for the party...so...thank you." A grubby hand wipes across a tired eye. The braids have come a bit undone. Wisps of hair illuminated in backlight from the fire form a soft halo.

Leaning over as she holds his hand, she whispers in his ear, "May I give you a good night hug...and can I have a kiss?"

"Okay," barely audible, "if you want."

"I do want," she says and scoops him up for the hug. Marshmallow sticky hands hold her face as he kisses her cheek. Joy suffuses her heart.

Fancy's content. Party a success. No, no regrets.

Friends and Lovers

In a culture brought up on western films, a ranch is a major attraction. Friends from around the world, and international clients, feel the pull to come and stay in the guest apartment or one of the boutique hotels in the area. Most have never been anywhere near actual cowboy country, a chance to experience what they have only seen in the movies.

Friends arriving for dinner in western garb, ZZ Top look-alikes, local ranchers and Native Americans spill out of pick-up trucks to crowd out horses bringing neighbors for the piles of meat served at the barbeque dinners Fancy prepares. For Fancy it's just another day, for a new visitor...better than movie magic.

Fancy and Polly have a deal. When Fancy brings a new face into the bar, if she nods, their routine begins. Polly leans over the bar with her best movie western drawl, "Howdy pardner, what kin I git ya to drink?"

The result is generally a startled look to Fancy for help. "He'll have the usual, Polly, and neat, if you please."

Polly pours a tequila shooter and, taking aim, slides it down the bar to where Fancy has strategically placed the visitor— far enough away for the shot to slosh a bit on the bar as it glides into their hand. Gotta have the whole western bar experience. Add in the locals in boots, hats and western garb for atmosphere. No guest ever left without feeling a bit like John Wayne, or maybe a little early Eastwood thrown in for good measure.

Word gets around the industry, if you make a deal with Fancy, be sure to finalize it at her office, but only if you don't mind getting mud on your shoes and dog hair on your suit. Better still, wear boots and blue jeans.

Fancy likes men. She likes the way they look, the way they smell and the way they feel. She likes the look of a tight butt and strong back getting out of her bed and pulling on their jeans. And leaving. Fancy can't keep interested in any romance for too long. Not in her DNA.

No patience. Fancy gets bored. Pissed off. On to the next. Been married three times, won't do that again. She's sure. But sometimes she misses the feel of a man-body under her fingers, the tangle of chest hair she can rub against, the soft skin of a hard dick in her mouth. Yeah! She really likes men—but not for long. No way's she giving up the remote.

After Fred—cowboys, friends from Los Angeles, Europe, New York drift through her life. She knows that it's not the time for commitments, forever-afters. It's the time for 'you're-all-right-for-nows.'

A woman can have itches that need a good scratch once in a while, with no need for more. Able was a nice man, widower. Met Fancy at a party. Invited her for dinner. Then out for dinner again. Third time they ended up in bed. A good roll in the hay. Nice.

He called the next day. "So, what would you like for dinner tonight, sweetheart? I could bring over some tri-tip and we can barbeque."

She thought for a moment. He hadn't asked if she had other plans, or even wanted to have dinner with him. Hmmm...and 'sweetheart'? "No thanks. I've got things to attend to. Bye." And she hung up.

Next day he called again. Different approach. "Hello darling. I was missing you, couldn't stop thinking about you all day today. How about I pick you up at six for a cocktail at the Mustang and dinner afterward."

Darling? What is this man thinking? "Sorry, can't. But thanks for the invite."

Hard to explain to a man a woman might not want to commit to more than casual.

Once everyone who works in the office, the yard or with the critters is gone, on their own, or in bed, the ranch belongs to Fancy.

She often sits on the porch in the dark, listens to the owls' soft hoot from their nesting place high up behind the barn. Cats mate at the ranch next door, their screams carry into the night silence. A hawk's black silhouette clear against the indigo sky as it hunts.

Damp night on grape vines, a special fruity yet acid fragrance drifting from the vineyards across the ranch to blend with the pungent odor of things growing in the rot of others dying. Fall brings the scent of ozone to clean the air, and summer brings dry dust mixed with ripening fruits on vine or tree.

Years ago, the smell of summer might have brought Fancy out hunting too. For sex, for love, for the touch of male skin against hers. The rush of hormones inflaming hints of the wealth of possibilities the world might have to offer. The mystery of what might be waiting at the next bar, or party, or just around the corner. Enough to bring out the wild child, the creature let lose to hunt the city night with the abandon of her beast within.

But her feral huntress is quiet. Nothing is needed beyond her porch. If she wanted sex, it's available less than three miles away at the Mustang.

Peace is what she seeks, the kind to bathe the mind, rejuvenate the soul. After all those years of rush, rush, college, law school, when she wasn't studying she worked to pay the bills. She hadn't taken a vacation since she couldn't remember when. No time. Hadn't stayed in a hotel that wasn't for business in forever. When she thought about it and tried to give it a time she couldn't remember.

166

Sometimes she closes her eyes and dreams of sitting at a sidewalk café in some distant city. Somewhere she can just sit, savor an espresso or a glass of wine, and watch. A magic time with no necessary end.

She imagines holding her cup or her glass in both hands while she studies people scurrying by. Time to see what the women were wearing. Time to imagine where they were going. What were they like? Was that man off to see his mistress and were the flowers he was carrying for her? Or were they for a beloved wife? Odd, she might think—how come she put the mistress first?

On her porch she can feel the temperature change, the evening mist gathering below the mountain peaks. The mist that makes Santa Isabelle so desired as wine country, kissing the vines with tender moisture-giving lips after hot sunny, arid days. The damp embraces her shoulders, cool against her cheek and neck, like ghost fingers bringing a sudden chill.

Some nights she goes inside, sits in front of the television, no idea what she's watching. Tom on her lap, Ethel next to her on the floor, paws twitching in dreams. The ranch house quiets around her, the creaking sounds of wood roof cooling, squirrels or quail skittering across the back patio. The refrigerator turns on, the washing machine goes into another cycle and a truck rumbles by on the four lane. One of the dogs scratches. Small breezes sighing across the chimney whisper memories of bygone wood smoke. The sounds are her company, her friends. Home.

Often, people ask if she's afraid to live on a ranch out in the country. All by herself. Are they mad? Afraid?

Her business was traveling the world; on her own. Been held at gun point in foreign countries, car stopped by Uzi toting youngsters, roses still blooming in their cheeks. In Spain she was caught in a riot in the Basque country. Several times in Paris, she landed in the middle of political manifestations so powerful armed military was on every corner.

Fancy is a fatalist at heart, she had to be, flying across the world as she did.

When a threat appears, her mind takes her to the places she's traveled, people she's met, art she's seen, lovers, friends, and she feels grateful to have been gifted with a such a life.

The plane can leap and plummet in a downdraft, the barrel of a gun yawn at her, and the smile she gives back is true. She's showed up for whatever life had to offer, and she's still ready for what comes next, even if it's the end.

As ghosts of the past, will 'o the wisps of what had been or might have been, twirl through her mind, she accepts her gifts— been luckier than most. Not as if she was entitled to anything. No, no way. But she's chosen well when it mattered.

Reaching down, there's a dog to pat. She lives in a privileged place, and she's learning to appreciate what she has. Maybe someday she'll even forgive the loss of her position, her corporate status. Maybe someday she'll even begin to forgive herself for the mistakes she's made, the people she's hurt. Maybe...someday. Just not quite yet.

At times, a sudden urge for people crawls up her spine, the need to know they're there if she wants them. A confirmation she's not as alone in the world as she is in her head.

If it isn't too late, she heads to the Mustang. Polly is always happy for company later in the evening. After their night with Timmy, she doesn't much like to be there alone. Especially in the winter when the place empties out.

Fancy sits at the bar, has her rum and coke and gabs with Polly. Other ghosts wandering through the evening mist join them. Seekers of company on nights when unwanted memories slip into the mind like unknown terrors scrabbling out of dark cupboards under the stairs, or slithering from behind dusty velvet drapes in an empty room. All to trouble the mind.

Hank often comes in late nights. Tall, handsome, artfully carved face filled with haunted fear of sleep. Sometimes he sits

168

next to Fancy and Polly. Doesn't want to say things to those who might talk. He knows the women will listen, closed-mouth, neither one much for gossip—except to each other. No further.

Hank saw two tours in Vietnam. Tunnel rat. Then First Lieutenant. Expected life span—minimal. One of the survivors. If you can call it that.

The women listen as he tries to exorcise his demons.

"...the fucking Cong got Tony, don't know why he was out alone, maybe a woman? ...some other bait?" He draws on his cigarette, so deep it visibly expands his lungs. "...we could hear this screaming...loud...knew it was an American by the voice. Then...saw Tony was missing. Damn fool! He'd a' gone to rescue a puppy. Cong did all sorts of tricks to lure us out, hurt something—kittens, dogs, kids. Didn't matter none to them, knew everything and everybody'd be dead anyway."

He looks around...fast...almost as if checking to see if the Cong was at the Mustang door. Satisfied, he continues. "The Captain, he sends a sniper up a tree... see if he can see where them screams is coming from." Silence. Another deep draw, slow exhale. "It was Tony all right. On a Punji stick and screaming for help. We all knew there's no help, them Gooks, they shit on the stick first...every damn germ in the world will get you if you don't bleed out fast enough."

Twenty and more years later, he still screams at night over the same scene, visions of explosions, flying body parts, begging for death cries from his friend Tony—all still vivid.

The story ends as the women heard so many times before. "Captain ordered the sniper, 'Take the shot.' We all knew it was righteous, a clean fast death. We'd all 'a wanted the same."

Tears roll down his cheeks as the words come to him like bits of shrapnel buried deep in his subconscious, fighting their bloody way to the surface.

Fancy puts an arm around him, hugs him like a sister while Polly pats him on the hand. Neither of them have words to lessen such pain.

Survivor guilt? Fancy doesn't know. PTSD for sure. All she can do is listen, sometimes on the porch of the Mustang; the fog surrounding them in silence while mortar fire and screams roar in his head. She'd suggested he see someone for help, knew there had to be some head doctor could lessen the memories, the guilt, but no—his choice is booze and speed.

Times when memories are too painful, he slaps money on the bar and runs. The roar of his Japanese crotch rocket firing up fills the open doorway. Late night, country roads, he opens it up as far as it will go and hurls himself into the unknown.

As the roar of his motorcycle fades into the distance, Fancy and Polly look at each other. Only a matter of time, they figure, before he'll hit something full speed. End the torment. Whenever he leaves like that, they spend the next hour at the bar, quiet over the juke box turned low, and wait, fearful—listening for the sound of distant sirens announcing a crash on some back road winding up the dark mountains. Into the cold, as far away as anyone can get from the steaming jungles of the mind.

No matter how fast you go, no way can you outrun that old devil when he's taken up residence in your head. Fancy knows.

Visitors From Afar

Fancy has a new gig—consultant for a European company. They want to produce programs, do business in the States. She's back and forth to Europe on their dime and hates every moment she's away from home. But rice bowls need filling, and the ranch has a myriad held out in front of her face.

First time she meets the head of the company, he comes to Santa Isabella.

Nice looking guy. Pleasant. Brings artwork and minimal business plan. She starts to suggest the first steps to take until she realizes he has absolutely no interest in what she's saying. He's looking around the ranch, playing with the dogs. She's trying to talk. Okay, she'll stop, he's paying the freight, what's he here for? Might as well find out.

Conversation starts out hard to fathom.

Fancy begins. "Michel, it's good to have you here. Would you like me to make appointments at any of the studios? Anyone you would like to meet with." Still disinterest.

Maybe she can try another tactic? "Is there anything special you might like to see...or do? There are wineries we can visit, an interesting tourist village nearby, or perhaps you'd like to see some of the horse ranches?"

He looks relieved the conversation about business has stopped. Lights up a cigarette. Takes a sip of wine. Coughs. "Are there stores in the area that sell western boots?"

Okay, we're getting to it. "Sure, several close by, others a few miles up the road. Anything special you're looking for?"

"Well, yes. I'd like a pair of hornback crocodile or Caiman boots. Good ones. Do you think we can find them?"

A bit of calculation. Probably cost him close to a grand, maybe more. Not her problem. "We can certainly check it out. With a little looking, I'm pretty sure we can find what you want."

This guy is paying Fancy by the day. She doesn't mind being his personal shopper if that's what he wants. And he does want. They spend the next three days in search of his boots. All over the Valley, even thirty miles up the road into serious cowboy country. Damn boots are hard to find. Fancy finally tracks them down in Los Angeles. Michel is overjoyed. While they're in L.A., she tries to take him to several studios to discuss business. He's not interested. Not her problem, she keeps reminding herself.

At LAX, she hands him her invoice for five days of her time before he gets out of the Suburban. He looks as it, opens his briefcase and hands her ten banded packets—ten grand in neat new hundreds. She hopes it's not counterfeit as she places it in her oversized handbag. "Thank you, I hope you had a successful trip. Would you like a receipt?"

"Yes, it was. Just what I wanted to accomplish. I appreciate it. And no, a receipt isn't necessary now. Just send one to the office when you have a chance."

Fancy drives back to the ranch with a big smile on her face. Damn if the consulting business isn't interesting. Sometimes it even pays well. But not regular.

Her next guest is Joan, a friend from the Europe. She's come to the States for a convention and has taken a week vacation after to visit Fancy at the ranch. Short, pretty, dark hair and eyes that always hold a twinkle. She's coming for fun instead of business.

The first night, Fancy introduces her around at the Mustang Saloon. New females are always welcome and Joan is no exception. Especially when the cowboys hear she's from Spain. Exotic. Good looking. The line forms to the right. Free drinks abound. Fancy

172

stands back to check out the action. There is plenty.

As the night goes on, the line thins as the guys give up hope. Joan is in deep conversation with Buddy, a cute looking cowboy, well built, blonde, freckled turned up nose, not too much taller than she is. Guy can't keep the shit-eating grin off his face. Last man standing.

Finally time to go. As they leave, he hands Joan a napkin with his phone number on it. "Don't forget to check with Fancy. Whatever night you're free is all right with me."

As the women get into the Suburban, Fancy laughs. "Joan, do you realize the stir you caused." She stops and thinks for a moment. "Stir isn't right, it was more like a stampede. Never saw those guys move so fast or try so hard."

"What do you mean? I thought they were nice. Polite too."

"Yes, they were, but they were all in love with you...or maybe just in heat." Fancy can't stop chuckling. "Did you like any of them?"

"Well, I thought Buddy was sweet." Pause. "He wants to take me out, but I told him I had to check plans with you first."

"Do what you like; we have nothing special on our calendar."

"He wanted to know about tomorrow night. For dinner. Would that be all right?"

"Sure. Go for it."

"Okay, I said I'd call him when we got home and let him know."

The next morning Joan is a bit doubtful. "What do you think I should wear? I don't have anything other than jeans and clothes I brought for the convention."

"Have you got anything like a black dress for one of the convention dinners?"

"I have two of those."

"Good, let's take a look."

One of the dresses has a low crossover bodice. Fancy surveys her friend when she tries it on. Sexy. Just the right amount of cleavage. Elegant. Sophisticated.

Fancy giggles to herself. Buddy will lose his mind. Think he's found himself in cowboy heaven.

All day Joan keeps asking, "What will I talk to him about?"

"What did you two talk about last night?"

"I can't remember, I was too overwhelmed by all the men around."

"Just play it by ear, you'll be fine. Don't worry so much."

A trip to the beauty parlor for a cut and a style, manicure and pedicure does nothing to calm Joan's nerves. Fancy is losing patience. "Calm down. It's just a date for dinner. He might only take you to the local chew and choke, who knows?"

Joan is lovely. The black dress fits to perfection, her dark hair shines and her eyes glow. She and Fancy sit on the couch in the living room as she picks at the fringe on a pillow. Fancy chases Tom off Joan's lap, white dog hair on the black dress will not do.

The chugging rumble sound of a diesel truck pulls into the driveway. Lars, Fancy's nephew, is walking up from the office and flings open the door. He's been hanging around day, teasing the women every time he sees them. Seems the rumor of the big date is all over town. "Ladies, Joan, your chariot has arrived. And it's been washed and detailed from the looks of it. In cowboyland, that's serious. Be careful Joan, there may be a proposal in the air." The brat is laughing as she turns pale.

Buddy knocks as the door, even though it's wide open. Like a well-trained cattle dog, he won't come until he's invited. Fancy comes to his rescue, "Come on in Buddy. Good to see you."

He's resplendent. White, knife pressed Wranglers, pale gray Resistol Big Spender, pink, green and white checked western shirt, shined alligator belly Lucchese boots. And the topper—six pink roses and white baby's breath wrapped in cellophane, tied with a dark pink ribbon that almost matches Buddy's cheeks. Maybe a bit lighter pink.

174

Buddy's welcoming committee is speechless. Joan graciously takes the roses. "Oh Buddy, you didn't have to…but they're beautiful…and my favorite color. Thank you so much…so thoughtful."

Fancy can see he's starting to breathe again. Joan is going to be just fine.

Joan puts her nose into the bouquet, inhales, and asks Fancy, "Do you have something to put these in? I'd like to keep them in my room. Near my bed." The flush is back in Buddy's cheeks. Fast.

Lars steps in. "Joan, come with me, I know where the vases are. You can pick the one you want." He takes her arm and leads her to the pantry while Fancy motions Buddy to the couch. Offers a drink. Politely refused.

As soon as Lars and Joan are in the pantry, he whispers in her ear, "This is serious; Buddy has obviously gone to great lengths to dress up and prepare for the occasion. He's dressed in cowboy-formal, very elegant, and *detailed his truck!* That is huge! The guys never do that. Consider it a monumental compliment to you. And flowers? Never saw that before in the Valley."

Joan's eyes are wide. This is a different culture and one she has no understanding of. But she does understand the flattery. As they come back into the living room, her cheeks are the ones flaming.

Roses in vase, Buddy takes Joan's arm and leads her to his truck. Solicitous, he helps her up the high step, throws a smirk back at Fancy and Lars watching from the doorway. As the truck rounds the circular driveway, they high-five behind the closed door, pleased their friend is out for an exotic evening—part of a lifestyle she's never seen outside of the movies.

Even coming from the heart of Europe there are always new customs to be learned.

Buddy comes for Joan for lunch or dinner every day until she leaves. As he heaves her big suitcases into the back of the Suburban for the trip to the airport, he holds her hand and looks into her eyes. Fancy makes herself scarce, leaving the two to their goodbyes.

When the women are finally alone in the car, silence prevails. Fancy doesn't want to intrude on Joan's thoughts until she's ready to break the silence. When that time comes, it's a surprise. "I really had a nice time with Buddy. He was pleasant—quite a polite gentleman.

"We toured all over the Valley, various wineries, out to visit friends on both horse and ostrich ranches. He even brought me to meet his mother and father. We had a wonderful lunch at his house with the family. They were very nice people...kind." She paused and looked at the window for a moment. "But at the end, I'm glad to be going back to the Basque Country. I liked him, but sometimes differences are too much to overcome."

Joan withdrew again to the window. Silent and thinking for a few minutes before she turned back. "I hope I'm not going to sound like a snob, but his education stopped at high school, the biggest trip in his life was to Los Angeles, which makes him a world traveler compared to the rest of the family.

"Fancy, you and I have traveled the world, we are both well educated with several degrees. How many years have we spent dealing with top executives in international business? You know what I mean." Joan looked down for a moment. When she looked up, her face was sad. "I liked him a lot, but it's as if we were from different planets. Then I understood, we *are* almost from different planets...or maybe only similar species but different branches. There was no point in leading him on, no matter how appealing the idea of life on a ranch with a handsome cowboy...something girls dream about...a movie story wish come true. But I knew there was no chance for us beyond a wonderful few days. Just a vacation I'll remember for the rest of my life." She was close to tears. Obviously the chemistry wasn't lacking.

As Fancy listens to her friend's words, she's struck by her own question. How much of those thoughts also apply to her? How long can she hang out at the Mustang Saloon and forget about what she'd done all her life? Not as if she'd accomplished anything of meaning, the entertainment business wasn't exactly save the planet stuff. But she had been a success at what she did.

Was there a way to reconcile such diverse lifestyles, or just another conundrum to consider? Knowing humans are not mono-dimensional, but have many sides, many diverse interests, is not a comfort. Doesn't help in making life decisions.

Sometimes when she speaks, she hears the Valley in her choice of words, the way she puts phrases together, her 'new' accent. The New York in her voice has almost disappeared. She only realizes it when she calls Mother or the Sisters and their East Coast comes through loud and clear. Does that mean she's losing herself? Or just adding another one of those dimensions?

John

Some memories can't be shaken. Some old loves are never forgotten.

When the internet arrives and people can find lost friends, distant family, past lovers, Fancy is inspired.

John, where are you? She thinks about him all the time, wants to find him. Not to start up a romance again. No. To purge her guilt and say "I'm sorry." Because she remembers. Much too clearly.

Once she searched the Vietnam monument in Washington for his name. Telephone books in every city she visited. Now the internet. Futile. Even a death notice might quiet her.

It seems only a short time ago she got up from the bed where they made love, sheets damp from their bliss. His flawless body smooth muscled, patches of silken black hairs twirling around aureoles, movie-star perfect face in despair as she left.

He was in panic mode, reasons over which he had no control—older parents selling a big estate, leaving the cold northeast for southern warmth. John's father demanding he finish law school and follow in his footsteps like any good son should. John hated it. He wanted something else.

What did he want? Fancy can't remember, one of the many things slipped from her mind as she rushed through her life those long years ago.

He clung to her for security. Wanted answers she couldn't give. Her own panic thrummed at the thought someone might want to depend on her when she wasn't sure she could depend on herself. She remembers the scene, the place. The fear in the emotion survived. Too clearly.

They were in the hotel where she stayed during college. A transient in a big city. Gramercy Park, high floor overlooking verdant park greenery fenced with wrought iron, tall enough to keep interlopers out.

First he spoke of suicide; wishing he was dead. She saw the melancholy in his eyes, the fear of a life trapped by circumstance, consumed by the need to flee to freedom. Cold fear touched her spine. No idea what to do, how to help.

She talked with him into the night. Made love again, hoping the joy of their flesh together might keep him from the tigers lurking in his dark.

But morning came and, clinging to her, once more in panic state, he told her he loved her, wanted to be with her always, wanted to marry her, to run away together. Words flowing in a boiling lava of fear and anxiety. She would be his rock in this world of change and inconstancy.

Fancy remembers the touch of his skin, velvet smooth and white, so pale in New York winter morning light against the blackbird feathers of his wavy hair.

Easing from the twisted sheets, she remembers dressing, no thought of showers or clean clothes, just whatever floor strewn piece she found, flung on as protection. From John? From his love? Perhaps also from herself.

Was his emotion panic-professed or real? Desperate? She didn't know, only knew it was claustrophobic, frightening. Smothering. His need so palpable the panic transferred itself to her and, terrified, she felt its claws wrenching into her soul. At twenty-one she was no one's rock, only a pebble tossed about in a turbulent ocean while she tried in her own hopelessness to find her way.

Running out the door, she left him alone, abandoned in the bed already cooling from the furnace of twining bodies, the heat of

179

rut still misting the inside window panes as freezing air pleaded to intrude. Suffocating. She couldn't bear it.

Not waiting for the elevator, she ran down the stairs, eighteen floors, each one bathed with tears spilled in flight. She cared for him deeply, but knew it was not the right moment for them, for her, for him. To be together.

Hours later she returned. Bed pristine from efficient room service, sheets fresh without his scent. The room once again dressed in elegant gold and beige French striped décor. She looked in the mirror and saw her reflection. Alone. Empty. John gone.

Fancy never saw him again, no one knew or heard what happened to him. Family moved away, no friends in common. The business of life occupied her. College and law degree. Married. Had a family. Divorced. Worked. Traveled the world.

She never forgot John, never stopped looking for him in her quest to spill out regrets. Tell him she was sorry. She couldn't be his rock. Couldn't hold anyone in her arms and tell them everything would be all right, whisper things always work out for the best. Because she already knew the hidden lies buried deep within each hope.

Searching the Viet Nam wall for his name, she was fearful it might have been the path he had taken. Relieved she didn't find it. Wishing, wanting only for him to have had a good life, family, loving wife, children, success. The ingredients of happiness.

It's been thirty years or more. If she closes her eyes, sometimes she can still see his pale skin in winter morning New York City light, even though the contours of his face have dimmed. But Fancy remembers and she's still so sorry.

Just another one of her ghosts to be reconciled. She reaches down and rubs the ears of the nearest dog. Soft, companionable beneath her fingers. So many years she spent without memories, too busy to let them flow. He life on the ranch so simple and easy, her relations with friends uncomplicated, only the memories intrude.

Hard to go back and imagine those other women, those other Fancy Ladies who peopled her life: the student too busy to pay attention to the pain of a loved one; the driven woman shooting her cuffs as she strides down the first class aisle of TWA on her way to Paris; the executive so self-obsessed she can't see the emotions of those around her.

Different times, different lives. Someday she hopes she can forgive them all. She's trying, bit by bit.

Porkers

Wild pigs thrive in the nearby mountains. Hitch likes to hunt, and when he has a kill, he brings Fancy a haunch. She's amazed at how good the meat is, would think it'd be tough and stringy, but it's always tender and sweet tasting.

Hitch explains, "Gotta'hunt the sows, ya' know, try to find smaller, younger ones." She watches as he trims the tough outer skin off and then the membrane beneath. "Once 'pon a time, there's only the wild 'uns in the mountains, native they were, tough as I remember as a young 'un. Over the years, domestic porkers got loose, mated with 'em. The pigs today are mixed breed...more tender." Hitch cackles, "...kinda' like the rest of us in these parts."

Hitch's explanation is Fancy's entire knowledge of pigs, and she's always been quite happy in her ignorance if she ever bothers to think about it. Which she doesn't.

The dogs bark as a familiar truck drives up. Katie gets out holding a pink something squirmy in her arms. "Hey Fancy, look at the present I brought you. A piglet."

Huh? Fancy is down off the porch in a minute. Tom and Ethel come over to take a look. The critter is small, round and very pink. Scrabbling sounds come from the back of the truck. Fancy looks inside. Three more piglets. Two black with merle markings and another pinky.

"Where on earth did these little guys come from?" Fancy asks.

"My father and friends were hunting up the mountain... killed

182

the mother. Found these guys making a racket. Want one? I'm gonna take one home for me and the kids to raise…need to find a home for the others."

"Gee, Katie, no thanks. I think I've got enough animals to take care of without adding a pig. Don't know anything about how to raise them. It would probably piss off the goat, sheep and steer."

Fancy has no idea about farm animals other than to keep plenty of water and food around. She relies on the ranch manager for the rest, when to shear, any doctoring. She didn't want any more responsibilities. The pigs did look cute. She leaned over the truck and picked the other pink one up. It was about the same size as Tom. It squealed a bit and then snuggled into her arms. She almost relented. Then she remembered visiting a friend's ranch down the road. Linda had a four hundred and fifty pound pig who ate Oreo cookies out of her mouth. Four hundred and fifty pounds! No way. Everyone tried to convince Fancy how smart pigs were, how clean and how easy to train. Uh-huh. Handed the pig back to Katie.

As they drove away, Katie called back, "If you change your mind, I'll have them for a few days until I can find a home for them.

All Fancy could think of was, "Good Luck!"

Two months later, Fancy is at a picnic at Katie's house. When Fancy arrives, she's greeted by three pigs, all about the height of Ethel and about three times her girth. "Thought you were going to get rid of the pigs, just keep the one."

"Found a home for one, other people wanted the other two, but were going to eat them. Couldn't let them eat my babies."

"Katie, don't you think it's a bit unrealistic to find people willing to take critters as house pets that will eventually be close to five hundred pounds?"

"I don't care; no one's eatin' my babies." Katie's lower lip begins to quiver.

In a way, Fancy understood, she'd not let her dogs or the goat go to anyone who was going to eat them. Although she'd probably encourage any interested party to eat the steer. Mean old sucker, bet he'd be tough—only good for stew meat. Still…

Few more months pass. Fancy stops at Katie's to pick her up for a party. One pig left, a merle, its back now level with Fancy's waist. Probably weighs over two hundred pounds.

Katie buckles her seat belt and Fancy commented, "See one pig left, good you found homes for the others."

Katie burst into tears. "I don't know where they went to. I woke up one morning and they were gone. Dad came and took them away, the kids told him they were biting them and getting mean. I caught him before he put the last one into the truck." She wiped her eyes. "Won't tell me what happened to the others, just keeps saying over and over, 'Pigs do not belong in a house!'"

Fancy actually agrees with Katie's father, but she's smart enough to keep her mouth shut.

Couple months after that, she runs into Katie's dad in the feed store. Asks how Katie's doing.

"I don't know how that insane woman is doing and I don't care!" His face is red. Stomps his foot.

Wow. Not what Fancy expected. She has no response for the outburst, but he didn't need one to continue.

"Remember those dang pigs? …'member she tried to give you one? Smart woman, you didn't take it. I kept taking them away until she had but the one left. Stubborn as she is, like her mother, rest her soul, she insisted I leave it be. Got so big she couldn't control it, got so damn mean bit everyone who got near but her. Snapped at the kids a few times but they learned real quick to dodge it. Almost bit her sister's hand off, she's not so fast. I was ready to come in and take the thing out of the house but couldn't figure how to. Probably would'da had to kill it and butcher it right there. Don't want to even think of what Katie'd do. Probably take a gun to me."

184

He shook his head. "Damn near tore the house apart, and it was just a rental. Landlord threw her and the kids out in the street, pig and all. Last I heard he was suing for damages. I won't help. Tried to tell her. She and the pig are off to some ranch in the hills, does cleaning in return for rent and some food, few bucks here 'n there."

Fancy can practically see the steam rising from his ears. "Now I got her kids living with me. They're all afraid of the damn pig and don't like where she moved, too far from school. I got me a girl friend who won't come 'round 'cause she says it's a bad influence on the kids if she stays over. I'm stuck, can't leave 'em alone in the house. Don't know what the big deal is, I'm a widower. My dang daughter has destroyed her life and mine, and now the kids are suffering." He pounds his fist on a nearby saddle display. Fancy is speechless for a change.

He turns back for a moment. "Sorry, Fancy, didn't mean to lay all that on you. Not your fault…really mine. Don't know what I was thinking when I gave her the durned things to begin with." Shaking his head, he marches off.

When he's out of sight, all Fancy can do was congratulate herself. She looked a gift pig in the mouth and actually said, "No!"

Pranks

There's no one who's ever lived in a small town and hung out at a local tavern without learning about practical jokes.

Raul is so good natured he's usually the butt of them. Been passed exploding cigars, whoopee cushions put on his truck seat, pizza delivered with extra hot sauce. The guys even painted Rocko's underbelly red with beet juice once. That didn't go so well. Raul started to cry when he thought his best pal was hurt. Took a while to calm him down. A lot of apologies, and a few good soup bones for Rocko.

Fancy finally got her chance to take part in one, and it was a cure-all for the future!

Eddie likes to drink. He likes to hang out with the guys, play the big rough, tough cowboy. But he's a little guy. Probably no more than five foot two, maybe three with boots on. Weighs soaking wet about a hundred twenty-five pounds, maybe less. Never weighed him. Got a big mouth, bigger than his size, and likes to use it on the ladies. Mostly they ignore him. Mostly. Once in a while he gets on their nerves. Happened one night at the Mustang. He just came back from hunting and was feeling real full of himself.

Hitting on all the ladies, trying to get laid and with no success. All the women know he has a lady at home, aren't going to give him the time of day. He's moving up and down the bar, buying drinks for every available woman, even some that aren't. No one's paying him a bit of attention. Since he's been drinking a new drink each time he's hit on one of the ladies, he's pretty sloshed. Not that he can hold much to start with, lightweight in body fat, lightweight booze consumer.

After about an hour of rejection, he ambles up to Fancy. Puts his arm around her shoulders, looks in her eyes. She sees his aren't focused. "Hey baby, you are one good looking woman." So slurred she can hardly understand.

"What do you want, Eddie?" Soon as the words were out, she was sorry. Too late. Crap.

"I want you, you know that." He studiously examines her breasts as a small bit of drool slips out of the side of his mouth. Charming.

"That's not an option. Anything else?"

"Yeah, you got the Suburban here?"

"Yes. So what?"

"I'm tired darlin', just want to take a snooze across the back seat for a while. If you bring me home with you I'll sleep on your porch."

"You can sleep in the car, but you're not coming home with me. Okay?" No way will Fancy have him wake up and start knocking on her bedroom window with any ideas.

"All right, sweet cheeks, if that's the way you want it."

"That's it, and if you puke in the Suburban, you're cleaning it up yourself and then having it detailed…and the inside steam cleaned. Your cost."

"Ch'u got it. No problem."

Fancy practically carries him to her car, slides him into the back seat. He's out cold before she shuts the door.

Back at the bar, Polly asks her, "What cha' do with Eddie?"

"Nothing. He was so drunk he almost passed out here. I took him to the Suburban and let him crash across the back seat."

"Sure hope he don't puke in it."

"Me too. Told him if he did, he had to first clean it himself, then pay for detailing and complete cleaning."

Phyllis is sitting next to Fancy, listening to the conversation. "Say, why not play a prank on him. He's been a pain in the ass all night to every woman in here. Let's get even."

Polly and Fancy are interested. "What 'cha got in mind?"

"I don't know. Something. Put bugs in his shirt?"

"No way! He's in my car."

Phyllis leans over to Mary sitting next to her. Eddie has pissed off an entire bar full of women, most of them ready with ideas. "Hey, Mary, what do you think we can do to Eddie—as a joke? He's passed out in Fancy's car, dead to the world."

"We could de-pants him and leave him in the road."

Polly, Fancy and Phyllis all make faces. "Damn, I don't want to see him naked." Phyllis says.

Yuck!" Polly adds.

"Naw, me neither, don't want any part of that little swinging dick." Mary puts in her two cents.

"Let's think of something less offensive." Fancy's sentiments are echoed by the others.

"Wonder if it's big enough to even swing?" Mary seems about to reconsider.

Everyone else is shaking their heads and making faces.

Polly puts her hand up. "Got an idea. Heard today they were digging the cemetery up. How about we take him there and just dump him in the grass next to an open grave."

"On my God! What if he rolls in? He's so short he'd never get hisself out."

"We could put him far enough away so that he couldn't roll in?" She's not giving up easily.

Lot of discussion back and forth. Final decision, graveyard wins.

Polly asks Frank to sub for her behind the bar, and everyone piles into the Suburban. Even their laughing doesn't wake Eddie. Fancy drives into the cemetery, puts on the high beams, lights flashing on several graves being dug, gaping holes with big piles of dirt next to them. Polly points at one further back from the road. "Not only don't we want the little bugger rolling into an open hole, we don't want anyone running over him either.

The rest of the gang grudgingly agree.

Everyone out, the back door open, everyone takes an arm or a leg and he's easily out. Good thing he's a dead drunk light-weight. Carefully plunk him down on the grass a distance from the open holes; arrange his legs and feet together, cross his arms over his chest. He is so out of it, Fancy's afraid he's really dead. Then he gives a loud snore and a grunt. They all run back to the car, she revs up the engine and they're back to the Mustang.

Inside, one of the guys looks at the snarky smiles on all the women and knows something's up. "Where's Eddie?" He asks.

Fancy manages her brightest smile, the most innocent she can conjure up. "Oh, he's just resting. He wanted to be someplace quiet where he could get a good snooze and we took him there." Excellent deadpan. She turns back to find Polly has set a new drink out for her.

Every time she hears boots on the porch, she turns expecting to find Eddie. When he doesn't show up after an hour, she begins to worry. "How about it? I think we should go back and check on him...make sure he's okay?"

The other women are adamant. "Don't worry about him. Let him stew there for a while...serve him right."

Two hours later, Eddie is back in the Mustang. Raul behind him. Raul is laughing , Eddie steaming. "Who the fuck left me at that fucking cemetery? I'm going to fucking kill them!"

Raul can't stop laughing. "Come down the road and there he is, covered in dirt and hitching a ride. Had to stop. When he told me where he woke up, been laughing ever since."

"How'd ya get all the mud on you, Eddie?" Fancy's curious.

"Woke up, first thought I was dead. All I could smell was fresh dirt and pine trees. Figured it was the end for me. Rolled around to see where I was, but so fucking dark and no lights, no stars, had to feel my way. Ended up on a big ass pile of fresh dirt

189

'fore it dawned—might be in the cemetery. Then I was scared of dropping in a hole. I had to crawl around on my hands and knees to find the fuckin' road." With every word his face reddens.

The more he talks, the harder the women laugh. They're all crying, tears running down their cheeks, mascara making tracks. Too funny! They're trying to tell Eddie he deserved it, but can't get words out. The guys at the bar start to laugh. It's contagious. Eddie looks down at his clothes, mud everywhere. Then he starts to laugh too.

Raul slaps him on the back. "Hey buddy, from what I heard, you were up to making a real ass out 'a yourself. Better not piss off these women again, they can be real mean...and they do seek vengeance."

Fancy feels sorry for him. She really likes Eddie, that is, except when he's a drunken asshole. But she can see how upset he was. Feels guilty about being mean. Goes up and puts her arms around him, hugs him to her. Until she feels his tongue licking her neck. Yuck!

"Damn you Eddie, don't you ever learn?" Grimacing, she wipes her neck with Polly's bar rag and pushes him away.

"Aw, come'on darlin', how about a little pity fuck?"

Some guys never learn. She shakes her head. Maybe they should take him back to the graveyard.

Then he starts to laugh at her. Okay, if he can kid too, all has been forgiven.

"Polly, give the man a drink. On me. Make it a 'Sex On The Beach', if you please."

This time Eddie hugs her—no tongue. "Thank you darlin'...not exactly what I was hoping for...but it'll do."

Night Terrors

Business is slowing down. The stock market plunges in its usual cycle of crash and burn, this time with the Dotcom bubble popping. Advertisers, careful of their spending, pull back their ad budgets. The entertainment business clobbered, the doldrums take over as far afield as Fancy's small consulting business.

Her bookkeeper takes her aside in the office. "We don't have enough in the accounts to make this payroll. The ranch water bill due, here is the cut-off notice. The next European convention is coming up and we'll need airline tickets, apartment rental money, stand space and decorations." Fancy doesn't want to hear, but the death knell continues. "I'm sorry to be the bearer of bad tidings, but you're short about twenty thousand dollars, and that'll only squeak us through the month. Next month, who knows?"

Another dip into her shrinking retirement fund. Fancy shrugs her shoulders and writes a check to the company. All she can hope for is death before she retires. Otherwise, at this rate, she'll be looking forward to a future as a Wal-Mart greeter with the expectation of taking her last breath draped ass up over one of their shopping carts.

Nights, she wakes up in a cold sweat—clients late with payments, bills, obligations, the people she supports weighing down her peace. The part time secretary who does all the office work, car payments, auto and health insurance, ranch upkeep, bookkeeper, damn water bill. Trips to the East Coast to check up on family, buy whatever Mother needs, Sisters want. She takes a few dollars a week out as salary just to keep her Social Security alive and well, but not the maximum. That worries her too.

The bills and obligations roil around in her head; she imagines them as animated dancers, all with their hands out, looking to her for payment. The reality of losing the ranch threatens her hard earned tranquility.

Fancy never thought of herself as entitled to anything. Whatever she had, she worked for. Worked her way through both college and law school. No one gave her anything, especially Mother, and she didn't expect it. But this was hard. Before, she was only responsible for herself. Now, she's responsible for both staff and family.

She's about to put the ranch up for sale in the middle of a real estate bust when another consulting gig comes in. Big. Respite for a while anyway. But she sees the future, and it's not very bright. She knows bad times are coming. Fancy is, above all, a fighter. And she gathers her strength to fight on. She's learned a lot during her time at the ranch. Does she have still more to learn, or is it time now to let go?

Once again she pushes imminent doom out of her head and tries to sleep. So far she's been lucky enough to squeak through the last years, but how long can her luck hold?

Halloween

The last night of October is a big deal in Santa Isabella. In the Village, kids trick or treat in costumes with bags to hold candies and apples. No one wants to travel out to the ranches so the ranchers, cowboys, hands and families come into town. Their kids trek through the housing and apartment developments, the grown-ups go to the Mustang. In costume too!

The first time Fancy went to the annual Halloween party at the Mustang, four tall women in evening dresses were cautiously picking their way up the steps. Closer inspection showed circa1890's style ball gowns, lacy wraps around shoulders, big hats with ribbons and feathers. Long gloves. A tail-biter fox fur stole. Then one turned around. Had a beard and plenty of hair peeking out of his décolletage. Roper boots. Fancy's mouth wouldn't close. What on earth was going on?

Her costume was simple, long black skirt, turtleneck and tights, some black cobwebby stuff in her hair with spiders. Black nails and lipstick. Sort of Goth and almost witch at the same time. Not very inventive. Tom guarding the car with a patch over one eye she was sure he'd be rid of in a second.

The Mustang was resplendent, strung with orange and black jack-o-lantern lights, autumn leaves, white cobwebs in every corner, ghostly images floating from the ceiling. The honkey-tonk band in full swing. Figures crowding the dance floor, pool table crammed into the corner.

Fancy wanted to have a better look at the 'women' in their

'Gay '90's' finery. As she worked the bar, she saw them over in a corner, laughing. The cowboys she's seen at the Mustang for the last few months? Formerly dressed in Wranglers, western shirts and mud caked boots? Broad shoulders. Those cowboys? What in hell?

Another cowboy came over and asked one of the 'ladies' to dance. Gracefully, she put her tiny handbag and gloves on the table, squeezed onto the dance floor with 'her' partner. Soon everyone was dancing. Fancy's amazed. Was this the night gay cowboys came out of the closet? She didn't care about anyone's sexual predilections, but in a western and predominantly conservative redneck town it was a bit of a mind boggler.

The conversation in the bar stopped as if on command. The band went silent. Everyone turned to the door. Fancy flashed back to the entrance of bikers her first time at the Mustang. And in they came—bikers all right. This time—all women. Tight black pants, some leathers, some just tights, all in either biker vests or jackets, helmets under arms. Bandanas folded around their foreheads. Cobweb tats inked on their necks, and those with vests, tats covered their arms. Very sexy. The local cowgirls, raring for a night out.

Room opened up at the bar and the cowgirls crowded in. Noise resumed. Glad she showed up, Fancy settled in to see what else was in store.

After their first beer, the girls ambled over to ask the 'women' to dance. Soon the floor was filled with female bikers leading bearded men in ball gowns. The cowgirls twirled the guys around, once in a while copping an obvious feel of a sock-stuffed breast or grab-assing when the opportunity arose.

When Polly had a free moment, Fancy couldn't resist. "Does this happen every year?"

"Mostly. Depends on the weather and if the guys have to stay at the ranches in case of fire. Otherwise, yeah, they seem to like to dress like that."

"Are they gay?" Fancy had to ask.

194

"Nah. They just think it's fun. See the guy in the pale blue taffeta with the big hat?"

"Got red hair and a fluffy beard?"

"Yeah, that's the one. He's married with three kids, another on the way. Don't think he's gay. Some years his brother wears that dress. Belonged to their grandma. She must have been some size as neither of the guys are small."

Every year Fancy goes to the Mustang for Halloween. She tells friends from all over the world it's a must see and often has out-of-towners with her.

One year, Lars dresses as a 1990's drug dealer, Mohawk down the center of his head, the rest shaved clean either side, moustache and goatee. Looks real badass, black lens John Lennon glasses, a velvet smoking jacket and matching vest. Every cowgirl in the place is climbing all over him.

On the way home he's laughing. "Damn! Normally I can't get myself arrested in this place, women have no interest in me. Tonight I shaved my head and they wouldn't leave me alone. What's with that?"

"Sorry, kid, I've got no answers. The human condition is a mystery I'm not about to solve. But it's a lot of fun to watch, isn't it?"

The next year, Lars shows up as a cowboy. He wins the prize for the best redneck costume, butt crack and all. Not one of the women looks at him twice.

On the way home, Fancy say, "If you want my advice, which you probably don't, I'd suggest you shave your head again if you want to get lucky."

He shakes his head in disgust.

Gamblin' & Ramblin'

Fancy broke her leg. Fell over a fire pit on a camping trip. Not quite stone cold sober, but close. Still, not easy to see in the dark. She's been wearing a cast for three months, stir crazy and driving the Suburban with her left leg up and out the window, the cast like a white flag of surrender. But no way will she give up.

Shopping with a friend at Wal-Mart, the greeter brings out an electric chair for her to ride in and they pile it with it high with purchases. By the time they get to check-out, Fancy looks like a shopping cart moving itself. Her grocery shopping is confined to the one supermarket in town that has the same contraptions. Otherwise, she gets around with a walker.

Fancy is not the most coordinated of women, and her doctor pointedly suggested the walker when she tried crutches and immediately fell in his office. He came out to see the commotion in the waiting room and was greeted by Fancy, on her back beached turtle style, the leg with cast waving in the air, the rest of her tangled in crutches, and howling with laughter. Not a great advertisement for his services, other patients looking on in horror. Bad idea to break the other leg as well. Took the doctor and two nurses to finally get her upright. He found a walker in the back and hid the crutches from her.

Fancy doesn't like the walker, thinks it makes her look like an old lady. She hobbled into one of the stores in town and a young clerk came over to her, solicitous. "Awww, here, let me help you."

196

Fancy shook her arm off, scowled and growled, "It's just a BROKEN LEG!" The poor girl fled. Probably still wondering what she did wrong.

Broken leg or not, business calls and she has to attend a convention in Las Vegas. Hitch is ready to go anyplace with her, even though he's recovering from hip replacement surgery. He won't use the walker, looks at hers with distain as he hobbles about with two canes.

The hotel in Las Vegas has a motorized scooter waiting for her on arrival and she plans to work the convention with it. Offers to get one for Hitch too. Two for one deal. He won't have any of it. Too independent. Stubborn? The major problem is to move it from one hotel to another. She orders a special taxi to take her and the scooter to and from the convention. No way can she and Hitch muscle the scooter into the Suburban by themselves and the valets seem to disappear when they see it ready to be unloaded.

After the first day at the convention, Fancy realizes she's hit on a good deal. All the hostesses at the various stands take pity on her—motorized conveyance, cast and all. Any promotional items they're giving away are thrust at her. So far she's scored several "Star Wars" tee-shirts, "Star Trek" watches, goodie bags filled with toys and DVDs, more tee-shirts and pens, flashlights, business card holders and calculators. She's been fed filet mignon in the VIP area of one stand, and baby lamb chops in another. And, she's learned to stop growling and to say "thank you" instead to the kind women.

Convention over, she and Hitch head to the outskirts of Vegas to hit Sam's Town for a taste of the old west and some gambling. Parking the car in a disabled spot and heading into the casino, Fancy humps along with her walker and Hitch with his two canes. No scooter. She goes to the nickel slots, he looks for the quarter ones. Big spender.

It's afternoon. Weekday. The place is dead empty. Any machine they want. Not even a floor boss in sight. They pick their machines and settle in. After about twenty minutes, Fancy starts to yell, whoop and holler. She's hit a jackpot on the nickel machine and nickels are pouring out all over the place. She fills one bucket, then another and another. The nickels keep coming. A hundred dollars in nickels. Almost three big buckets. They're both giddy. A jackpot!! After getting the money all tidy into the buckets, to cash out, they have to take them all the way across the casino and up to the far end where the cashier is located. No way. Neither one of them can carry one bucket, let alone three of them. No one to help them. Fancy checks out the casino while Hitch guards the buckets. No luck.

After about forty-five minutes, Fancy is pissed off. She tries yelling a bit, still no response. Have they all died? On break? Then she gets the idea to push the service buttons on all the machines. Screw ruining their cigarette break, she'll wake everybody up.

Lights flash on all the rows as one at a time they hobble up and down the aisles button pushing. Five attendants run in from various directions. She and Hitch grin at each other as they form a procession to the cashier. Must have disturbed a lot of smoke and lunch breaks.

When she's handed five crisp new twenties, Fancy's overjoyed. Couldn't be happier if she won a million bucks. She folds the bills into her wallet and they head out to spend it on big steaks—The Palm next on their agenda. What better way to enjoy winnings than a good steak dinner with a friend?

All the rest of the trip, they laugh at the image they must have made—two old codgers, one with walker, the other on two canes. Hitch says, "...should'a asked to have them nickels weighed before they went into the counting machines...bet it was a few good pounds." He cackled about it all the way home to Santa Isabella, "First time I ever led a parade—with three attendants toting our winnings ....kinda' felt like royalty." He was quiet for a moment as he looked for something in his pockets, started cackling again. "Best part was them steaks though."

Old Heelers Never Miss

Hitch insists he's going to rope in the local rodeo the year he hits ninety. "Done it ever' year before, don't see why not now."

When it's time for his event, Fancy walked back with him to the stable, took the borrowed horse outside the stall for him to get on. Didn't look like it was going to happen, his new hip replacement wasn't about to move enough to let him get one foot in the stirrup so he could push the other leg up and over. She could almost feel his heart sink, knew he was looking forward to the event.

He takes the reins from her, nods. "Be right back, got something to do. Stay right there." He walks off, around the corner of the stable, out of sight.

What on earth is he up to? She wonders but stays put as ordered.

Comes back in a couple of minutes. On horseback, big smirky smile on his face.

"How did you do that?" She asks.

"Magic." Smirk grows.

"Come on. Tell me." She wants to know.

"Saw a tree stump over 'round the stable, took the horse over, climbed up on the stump and easy from there. Durned new hip don't move the way the old one did."

She goes back to the stands, front row in the middle. Watches as he rides in. Proud. He's a heeler, and sits tall in the saddle as he coils his rope just the way he wants it.

As he rides into his place in the chute, the announcer tells the audience it's his seventy-sixth consecutive rodeo.

His buddy, the header, nods they're ready. Chute opens and the steer launches out like it's been shot from a cannon. Takes the header by surprise and he's a fraction of a second slow to break the barrier rope. Hitch right behind. Header takes his throw. Misses. Coils the rope for another try, misses again. Hitch takes his hat off, smiling, waves to the crowd. They wave and yell back, cheering the two old cowboys. The applause deafens.

Just before the exit gate, Hitch reins his horse right for another turn around the arena, still waving to the crowd. Big smile on his face. They love him, everyone on their feet, shouting and clapping.

Fancy meets him back at the stable where he's taking the saddle off and hanging the tack up. "Hitch, you were so handsome out there in the arena."

He breaks into a huge grin, "Yep. And didn't have to embarrass m'self by missing, neither. Never felt so grateful before when my header missed." Fancy hugs him as he breaks into the familiar cackle.

After the rodeo and late dinner at Buffalo Pete's Original Steakhouse down the road from the arena, Hitch and Fancy are quiet in the Suburban as she winds up the mountain through the puffs of fog decorating every depression in the pass.

He's too quiet, she thinks. Must have something on his mind. Figures she'll start the conversation. "Did you see all your buddies you expected to be there?"

"Yep, I did...mostly. Chico wasn't there, Bonner says he's in the hospital, ICU, all hooked up, tubes 'n all. Lung cancer. Ever'one told him to ditch the Camels, he don't listen to no one." Silence again. She'll wait.

"How 'bout you, Fancy? Been in the Valley close on 'ta ten years now, when ya goin' home?"

"Hitch, I am home. I love my ranch, love you and love Santa Isabella. This is my home now."

"I know you like it here, like the people too. But this ain't your home. Most folks don't know much 'bout you, you never speak of what you did 'fore you came to the Valley, but I know. Fred told me, he's real proud 'a you and what you done."

Fancy's taken aback. They seldom speak of Fred, and especially in regard to her. That was over and done with years ago. Ancient history.

"It doesn't matter what I did, what jobs I held in the past. It is the past. This is now, no point in dragging up old news." She adjusts the seat belt, feeling a little constrained.

"Don't get it, do you Fancy? This ain't where you should be. Not that folks ain't happy to have you here, fact is, they like you a lot. But it ain't your rightful place." He's quiet for a moment. She knows he likes to say things just right. One of those people of few words, but when he get's them out, it's time to listen."

"I been to those conventions with you, seen how you been treated. Respected. Must 'a earned it to have the top dogs remember you, still like you. That's what I mean by your home. Not back East, but your business home. That's where you belong.

"You worked hard to get there, even your ma gives you that. I know you got a lot of education, did it yourself. Must not 'a been easy, woman and all, even in these times, that business. But you did it, earned their respect, made them pay you big like all the other big wigs. Don't give up the things you worked so hard for...and fore it's too late. Those doors don't stay open forever. Time moves 'long—rope the old steer by the horns. Remember, you gotta get out of that chute fast to make your winning time." Reaches over and pats her on the shoulder. "Look at me, ropin' all those years 'n now cain't hardly get my tail in the saddle." He laughs at his own joke.

Fancy drops him at his door, gets out and give him a hug. All way the back to the ranch, tears threaten. Sometimes the truth hurts. The pile of bills keeps growing while she watches the

201

depletion of her savings. Soon. Soon she'll either have to sell the ranch or declare bankruptcy. Mother hints about the big screen television she wants, how a new air conditioner would be nice in her room.

Salvation is not far away, just one hundred and fifty miles south-west, waiting for her in the City of Angeles. She's just not sure she can fly that far.

Is The Future Calling?

The phone in the office won't stop ringing. Fancy's alone and runs to answer it. Glad she did, it's a friend calling from Los Angeles. Seems one of the studios is looking for someone to oversee all their business interest—what she used to do. Her name came up in the conversation and he said he'd call and find out. Is she interested?

It stopped her in her tracks. Interested? She'd have to move back to Los Angeles. Or at least find a place to stay there. Travel, plenty of it, back on the road again. Months every year.

Big salary for sure, bigger benefits. She'd have to close her consulting business, her office. Sell the ranch. What the hell? Her mind went back to the past weekend, her conversation with Hitch. Is he clairvoyant? Or was it only fortuitous?

It was agreed; she'd come in the end of the week and meet with top management. See if they all got along. See if she thought she could do what they had in mind. See if they liked her and if the chemistry was all right. See if she liked them. She hung up the phone and looked around at her office. Funky.

Her desk looking out on the lower part of the ranch, the sheep munching in their pasture, the steer back towards the road in his. Dogs sleeping on the office floor. Myrtle outside, eating the roses. The usual.

Been a lot of rain the past winter; too much. The weeping willow in the center of the lawn is dying. Leaves no longer verdant

203

green but yellowing and curled. Fancy knows it will have to be cut down, but has put it off in the hope it might decide to survive. A futile hope, but one she clings to. To her, the willow was why she bought the ranch. Some people might equate weeping willows with cemeteries and death, but she was attracted to its graceful shape, how it dominated the entrance, first thing you saw when you turned in the gate. So many parties and barbeques under its shade, so many times she felt her heart lurch with joy when she saw it after a long trip. Home.

So far, she's survived for years. Not easy with a small business and a ranch that's sucked up money faster than the willow could suck up the too abundant water. The tree is dying. It had no choice. More water than it could absorb has rotted its roots. Debt is threatening hers.

That night, Fancy sits on the porch, looking out over her ranch, the dying tree, the critters in the pastures. She imagines Heap Big Chief and his marshmallow hands, now a teenager swaggering as he walks through the Village, taller than his father, shoulders broad and so handsome all the girls turn and look.

The phone rings again, interrupting her thoughts. It's Polly.

"Hi, Fancy, wanted to let you know. Sorry to bring you the sad news, but Hitch passed away last evening. Just got a call."

Tears fill her eyes, her throat starts to close. "What happened? How?" Was there something she could have done?

"He was hunting with the guys. Wild pig."

"Way back off one of the fire roads. They had him in the truck, parked near spore, left him quiet, hoping a sow'd come within range while they went out to follow tracks. Sure enough, one comes along and he pops her clean. By the time they get back, he's already gutted her and is working on the butchering.

"They spent the night out, supposed to be gone a few days. Got him fixed up to sleep in the truck bed, keep him off the cold ground." Fancy hears noise, something slams. Polly's voice yelling at someone. "Hang on a minute, wait, I'll call you right back."

Fancy heard voices in the background, figures Polly's in the Mustang with customers. It gives her time to collect herself. She can't stop the tears as they flow. And then she realizes it's the first time she's cried for anyone. Got through the death of her father, grandparents, friend Pat, a Sister, friends, never shed a tear before. Wouldn't allow herself to open up to grief.

The phone rings again—Polly. "Got a few minutes. Anyway, old Hitch, he fixed a haunch for dinner, set out a nice barbeque, got his chair next to the spit he arranged, and he's warm and wrapped up, turning the spit and looking forward to dinner. The boys are messing with their gear, one says 'Look, Hitch fell asleep'. When they come back to the fire, they see he'd passed. What a cool way for him to go." Polly sounds tearful, a catch in her voice.

Fancy thinks, quiet for a few seconds. Stops crying. Damn! "What a beautiful way for him to leave. Really amazing. Fitting. There he was, his friends around, doing exactly what he likes to do best. Fixing something for his buddies to eat!"

When she hangs up the phone, she understands how someone deeply valuable in her life has gone. He's been her rock, the anchor to keep her in Santa Isabella. Hitch has been her chosen family, like both friend and father to her, as well as her connection with the community.

Her status has never been given to her by her former executive career. No one in Santa Isabella could care a rat's ass about that. She's Hitch's friend. And it's the most important title she's ever earned.

The air cools around her, she gets out her PRCA National Finals jacket and hugs it around her shoulders. She was at the National Finals in Las Vegas with Hitch when she bought it. Still has one of his old baggies in the pocket. She takes it out. Opens it. Crumbs of beef jerky fall out. Tom crawls onto her lap, Ethel comes over and lies at her feet.

As she remembers who she once was, it becomes clear to her what she's been given by her time at the ranch. When she came, she was a doer, so driven she saw nothing around her—past self

205

obsession, beyond narcissism, to the point of oblivion. Everyone and everything sliding by her in a blur, her attention focused on success, business, work, and education. Nothing human or breathing mattered. Not really her fault, just the culture she grew up in, too fast to think about simple immaterial things like emotions, love, families, enjoyment.

The ranch slowed her down. Gave her time to think, to look at the people who were important in her life. Gradually, she's learned to see life from different perspectives, through the eyes of those around her. The time to sift through her memories was like cleaning out her garage, still packed with junk from when she moved in. Time to dredge through unopened boxes filled with 'stuff' unused and unremembered for years.

Perhaps it is time to go back to the life she worked hard for so many years to obtain. She loved the work, the hustle and bustle, the endless mind games of deal making. For her, in the past, her business was her life, her reason for getting up every morning. But now she doesn't have to let it suck her dry, to be obsessed with control.

One thing she knows for certain. The company, the title on her door—no longer important—only sign posts for those who require labels to know who they are. Validation no longer needed, …that is, unless it's for her parking ticket.

As she hands the dogs their goodnight treats, she understands she's learned who she is—Fancy Lady: Survivor. The best title of all!

Squash Blossom Finery

Fancy parks the Suburban in the visitor parking, the candy apple paint sparkling in the sun, clean and detailed for the first time in years in honor of her trip to Los Angeles.

Her black pants suit is off the Rack at Nordstroms, fits well, white silk tee shirt beneath instead of custom shirt with monogram. She's given up shooting cuffs. Italian loafers are exchanged for polished Ariat boots. Squash blossom necklace, a birthday present from Hitch, around her neck for good luck. No diamond rings. No gold chains. Simple Ebel watch. No longer anything to prove. Take it or leave it as it comes—her new motto.

The receptionist checks her name off an appointment list, asks her to please wait a moment while she advises everyone of Fancy's arrival.

A long purple couch beckons Fancy to sit, look at the framed movie posters lining the reception area walls. Modern furniture. Very young woman at the desk speaking quietly into the phone as she looks Fancy over.

Fancy is Zen quiet. Stares out the wall of windows where she knows the hills of Hollywood reside, only slightly blurred by smog. No longer the smell of cigarettes in the reception room. Instead, Windex and furniture polish; she prefers them to the stench of old dead cigarettes permeating the offices she remembers. Not politically correct to smoke anymore in Los Angeles. Glad she gave it up years ago.

Dior's Chance wafts by Fancy's nose and she realizes the

young woman is waiting for her to get up and follow her into the meeting. Long legs, miniscule skirt in bright orange, black décolletage decorate the slim frame leading her into the conference room, motions her into a chair, turns and closes the door behind.

Time to strut your stuff, Fancy tells herself. She sits down, puts old faithful Gucci handbag and briefcase on the floor next to her chair, and begins to do what she does best. Sell. Herself this time. Talk. Smile. Charm. Done it for so many years, like learning to ride a bicycle, no reason why she can't do it again.

After lunch in the commissary, the president takes her arm and leads her to a large office next door to his, one wall all window, this side facing Olympic Boulevard to the ocean sparkling far beyond in reflected sunlight. Leather sectional, L-shaped desk, wall to wall bookcase behind. Leopard printed carpet. Interesting. She smiles, likes it. Her contract will provide she only has to come to the office three days a week, available by phone or e-mail the other times; can bring her dogs to work with her. Dogs were a deal breaker. New rules in Los Angeles: smoking no, dogs yes. She approves of that too.

On the drive back to the ranch, Fancy understands her life has changed. The mental to-do list grows with every mile from Los Angeles to the ranch. Call the real estate broker, put the ranch on the market, close up the office, send the sheep and steer to the auction house. Give Myrtle to Eddie, he's got plenty of room on his ranch and he and the goat are friends. Clean out all the junk collected over the last years. Send her family anything they want from the ranch. The rest into a big yard sale. Open her mind up to once again be an active participant in the business she loves. Pack up. Move on. Say goodbye to all her friends in Santa Isabella. She knows how much she'll miss them and how appreciative she is they took her into their hearts.

No house in Beverly Hills this time around. Thinks she might take one of the ranch trailers, hook it to the Suburban and drag it up to a trailer park she's noticed in Malibu. High on a cliff overlooking the ocean. Might be nice to walk the dogs in the morning and watch the dolphins play in the turquoise deep framing the beach below. Maybe even see a whale or two. Think of her father fishing in the Everglades.

Never lived in a trailer in Malibu before. Time for new things. Make life simple. She's looking forward to it all.

Her hands move to touch the squash blossom necklace as "Me and Bobby McGee" blares out from the radio and she heads back over the pass towards Santa Isabella.

…just one more rodeo.

About The Author

Alice Donenfeld-Vernoux, a veteran in the entertainment business, spent more than 40 years working in Broadway theatre, films, television and New Media as attorney, producer, studio executive, creator of over a hundred television programs, distributor, consultant and consistent exhibitor in the world television markets.

While Vice President of Marvel Comics she headed international television, video and licensing for "Spiderman," "The Fantastic Four," "Captain America," and "The Incredible Hulk."

As Executive Vice President of Filmation Studios, she launched the world-wide television and product licensing for "He-Man and the Masters of the Universe," "She-Ra Princess of Power," "Fat Albert and the Cosby Kids," and "Brave Starr." Her own company, Alice Entertainment/Alice4TV.com produced and distributed over 100 episodes and distributed thousands of additional programs for independent producers.

Her five-star reviewed first novel, "Cave Dreams" is available in print and Kindle on Amazon.com.

Currently she is at work on her memoir, "Behind the Spandex, Globetrotting With Superheroes" spanning her travels with superheroes as the first woman heading a global television distribution company. Two other novels are also in the pipeline.

She lives in Baja California, Mexico and Laguna Hills, California with her four dogs and can often be found in local French restaurants enjoying a *kir vin blanc* and is always in search of the perfect red wine to go with wild pig.

www.ingramcontent.com/pod-product-compliance
Lightning Source LLC
Chambersburg PA
CBHW021033130626
46552CB00005B/1817